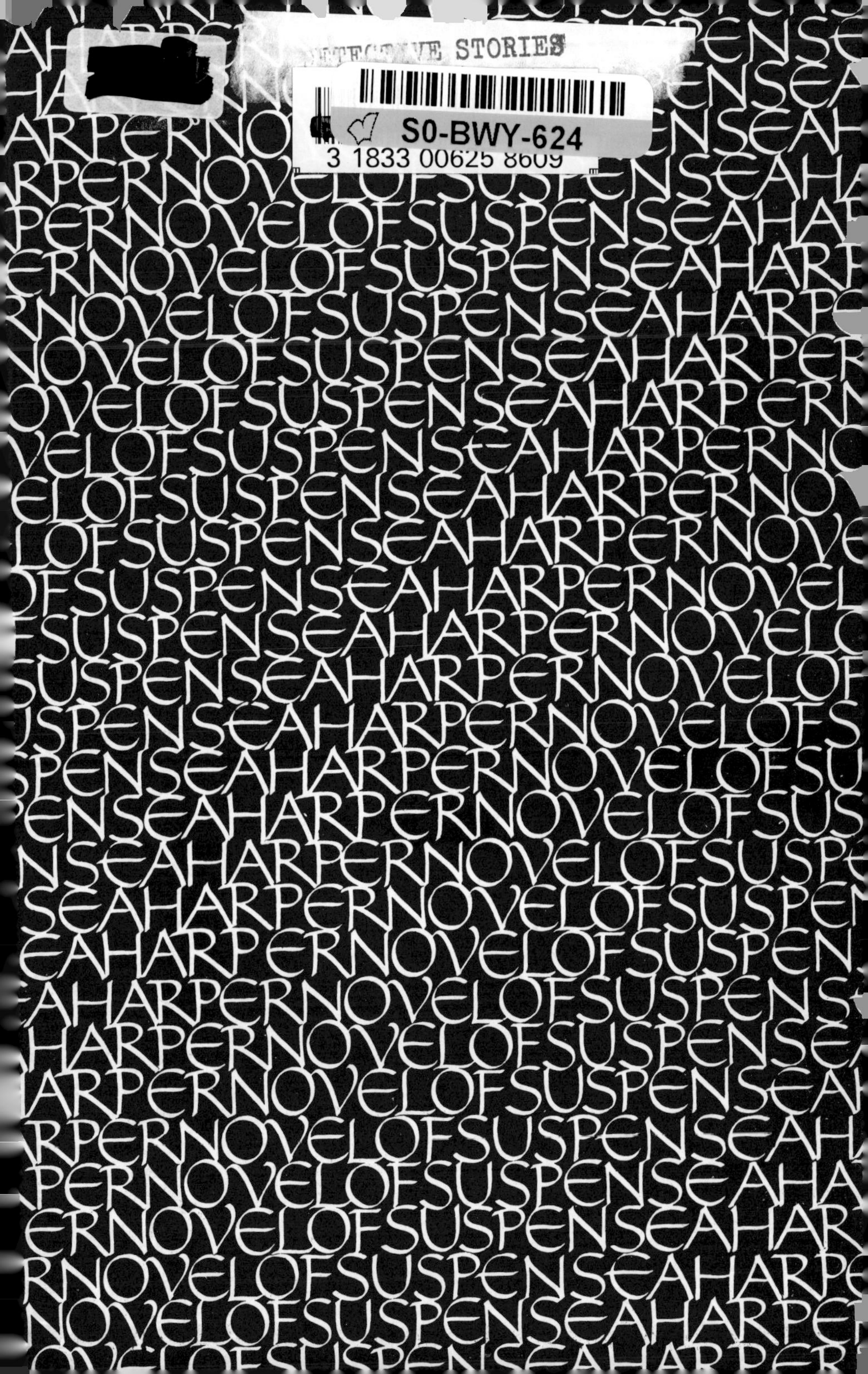

DETECTIVE STORIES
S0-BWY-624
3 1833 00625 8609

C I P H E R E D

HARPER & ROW, PUBLISHERS

NEW YORK

Cambridge
Hagerstown
Philadelphia
San Francisco

London
Mexico City
São Paulo
Sydney

1817

SCOTT KEECH

CIPHERED

CIPHERED. Copyright © 1980 by Scott Keech. All rights reserved. Printed in the United States of America. No part of this book may be used or reproduced in any manner whatsoever without written permission except in the case of brief quotations embodied in critical articles and reviews. For information address Harper & Row, Publishers, Inc., 10 East 53rd Street, New York, N.Y. 10022. Published simultaneously in Canada by Fitzhenry & Whiteside Limited, Toronto.

FIRST EDITION

Copy Editor: Mildred Maynard

Library of Congress Cataloging in Publication Data

Keech, Scott.
Ciphered.
"A Joan Kahn Book."
I. Title.
PZ4.K2539Ci [PS3561.E333] 813′.5′4 79-2737
ISBN 0-06-012294-3

---

80 81 82 83 10 9 8 7 6 5 4 3 2 1

2096103

For Catharine and Steven

[Einstein] mentioned a fairly recent and controversial book, of which he had found the non-scientific part—dealing with comparative mythology and folklore—interesting. "You know," he said to me, "it is not a bad book. No, it really isn't a bad book. The only trouble with it is, it is crazy."

An Interview with Einstein, *Scientific American*, July, 1955

CIPHERED

CHAPTER 1

During the Memorial Day weekend of 1968, Kate Shaw suffered a robbery that was, she conceded straightaway, "all my own fault." Living on one of the few privately owned pieces of lakefront property in Thorpe, she had permitted a young hiker to spend Friday night camped on the shore. The next afternoon she went shopping. When she returned, the hiker was gone, and so were her typewriter, camera, and radio.

Inspector Adams resisted the urge to lecture on the horrors that might have befallen an attractive young woman alone with a stranger in an isolated house. He commented that she was lucky her stereo was too big to carry, and warned that the collegiate secondhand market would probably swallow her goods without a trace.

The End, he thought, and as far as the case was concerned he was right. But two days later he passed her in the University library where she returned his greeting, although her expression suggested she wasn't sure who he was. On Saturday, at Professor Lacey's end-of-term party for present and former students, she not only recognized him but sought him out.

"Hello, Inspector," she said with a smile. "You're like a new word." He raised his eyebrows inquiringly. "You know, once noticed, you turn up in all sorts of odd places— Oh, my! That sounds awful."

He was in fact sensitive to implications that he was out of place among the academics, but her flaming blush looked so painful that he went quickly to the rescue.

"I know, like the well-known ill-fated groundnut scheme in Tanganyika."

"What on earth is that?"

"A phrase I encountered in an article and then seemed to meet again in everything I read for months afterwards."

"But what was the ill-fated groundnut scheme in Tanganyika?"

"The *well-known* ill-fated groundnut scheme in Tanganyika," he corrected her solemnly. "But you really don't want to know. Three double-barreled words in a row have a transcendental allure that the facts lacked."

She laughed, her color back to normal, and said, "That sounds like pataphysics to me."

"Oh, ho. You're an initiate, are you, of the science which is as far beyond metaphysics as metaphysics is beyond physics, but in the opposite direction?"

"I am the merest tyro, sir, at analyzing the infrangible, explicating the ineffable, stabilizing immutable modalities, and, of course, vice versa."

"I'm no match for you in the rhetoric of obfuscation. Can you do that again, and keep a straight face?"

She tried and failed, and they chuckled companionably.

"Tell me, what do a mysterious scheme in Africa and pataphysics have to do with law enforcement in Thorpe?"

"I'm still trying to find an answer to that question," Adams said.

What she really wanted to know was what he was doing at this party, so he told her.

"Several years ago the Department began encouraging policemen to increase their educations. I had dropped out when my father died—"

"Chief Adams, you mean?"

"Yes, but I'm a cop in spite of him. He had intended to be a lawyer until the Depression and an unplanned set of twins came along. He wanted his children to do better. By way of setting me on the path to a career in history, he saddled me with the name Thomas Jefferson Adams. Not too surprisingly, I rebelled. First I demanded to be called Jeff, not Tom. Then I decided to become a cop, and set off a feud that lasted for years. I guess he would be pleased with me now, or maybe just amused.

"I went back to school planning to take useful courses like prelaw and accounting, but the University required me to fulfill various requirements, including one in American history. John Lacey was teaching the introductory course, and he got me so interested that I changed majors and finally got my bachelor's degree. John seems to think he can make me earn a master's, too, but I'm not so sure. The truth is that I'm a sort of addict, not a serious student. I read history for high adventure and low comedy."

"Why, this is wonderful," Kate said. "John has been my mentor for years, and I, too, have a father whose plans for himself and me went agley. He ended up teaching only because of a severe case of writer's block—Oh, now, that's unfair," she reproved herself. "He was an exciting young author in the thirties but Spain and the World War did something to him."

"Mark Shaw? The head of the Drama Department?"

As soon as he asked, Adams regretted it. Shaw was one of Thorpe State's luminaries, and Adams felt he should have known. He was still more embarrassed to realize that somehow he had embarrassed her.

"Sorry."

"No, no. It's only my insecurities showing. I've spent years struggling to escape the label, 'Mark Shaw's daughter,' and then I drag him into the conversation at the earliest opportunity.

"Anyway," she rushed on, "I only brought him in because his dream was to make me a novelist or playwright. *My* dream was to be a historian—how's that for coincidence?"

"Reviewers would pan it," Adams judged. "And I hope you aren't going to tell me that after a day's labor in the archives you pursue an avocation in amateur theatricals."

"No, no more parallels. As a matter of fact, I didn't become a historian—not a proper one, at any rate. I stopped short of the Ph.D., and I don't do original research. What I do is rummage around until I find a character who intrigues me, and then I write him up."

Her insecurities certainly did show, Adams thought. He recognized an I'll-put-me-down-before-you-can defense when he heard one. He wondered if scholars had sneered at her writing, but this didn't seem the right time to pursue that question.

"Do I hear faint quotation marks around the word 'character'?"

"You may. My current subject is Ignatius Donnelly."

Adams cast about for a non-discouraging way to admit that the name meant nothing to him, but she saved him the trouble by going on without waiting for a comment.

"You could call him my personal groundnut scheme, with the emphasis definitely on the second syllable."

"Was he well known and ill-fated?"

"Hardly ill-fated. He was and is well known among students of Populism and some other, rather more exotic fields."

Her air of suppressed amusement made him uncomfortable, since he didn't understand the joke. Fortunately, "Populism" let in a little light.

"Didn't Donnelly run for President once?"

"Vice-President, actually, but I confess that it isn't Donnelly the politician who attracts me as much as Donnelly the . . . well, the comic figure. The political aspect is important, of course. It gives him a seriousness that contrasts strikingly with other traits. On one side is his passionate commitment to reform, and, later, to radical change. On the other side is an enthusiastic theorymongering that has led one student to call him a man of 'desperate gullibility.'"

Adams was congratulating himself on having prompted her to unself-conscious absorption in her subject when she broke off abruptly.

"Oh, no. This is a terrible mistake. I've been reading galleys and mourning over the wounds my editor inflicted. If I get started, I won't stop till I've resurrected every lovely word he slew. Wouldn't you rather talk about the weather or something?"

"Unfair," Adams protested. "Nothing I ever heard about Populists struck me funny. Now you drop a tantalizing reference to a humorous one and try to leave it at that. It's cruel and unusual punishment."

"If you don't save yourself," she dropped her voice ominously, "I'll bend you ear like a pretzel."

"I have an idea. Come and have dinner with me and we'll see how flexible my ear is."

She hesitated about a third of a second. Then she smiled.

"I will, if we go Dutch."

"Agreed."

In the restaurant, shyness overcame them. Awkward silences ended in simultaneous bursts of speech. They asked questions that led nowhere.

"How long have you been a policeman?"

"Almost nine years."

"Oh."

"Are you named for one of Shakespeare's heroines?"

"No, for my grandmother."

"Oh."

Kate forced a laugh. "My father was still in his Spanish Civil War stage when I was born. He wanted to name me Dolores, for La Pasionaria."

"Umm," said Adams. His ignorance of Spanish history was nearly total.

"My mother put her foot down, though, and Daddy accepted defeat gracefully. He has never once quoted Petruchio at me."

"He certainly does manage to draw fine performances from his students."

It was what everyone said. Shaw's twice-yearly productions of Shakespeare were major events.

"Umm," said Kate.

A disaster was in the making. After the wine had been served, Adams said, "Could we make a deal? If I promise to stop you if I get bored, will you go ahead and tell me about this comical Populist of yours?"

"You must be a masochist, and I must have a sadistic streak," Kate said with a smile that cured all pain. "Well . . . I have to say first that I've misrepresented Donnelly a bit. His politics weren't funny, although many people have considered them outrageous. But when he turned to other fields he displayed a gift for illogic that Lewis Carroll couldn't have bettered.

"If I were utterly sadistic, I'd urge you to read the whole thousand pages of Donnelly's masterwork, *The Great Cryptogram.* Having a drop of mercy left, I'll give you the gist. The argument is that the plays attributed to Shakespeare were really written by Francis Bacon. Furthermore, the beauty of the plays is sheer accident, because they exist only to disguise the very, very great cryptogram in which Bacon recorded his autobiography."

"Are you making this up?"

"Not a word. And you ain't heard nothing yet. Donnelly was put on the trail by an article about a cipher that Bacon had known, and may have invented. Intuition blossomed. Donnelly went to work, and, by golly, he found a cipher—but not Bacon's. He couldn't find that because he completely misunderstood the explanation he had read, an explanation a twelve-year-old should grasp easily. I understand it myself."

Adams laughed. "Are you telling me that Donnelly wrote a thousand-page book about a cipher that wasn't there?"

"Let me put it this way," Kate replied with a solemnity somewhat marred by a broad grin. "Donnelly's cipher is, in its way, a tremendous achievement. It is so unlike any other known to cryptography that no one has ever reproduced it."

Adams shook his head wonderingly and opened his mouth to speak. Instead he emitted a sound like the alarm of an electric clock.

"Have you blown a fuse?"

"No such luck." Adams took a small plastic cube from his pocket and pressed a button to end the racket. "This is a wonder of modern science called a beeper, though mine buzzes. It tells me to call headquarters."

"Do you mean to say that you can be sent for at any hour of the day or night? I thought policemen worked scheduled shifts."

"Most of us do, but as the only unmarried inspector I'm usually the one called in at night or on holidays. This doesn't happen very often. Thorpe isn't exactly the crime capital of the nation, you know."

He won a smile, but she looked thoughtful as he went to the phone. He imagined her thinking: He could be in the middle of a bridge game, or meeting someone's parents, or making love, and that thing might go off.

He learned that there was no great crisis, only a few too many events at the same time—a fire, a three-car accident, and an apparent burglary at a Main Street jewelry store. But he did have to go to work.

Kate was ready. She had called for the bill, figured their shares, and got her money out. They told each other they had enjoyed the evening and should repeat it soon. Nevertheless, Adams drove away from her door feeling glum. She wasn't likely to continue an acquaintance with a cop whose duties might intrude at any moment, and with a loud noise.

"Pity. I was just learning to like old Ignatius."

Wednesday's mail brought a parcel containing a book, *Atlantis: The Antediluvian World,* and a note.

"Dear Jeff Adams—This is my favorite of Donnelly's creations. If I haven't exhausted your tolerance entirely, you may find it interesting.—Kate Shaw."

Trained observer that he was, Adams noted certain facts: the book was well worn; she wrote left-handed; he was grinning like an idiot.

He phoned his thanks at once, visited briefly that night, went to see Olivier's film of *Henry V* with her and her parents on Saturday. Sunday, they played bridge with Captain Vogel and his wife. (The Vogels had been surrogate parents to Adams since his mother died.) Afterward they sat up talking until well into Monday morning.

That was when she broke the news that she would depart in five days to take a post as lecturer for both six-week sessions of the summer term at a California State college.

"Twelve weeks?" Adams said. He was in love and she was going to be in California all summer.

"Yes, it's great! Last year I taught only half as long, and I need the extra money. I'm so broke I couldn't buy a plane ticket until I'd rented my house for the summer."

Great? Didn't she care for him at all?

He blurted, "My savings account is full if you . . ." He trailed off, feeling foolish. She would sooner sell everything she owned than ask for help.

"My weakness for hyperbole always makes trouble." She laid her hand on his. "Thanks, Jeff. I'm not in danger of starving, really I'm not."

One word made him despair. One touch elated him. It was ridiculous. Her quick gesture need not have implied any more affection than casual friendship.

In the few remaining days, he spent every free moment with her. There weren't many. She had friends and relations to take leave of. He gave himself stern instructions against mooning about like an adolescent in the throes of puppy love.

The night before she left, she gave him a copy of her last book, *The Enigma of Aaron Burr*.

"You don't have to read it. Few people did," she said. "Unfortunately, I'm the one Burr puzzled."

Adams came alert. Cautiously he said, "There's a lot riding on Donnelly, then?"

"Only life, liberty, and happiness," Kate answered, just missing the joking tone she had aimed for.

He couldn't help himself. His arm went around her and he said, "Oh, my dear."

"Jeff, I— Hell! I don't mean to be coy. I've got to get Donnelly out of my system before I can think seriously about anything else. I need these twelve weeks, Jeff."

So she had heard and understood the tone in his voice when he realized how long she would be away.

He managed a smile. "I'll try not to throw myself at you, but I have to say I'm going to miss you."

She leaned on his shoulder for a moment. "I think I'm going to miss you, too."

CHAPTER 2

It was a miserable summer. Appropriately, in Adams's mind, it was also the summer of what came to be known as the Great Stink.

Odors are hard to describe, and this one was different from any in Thorpe's experience. It wasn't the reek of low tide, rotten eggs, or burning rubber. Whatever the source, the result was impressively foul, and it brought Thorpe to the edge of panic.

The fetor blew away on an evening breeze, but the memory lingered. Thorpe wanted compensation for a long day of suffering, and a guarantee against repetition. What it got was a set of inconclusive reports from University, city, state, and federal investigators. No one knew, or admitted to knowing, what had caused the stench.

Most people in Thorpe blamed the University. They remembered other mysterious events.

The Big Bang had occurred late one night in February. A fire had broken out in one of the so-called "temporary" wooden buildings that had been erected during the rapid growth after World War II. The blaze spread swiftly. Before fire trucks arrived, the building had exploded. A campus policeman was injured, 243 windows were shattered, and just about everyone in town was blown out of bed. The Fire Marshal was unable to determine the cause of the blast, and, according to the Thorpe *Gazette*, he complained that the Chemistry Department "was not helpful."

The incident of the Cancer Bugs came in the spring. Someone from the University enlisted a fifth-grade science class as assistant naturalists, paying a dime a dozen for lightning bugs.

So far so good. Entomologists catching, releasing, breeding, or slaying insects was nothing new in Thorpe.

This scientist, however, had given his employees a rationale which, after editing in juvenile minds, was reported as: "They're for cancer."

Parents chuckled. The story went around. Laughter became hollow. Thorpe couldn't conceive of a relationship between cancer and the light in a firefly's tail. A good many people, gown as well as town, doubted that there was a relationship.

The *Gazette* interviewed scientists and published a lengthy article on bioluminescence, ATP, luciferin and luciferase, and the catalytic effects of calcium. Thorpe shook its collective head and wondered what was really going on.

Adams scarcely noticed these developments. He wondered what was going on in California. Kate wrote long, good letters. She said she missed him. Adams worried that she might have growing doubts about attachment to a man whose job prevented him from traveling with her, and who always had a little black box in his pocket. He told himself that he was being stupid, becoming paranoid. Nevertheless, he feared the worst, and, in a way, it happened.

Kate came home on the Saturday before classes opened at Thorpe State. The demonstrations began on Monday.

During registration week, students had noticed guards at University Research Center. Officially, U.R.C. was "semi-autonomous." Translated, that meant its Board of Directors was identical with the Board of Regents and its staff was drawn from the faculty, but the results of its research didn't have to be published.

An undergraduate reporter tried to interview Ernst Feith,

professor of biochemistry and executive director of U.R.C. His only comment was headlined on the front page of the college paper, *El Toro:* "'NONE OF YOUR BUSINESS,' SAYS FEITH."

That same edition of the newspaper informed students about the Great Stink of the summer and reminded them about the Big Bang and the Cancer Bugs of the previous school year.

Later in the week, *El Toro* reported that near the end of the preceding spring term the staff of U.R.C. had been required to turn in keys to the building and their offices. Some staff members had been interviewed by men reputed to be F.B.I. agents—they had short hair and wore jackets, ties, and blue shirts.

Unnamed sources asserted that something had been stolen by a foreign student. One said that the "something" was a classified document. Another said it was a test tube. The latter claimed that the thief had subsequently died.

El Toro didn't publish on Saturday, but the *Gazette* took up the story. Citing unidentified "police officials," it reported that a foreign student had killed himself while in the custody of federal agents.

The *Gazette* also printed a brief biography of Ernst Feith. He had emigrated from Germany in 1938. Two years later he married the daughter of Walter Nelson, president of what was then and until 1954 Thorpe State Agricultural College. In 1943 he went to Camp Detrick, Maryland, to work for the War Research Center. "War Research," said the *Gazette,* meant "germ war research."

Monday morning, a picket line ringed U.R.C. Several hundred students held a rally in Nelson Quadrangle at noon and appointed a delegation to go to the president's office and demand information. A vice-president distributed an old press release describing University policies on research, a policy that didn't apply to U.R.C. The vice-president declined to discuss U.R.C. The delegation sat down.

The sit-in continued past closing time, and for the rest of the week. Noon rallies grew larger. A student political group issued leaflets noting that Feith's earliest published work had dealt with raising and lowering resistance to infection in wheat. The handout went on to list frightful organisms and chemicals developed for military use against vegetation, and against people. It concluded by asking if the next leak or blast from a Thorpe State laboratory might be not just sickening or scary but lethal.

Friday afternoon, late but in time for the next morning's newspapers, the Public Information Office produced a statement. While the University was committed to unfettered freedom of speech, it warned students against circulating unfounded rumors intended to incite fear and distrust. All research at the University was conducted under rigorous safeguards assuring the safety of the academic community and residents of Thorpe. No hazardous substances were ever left unguarded at University Research Center or anywhere else in the University. The only materials that had been stolen from U.R.C. had been papers.

The press release asserted that the University was a defender of open science but that it recognized an obligation to the national welfare. Classified research was carried out at U.R.C. and only the government could release details. The guards posted at the U.R.C. building came from a private agency, not a governmental one. They would be withdrawn as soon as replacements arrived for the old locks, which had been removed.

Journalists who had been skimming stopped and reread the last line. "Well, I'll be damned," said one. "They couldn't even lock the door after the horse was stolen."

Admitting that the security effort had left the U.R.C. building unlocked and unlockable raised doubts about the importance of the research being guarded. Even among protesting students the admission might have raised a horselaugh—if it had been made in time.

This was election year, the year of law and order. Students and demonstrators were in distinctly ill-repute. The Governor ordered state police to end the sit-in. Before dawn, long before Thorpe had read its newspaper, troopers had cleared the president's office and arrested twenty-two students.

The next Monday, pickets paraded at every entrance to the campus. The mass of protesters grew so thick before U.R.C. that Professor Feith called for an escort to get him out. State policemen waded in swinging billy clubs and arrested nine more students.

Tuesday brought the first rainstorm of what was to be the wettest autumn in Thorpe's history. Picket lines shrank. The noon rally was canceled. Officials breathed a sigh and hoped the rain would keep falling.

It did, but some three hundred students occupied the library and shut it down. At midnight, fifty state police reinforced by an equal number of sheriff's deputies removed and arrested 246 students and one nonstudent.

The University virtually ceased to function. Students demanded amnesty. The Governor vowed to protect the state from "hoodlums and radicals."

The demonstrations went on.

The Thorpe Police Department was called upon only when the action spilled off-campus. Even so, overtime mounted and men were moved from night shifts to day shifts. Adams had to handle cases patrolmen would usually have managed. He was forced to cancel engagements with Kate. Several times his buzzer required him to leave her.

Was it his imagination, or had her manner cooled?

Once she staged a conversation intended to be reassuring. "Staged" was the right word. She had no skill at dissimulation and Adams was fully aware that she was leading up to something. Finally she repeated the crusher she had delivered to someone who made "cop" synonymous with "brute." He would have been more appreciative if he hadn't suspected that "someone" included most of her friends.

The demonstrations went on and on.

Desperate Gullibility: The Life and Opinions of Ignatius Donnelly was published October 29th.

Seventy-nine demonstrators were arrested that day. Shortly before noon, the wind changed and blew tear gas into an elementary school, which had to be evacuated. Rain caused a mud slide that carried away a garage and blocked Lakeview Drive for a couple of hours. At 2:55 P.M., three armed men wearing stocking masks robbed the First National Bank of Thorpe.

Adams was four hours late for the publication party Kate's parents gave that night.

Kate, who began to get sleepy after two drinks, was so heavy-lidded she could barely see. When she thrust a copy of her book at Adams, her other arm swung and splashed liquor on both of them.

He disengaged her from the glass. Dabbing at wet spots with a handkerchief, he tried to apologize. Kate paid no attention.

"The beautiful new man in the Drama Department has been making such a play for me that I feel like a *femme fatale*," she said dreamily. "I can visualize a succession of lovers. Some end brokenhearted. Some break my heart. A few, very few, part with farewell and amen." She giggled drunkenly. "And in old age I shall write lavenderish poetry."

She wasn't going to accept excuses, at least not yet.

She yawned. "Take me home, please."

In the car she fell asleep and woke at the end of the drive only enough to walk indoors and head more or less straight for bed, where she passed out instantly. Adams took off her shoes and covered her with a blanket.

The very next day, Kate left for a symposium on Populists at the University of Minnesota. From there she went to New York for a round of appearances publicizing her book. The *Times* had given it a rave review.

The next week, the Governor let it be known through spokesmen that he would not object if prosecutors dropped charges against most of the nearly six hundred students who had been arrested by then. The University announced that it would establish a committee of administrators, faculty, and students to re-examine research policies. More than a thousand students voted overwhelmingly at a noon rally to cancel further demonstrations.

"PEACE DECLARED" was the headline in the *Gazette*, but there were many who were less optimistic. The Board of Regents need not accept recommendations from the new committee. State and county attorneys were still free to decide to drop some charges, to reduce others, and to prosecute the remainder to the extreme. By the time Regents and prosecutors had acted, students would be rested. Then, perhaps, the *Gazette* would rue not having limited itself to "TRUCE DECLARED."

Kate returned on Wednesday, November 27th. Adams couldn't meet her plane, but she phoned him at the office a little after noon.

"Hi, I'm back."

"Welcome home. When can I see you?"

"When you like. I've cleared my calendar for the weekend."

Morale soared. "Admirable woman. May I take you to dinner tonight—my treat, for once?"

"You may, this once," Kate said with a chuckle. "Look, what I really called for was to say I'll get a turkey if you will spend Thanksgiving with me."

"I'd love to. What should I bring?"

"Just yourself. I plan to put you to work on stuffing and things."

"Fine. I'll pick you up about seven, okay?"

"I'll be ready."

"I'm glad you're back, Kate."

"So am I."

CHAPTER 3

"Oh, when constabulary duty's to be— Dunce! This is a hell of a time to think about a policeman's lot."

Adams stuck his head under the shower jet and finished bathing in sober silence. Clean, combed, and dressed, he was halfway down the stairs from his apartment when he realized he hadn't put the notorious buzzer in his pocket.

"A textbook Freudian slip," he said, turning back. "And if I had a mystical bent, I might see a sign."

But no. The night before Thanksgiving wasn't one of the desperate holiday eves. Christmas and New Year's were occasions for wrecks and fires and violent outbursts at family gatherings. Thanksgiving, at least in Thorpe, was a quiet time.

There would be burglaries, of course. Empty student apartments would attract the larcenous. Adams didn't have to worry about that sort of thing, though. Most of the thefts wouldn't be discovered until the end of the weekend, and the remainder would be handled by the uniformed men. Adams could look forward with some confidence to four days of vacation.

And Kate had made it very clear that these four days were for them alone. He was hoping to be truly thankful tomorrow. Very appropriate and corny, that would be. It would be just as corny, although ironic, if Kate dashed his hopes, but he didn't think she would. For the first time in months, he felt sure he knew her mind.

He went out. Rain had come again.

"No. I refuse to see omens."

He drove away, whistling "You Are My Sunshine."

Kate opened the door before he knocked. She was vibrant. Ebullient as he had been since her phone call, he felt anemic beside her. She was radiating energy like a dynamo.

He held her at arm's length, looking her over. "What kind of uppers are you taking these days?"

"Don't be a bear." She hugged him. "I'm happy."

"Then I am, too. Donnelly is doing well I take it."

"That's not the only reason. But he is, as a matter of fact. A second printing has been ordered, and paperback rights were sold the day before yesterday."

"Kate, that's wonderful. You're going to have a best-seller."

"Ooh, I'm going to be rich and famous and people will ask for my autograph. Do you want to be the first on your block to own a genuine Kate Shaw scrawl?"

"It's not mementos that I want from you, Kate."

She gave him her hell-raising look. "Whatever can you mean by that? No, don't answer. Not yet. Come on, I'm famished."

They were in a mood for laughter at dinner, and everything either of them said seemed marvelously comic. He made a bad pun; she capped it with a worse one; and they ended with such terrible ones that they were both convulsed. Disapproving stares from other patrons only heightened their merriment.

The rain had stopped while they were in the restaurant. A stiff breeze was scattering the clouds.

Kate said, "Lord, it's cold. Let's go to my place and have a fire."

The night air couldn't cool their exhilaration. Kate had hardly passed the threshold before she flung off coat and shoes and went dancing across the room to start a record playing.

She swooped back and he caught her. Together they whirled and stamped to the hammering rhythm of a Beatles' tune, until he exerted his strength and wound them down to rest.

"Rat!" she gasped when he pretended to let her fall. "Rat," she breathed indulgently when he drew her close.

He built a fire then while Kate changed records and the mood. She chose Schubert's cello quintet, with its slow development and long-delayed climax. At the first notes, Adams glanced up at her, and they smiled in shared appreciation.

She came and sat beside him on the rug before the hearth, her hip and shoulder just touching his. Content to prolong the moments of not yet insistent anticipation, they sat quietly absorbing warmth, sweet sound, and each other's nearness.

Adams felt . . . safe. The long months of doubt and awkwardness had not deprived them of each other. He turned his head and found her gaze on him. In an instant, gentle expectancy became urgent need. With fingers that weren't quite steady he touched her hair, her cheek, her lips, her throat. She sighed. Taking his hand in both of hers, she pressed it to her breast.

The telephone rang.

Kate stiffened. "Blast. I forgot to disconnect it."

At the second ring, Adams said, "It can't be for me. No one knows I'm here."

After two more rings, Kate stirred.

"Let it go. It's probably a wrong number."

The ringing kept on, demanding and disturbing.

"Hell," Kate said finally. She leaped up. "I'll get rid of whoever it is, and then I will unplug that thing."

She went to the kitchen. Adams heard her speak briefly. She returned with a frown.

"It is for you, but it's my father."

"Your father?" Adams said stupidly.

"He sounds strange, Jeff. Something's happened, something serious."

Adams rose reluctantly and went to the phone.

"Jeff? I'm sorry to bother you—What idiotic things we say out of mistaken propriety!"

Shaw sounded like a man struggling to retain control of himself.

"What is it, sir? Are you hurt?"

"I? No. Feith . . . he has been murdered."

"Feith!" Adams exclaimed.

"Yes. Ernst Feith, the biochemist."

"I know, I know. But murdered?"

Kate inhaled audibly and moved away from his side.

"He, I . . . There's no doubt of it." An odd sound came over the wire, as if Shaw had gulped. "They're terrible—"

"They? Who?" This was something out of a nightmare.

"Both of them. Mrs. Feith, too. They were shot, and I—"

"Where are you now?" Adams interrupted brusquely.

"At home. They live—lived just across the street."

"Stay there. I'll send officers as fast as I can."

Adams slammed down the receiver, cutting off Shaw's attempt to add a word. Then he dialed the unlisted number that put him straight through to the duty lieutenant, and gave a swift résumé of Shaw's news.

As he hung up, Kate returned, wearing her coat and carrying his.

"Will you take me with you? To my parents' house, I mean."

"Yes, of course— Oh, Kate."

For a moment, they embraced. The fire still burned on the hearth. The quintet's second movement had not yet drawn to a close. They went out into a wintry night.

The Shaws lived at the top of what Thorpe called simply The Hill. Isolated from the distant mountain range by an ancient glacier, it was now a geological curiosity and an expensive residential area.

By crow's flight, Kate lived less than two miles from her parents, but The Hill's lower slopes on the west, toward the lake, were too steep for roads. Adams must first head south on Lakeshore and then east on Main before turning north on University.

He drove carefully, aware that he had no siren or light to warn motorists and pedestrians at intersections. Throughout the length of University Avenue, they saw no other traffic.

At the foot of The Hill, University ended in a fork. On the right was Elm Street, with a stop sign. On the left was Lakeview Drive, with the right-of-way. Adams was preparing for the left turn when a car shot out of Elm and sped across in front of them.

They decelerated sickeningly, skidded on the wet pavement, straightened, began to spin, straightened again. Somehow, the two cars passed without a crash. Out of the corner of his eye Adams saw an already scarred fender flashing by. He downshifted brutally and twitched the wheel far enough, but not too far. They missed the tree on the corner and the parked car that appeared suddenly in the glare of the headlights. The rearview mirror showed the other car racing away.

Adams cursed. Kate whispered, "God." He extended a shaking hand and gripped hers. The gearshift stayed in second the rest of the way up The Hill.

Every light in the Shaws' house seemed to be blazing when Adams pulled into the driveway. Across the road a patrol car was parked, the red light on its top revolving slowly. Adams had come to similar scenes many times. From habit, as soon as he took the keys out of the ignition he bent down and unlocked the chain securing his revolver to a bolt under the seat. Strictly speaking, he was supposed to carry the gun, off-duty or not, but he'd be damned if he would wear it with Kate.

He had the gun in his hand before he thought to look at her. She was staring at the weapon with wide eyes.

"Kate, I . . . In nine years I've never fired a shot except on the range. I've never been shot at, either."

"I'm sorry, Jeff. I do know that policemen are armed. I just hadn't stopped and realized that that means you, too."

She leaned over and kissed him. He held her, wanting never to let go.

"It's going to be a long night," he said at last. "You'd better take my keys so you can drive yourself home."

He dragged himself away and crossed the street without a backward glance.

CHAPTER 4

"Evening, Kovallo, Parker." Adams felt shaky, almost ill, but his voice betrayed none of his emotional state. He spoke in the flat tone of a police officer taking charge. "Are you the first ones?"

"No, sir. We heard Petersen and Waite report they were going inside a few minutes ago."

Adams nodded and looked around. He had visited the Shaws three or four times without noticing the Feiths' house, set far back from the street, or their driveway, which entered Lakeview under a streetlamp directly opposite the Shaws'.

"All right. One of you stay here and direct traffic. I want the next patrol that arrives to go back downhill, around the loop in the road, to see if there is any sort of entrance to the Feiths' property on that side. And one of you go to the house across the way and stay with Professor Shaw. He's the man who reported finding the bodies."

"Okay, Inspector."

So he began the routine, but his mind was elsewhere. Only the need to pay attention to his path drew his thoughts away from Kate. He became aware that it was unexpectedly dark. Heavy old trees stooped over him on each side. In other seasons they would completely mask the house from passersby. Even leafless as they now were, they made the driveway a black tunnel. The streetlamp behind and the house lights ahead cast only sufficient illumination to create deceiving shadows.

This must have been a damned unpleasant walk for Shaw. Adams would want to know what had prompted him to stroll this way.

And why tonight, of all nights?

Adams shook himself, took himself firmly in hand.

"Long driveway," he said to himself, and realized that in fact it was surprisingly long. Three hundred feet or more, it seemed to be. Adams would not have expected to find such an expanse of level ground anywhere on The Hill. He would need to find out just how much land the Feiths had owned, and what it was worth in dollars.

Adams came to the open front door, took half a step inside, and stopped suddenly. His stomach reacted first. For once, he was grateful for self-consciousness which made him sneer at himself, a squeamish cop, and converted a gulp into a snort of self-derision.

At the sound, the patrolman standing in the hall where he could watch every door but this one whirled about, hand flying toward his gun.

"It's Adams, Pete."

"Inspector!" Petersen said in an abashed voice. "I didn't hear you coming. I was worried about the rest of the house. Waite is at the back. We couldn't make a proper search with just the two of us. There are doors and windows all over the place that somebody could have gone out of while we wandered around."

"All right, Pete. I don't suppose the killer is still here, though."

Adams was a little consoled to hear Petersen, with fifteen years' experience of the frightfulness of accidents and fires, displaying his own shock in unaccustomed garrulity.

Adams completed his step over the threshold and closed the door carefully behind him.

It was the spatters, he decided, that made the scene so gruesome. The eye could not escape signs of carnage. The floor, the bodies, the creamy-white wall on the opposite side of the wide entranceway—all were splashed with blood, and other things.

Routine called for a slow survey. Adams looked around, and became aware, as he had outdoors, of spaciousness. The foyer was two stories tall, and—he stepped to his right in order to see through the door across the hall—yes, so was the living room. A pair of wooden staircases ascended to left and right on the inside wall, leading presumably to wings of bedrooms. The outside wall was unbroken, except for the entrance, up to four or five feet below the ceiling. The rest was leaded, pale-tinted glass. Below the window, most of the wall was covered by an enormous tapestry of brilliant hues.

To the left, Adams saw a kitchen. To the right, he saw books. Picking his way carefully in this direction, he discovered a room in which three walls were almost completely lined with shelves holding, at a guess, a thousand volumes. Through a door in the back wall, he saw part of the living room and a baby grand piano. Along the front wall, under a single, large window, was a desk flanked by a pair of tall filing cabinets. Desk and cabinets had been ruthlessly ransacked. Drawers stood open or lay overturned on the floor. Papers had been strewn over half the room.

With no transition, Adams was wholly a policeman at work, observing coldly, feeling nothing at all about the bodies behind him. The vandalizing of the room might prove trivial to this case, but it had elicited his trained responses and restored his balance.

Now he scanned the room quickly, seeking any detail the chaos hid or was intended to hide. He found none, but a flicker of motion attracted his eye to the window. He stared, then nodded. Someone—Kovallo or Parker, no doubt, although Adams could not make out features or details of dress at this distance—was walking across the end of the driveway.

So. The streetlight would have made it possible for the killer, rummaging through the desk and files, to see Shaw crossing the street and entering the driveway.

Adams turned back to the hall and, again treading carefully, approached the nearer body. This was Ernst Feith, probably, but no one would ever identify his features. His head had been blown apart. His face was gone.

Beyond him, sprawled at the foot of the left-hand stairs, lay a woman's body. This might be Mrs. Feith, but she was as unrecognizable as the man, and for the same reason.

Was there significance in that? Were the bodies meant to be unrecognizable? Or had the killer merely intended to make very sure of his victims? Shooting them at the base of the skull with a large gun would achieve either purpose, or both.

And what a gun it must be!

Adams knew how deceptive head wounds can be. A shot fired very close to a head may cause appalling wounds that appear far out of proportion to the size of the slug. But the woman had been shot a second time, in the body, and the exit wound in her back was monstrous.

Shaking his head, Adams turned back to the man. The dark, rough material of his jacket had disguised the fact that he, too, had been shot in the body, but from behind. The jacket was charred, indicating that this shot had also been fired at close range.

At first glance, it seemed that Feith had been shot in the back by someone he had just admitted through the front door. Hearing the shot, or shots, Mrs. Feith had come running and was shot as she rushed down the stairs. The killer made certain she was dead with a second bullet, did the same to Mr. Feith if he had not done so before, and went to the study whence he was frightened into flight by the approach of Mark Shaw.

Adams frowned and stooped to peer closely at the man's body. Around the head wound was a circle that was black but not burned. It was the characteristic trace of old-fashioned, slow-burning gunpowder. The black stuff was powder that had failed to ignite and had been blown out of the gun with the bullet.

Now, surely, no one but a collector of old guns had black powder these days. It would have to be specially ordered from one of the few companies that still made it, and such an order could be easily traced. If the killer had set out to narrow the range of suspects, he could hardly have found a better method.

"And what the devil were they shot with?" he said aloud. "A blunderbuss?"

"Soft-nosed slugs," Petersen suggested. "Or something awful big. I wouldn't have thought a thirty-eight would do so much damage. Maybe a forty-five would."

"Godalmighty!"

Adams and Petersen spun around simultaneously. Two men with metal cases in their hands stood in the entrance.

"Jeez," said one, "it's a bloody massacre, and do I ever mean bloody."

Adams and Petersen breathed deeply. The laboratory detail had arrived.

"Hello, Turner, Warren," Adams said. "Shut the door, will you? I don't want anyone else in here until you two have finished.

"I want color and black-and-white pictures of everything, from every side, angle, and altitude. I want every fingerprint and samples of every bit of dust and anything else you find on every surface you can reach, here and in there," he added, pointing toward the study.

"Are we looking for something in particular, Inspector?"

"No," Adams said slowly. "I just want to be sure we have all the evidence when we know what evidence we need."

As he spoke, the cameras, the midget vacuum cleaner, several sizes of plastic bags and glass vials, and all the rest of the lab squad's paraphernalia emerged from the metal cases. As he went out the door, a thousand-watt bulb was cruelly baring the crueler wounds.

Yet it was outside that he blinked. A traffic jam had evolved, and he had heard none of it as he concentrated on the scene inside. The technicians' panel truck and four police cars were parked on the driveway and lawn. The ambulance used especially to carry away the dead was just coming to a halt nearby.

"Inspector?"

"Crane. Glad you're here," Adams greeted the uniformed sergeant who hurried forward. "Take charge, will you? Get those cars out of the way. There must be space to park over there, where the driveway goes around the corner.

"Then I want you to go through the house, top to bottom, but fast. The killer must be long gone, and I hope there are no more bodies, but we have to look. Take somebody with you, just in case. Don't try to do a full-scale search. The house is big. Keep your eyes open for anything that ought to be examined closely and soon.

"Take a good look at the bodies, the hall, and the library. I can't tell you what to look for, because I don't know. But I don't like the setup and you'll see why.

"The lab squad has just started, and it will take them some time to finish. Don't let the medical examiner in until they are done, and don't let him or them leave until I return.

"I'm going over there." Adams pointed. "You can see the lights of a house up The Hill. The man who found the bodies, a professor named Mark Shaw, lives there and I have to get his story.

"Questions?"

"No, sir."

CHAPTER

5

Mrs. Shaw and Kate were not in sight when Officer Kovallo opened the door. Half regretful and half grateful for Kate's absence, Adams thought: She must guess what her presence would do to my composure.

Kovallo led the way to Shaw's study. Here, as in Feith's, there might be a thousand volumes but, with less shelving and a different controlling temperament, Shaw's books were stacked in corners, piled on and under chairs, lying open amid a clutter of papers on the desk. It would be hard to tell if vandals struck, impossible to discover a small-scale theft.

Another contrast struck Adams. Shaw's was not a small house, yet it was probably no larger than the ground floor alone of the house he had just left.

He became aware of Shaw's questioning glance.

"Sorry. My mind wandered." He considered briefly. "It's none of my business, of course, but would you mind telling me what your house cost?"

"Ah," said Shaw. "The palace."

Giving his full attention now to Shaw, Adams was shocked. Not because Shaw had understood immediately. He would. Nor by his style. That was quintessential Shaw, perfectly to the point, and somehow declamatory and joking at the same time. But the voice reminded Adams that Shaw had seen the bodies across the street. It wasn't the voice Adams had known, with its actor's resonance and projection. It had become weak and toneless. And the smile, the famous little twist of the lips, was a pathetic parody of itself. Shaw looked old; his face seemed to have shrunk; his skin was pallid and his eyes were shadowed. This night had not been kind to Mark Shaw.

Shaw, who had been following his own train of thought, said, "Strange, the things Feith and I had in common. We joined the faculty in the same year, we married in the same year, and we inherited properties across the street from each other."

His tone changed abruptly. "Stranger still," he said bitingly, "how maudlin a middle-aged man can become in the presence of death.

"To answer your question, I can't put a price on this house, because it was a wedding present. Land up here is expensive. I suppose I could sell for eighty or a hundred thousand dollars.

"As for your unspoken question, the Feiths inherited their land from Walter Nelson. I have heard that they spent fifty or sixty thousand dollars building their home. That was in 1954 or '55, and land and house together must be worth several times as much now.

"If gossip is to be believed, the Feiths also inherited a deal of money. Gossip adds, for what it may be worth, that Ernst Feith was a shrewd investor, and, which may be better, a lucky one."

"Umm," said Adams.

Who benefits? is ever the policeman's first interest. Gossip might exaggerate, but his own observations suggested to Adams that someone would inherit a deal of money and land now. He would want to see the Feiths' wills soon.

"Well, I think we had better have your story."

"Yes," Shaw said unenthusiastically. "I must say it is a tale I would prefer to know vicariously."

"I can believe it," said Adams, striving for a moderate show of sympathy combined with official briskness. "I'll try to keep this brief. Suppose you tell it straight through and I'll save the questions until later."

"Very well . . . I had been reading, and it was growing late. I'm not certain of the time. I think it was a few minutes before eleven, but I . . . my sense of the passage of time may have been distorted by subsequent events."

Shaw cleared his throat. "At any rate, it was late enough for my nightcap. I had just stepped into the hall when I heard what I took to be gunshots. You may ask why I didn't think of firecrackers or blown-out tires." He ignored Adams's shake of the head. "I can't say precisely, except perhaps that there were four explosions.

"The truth is," Shaw went on, as if he had reached a conclusion, "they sounded like nothing but gunshots. Four blown-out tires are scarcely likely at any time, and while fireworks are not uncommon when the University is in session, this is, because of the holiday, one of the rare nights when they, too, are unlikely."

Adams stirred. He preferred not to hurry or interrupt witnesses, but at this rate Shaw's tale would prove as long as Scheherazade's.

"I was concerned," Shaw continued at his stately pace, "so concerned that I went straight to the front door and out on the porch. I suppose I anticipated the sight or sound of some kind of stir, but my first quick glance around encountered nothing untoward. Then my eye was drawn by a sight that struck me as distinctly anomalous.

"I should explain that if you stand at the end of my porch, you can see the whole length of my driveway and the Feiths', as far as the Feiths' front door. What I noticed was that their door was wide open.

"Do you know," Shaw said in surprise, "it has only this minute occurred to me to consider that their door might have been opened by someone coming out to investigate, as I was.

Not that it matters now. At the time, I found that open door odd, and, in the context of gunshots, somewhat sinister. Illogically, but with unhappy accuracy, I concluded that the shots had come from there.

"Why, then, did I not call you at once?"

This didn't sound rhetorical. Adams decided that Shaw was asking himself a painful question.

"I don't know. I was convinced that shots—four shots, in fact—had been loosed off, and yet I was no more than uneasy. I made no deductions— What a thing for a scholar to admit! Least of all did I infer the possibility of danger to myself.

"Well," Shaw said in the tone he probably used on students who reasoned sloppily, "I proceeded quite openly across the street and perhaps two-thirds of the way along the driveway. Only then did laggard caution begin to assert itself, and then I attempted to dismiss it as childish fear of the dark.

"I was *not* relieved when the silence was broken by a sound, as of someone or something moving stealthily among the trees to my right. Rather than turn back—rather than turn my back, to be truthful—I made to hurry forward. When the sound came again, however, I stopped and turned toward it. Then someone shot at me."

"Damnation!" Adams exclaimed, utterly astonished.

Shaw, who usually delighted to cause a sensation, barely paused: "I saw the flash. I seemed to feel the explosion. I heard the whine of the passing bullet, the terrible thump as it hit a tree. I . . ." He took a rasping breath. "It is a long time since I was shot at," he said in an apologetic tone.

After another pause, Shaw went on, "I threw myself on the ground and lay for some time in a state that could be described accurately as abject terror."

Adams would have said something, but Shaw hurried on.

"At length I heard footsteps running away from me—and down The Hill, I think. A little courage returned. I forced myself up and went on. God knows I shall always regret doing that!"

"Yes," Adams said. He could think of nothing else to say.

"I should perhaps have telephoned from over there." Shaw shook his head. "I could not."

"Yes," Adams said again.

"I had intended to tell you about the shot fired at me, but I was dithering, I suppose, and you cut me off."

"I'm sorry."

"No. No. I only meant that my delays may have aided the killer to escape."

Adams could be reassuring on this point. "Probably not. In a car, he would have been in the center of town before you could get to a phone."

"I heard no car," Shaw said firmly.

"No? Well, even on foot he would have been far away before a search could have been started."

It was strange, though. While the distance from here to the center of town was not too great to walk, pedestrians were rare on The Hill at any time and especially rare when so many students were out of town. Adams couldn't imagine a killer choosing to walk those empty streets knowing that the police might be after him at any moment. He thought back to a gun that used black powder, and wondered if both oddities were evidence of stupidity, or bravado, or . . . what? Something he couldn't label yet. Its name might emerge after he had solved a few other puzzles.

"You heard four shots," Adams said slowly.

"Yes, not counting the later one fired at me. Of course, I was not listening for shots, and I might have missed one. No more than one, I should think."

"And they were loud? They sounded loud to you in here?"

"Yes, but . . . How can I explain? The absolute volume was less than would be caused by, let us say, slamming the door behind you. The relative sound was great, because I was indoors and because I received the impression that they were fired some distance away. I thought of something like a large-caliber rifle."

"And how did they come? All together—blam, blam, blam, blam—or spaced out in some fashion?"

"In two pairs, I think. Ah, as you say, blam, blam, pause, blam, blam."

"Did Mrs. Shaw hear the shots?"

"No, she was asleep. She usually goes to bed early. She didn't wake until I returned and had to change my mud-stained clothing."

"When you went out, did you turn on the porch light?"

"No. I left it off so that I wouldn't be looking out of brightness into darkness."

"Could you see lights, other than the one from the front door, in the Feiths' house?"

Shaw looked startled. "How very odd. I can see nothing but that door now, in memory." He shook his head. "But there must have been others. The scene would have been very much too sinister if there had been nothing but a gaping, brightly lit doorway at the end of an exceedingly dark path." Again he shook his head, impatiently this time. "This is stupid. Of course there were others. I remember now that I could see into the living room and into what I took to be a library from where I stopped just inside the front door."

"But you saw nothing of the person who shot at you?"

"No, but you see, he was behind me—that is, I had already passed the place where he was hidden among the trees when I turned toward him, and so he was completely out of what little light there was."

Adams gazed into space, trying to visualize the scenes and events as Shaw had reported them. He couldn't do it.

Adams sat in silence for a moment, unsure how to proceed. The questions that came immediately to mind all seemed too leading, and he was leery of prompting a witness to tell him what he showed he wanted to hear.

He reached a decision. Shaw's story could be re-examined tomorrow or the next day, or every day for as long as necessary to clarify it. There was another tack to take with this particular witness.

"You know," he said slowly. "I'm in a rather difficult position."

2096103

"You mean, because you are, shall we say, acquainted with the chief witness?"

"There is that," Adams acknowledged, "but I was thinking of something else. I mean," he went on in a carefully expressionless voice, "that you are such a liar."

Shaw and Kovallo, who had taken notes stolidly until now, both sat up with a start and stared at Adams. Then Shaw made a sound that might have been an attempt at a chuckle.

"Yes. Yes, I see. Who steals *my* reputation steals trash. At the least, it is not altogether amusing at this moment to be known as Thorpe's leading fabulist."

Shaw had fielded that one without difficulty, but Adams pressed on: "You understand, I never took your courses, but even I have heard that you fought in Spain, served with the merchant marine in U-boat-infested waters, parachuted into I forget which occupied country for the O.S.S., wrote a play that ran on Broadway, published a controversial novel—I'm getting the order muddled, but—"

"Enough. Enough." Shaw held up his hands in mock surrender. "I confess to having rather overstuffed my pseudobiography. But, by heaven, if you ever face three hundred undergraduates at nine in the morning, you may find yourself resorting to desperate expedients. Shakespeare complained, with cause, of distractions in the pit, but at least his audiences gathered in hope of entertainment. Mine, Lord help them, have no hope, and attend class only because the course satisfies a requirement for English and Drama majors.

"I have an active, not to say hyperactive, imagination and a certain talent for drama. So I entertain them. It keeps them awake at least.

"Over the years, they have learned that I tell them fantastic things. They must pay a little attention, if only to avoid the ignominy of missing, or being taken in by, Shaw's latest whopper. Besides, they can never be entirely confident the whopper didn't happen. Some of the least credible things I say are true, after all.

"I did go to Spain, though as a medic, not a combatant. I

did write what was unfortunately a very silly novel about a sort of schizophrenic, told in the first person plural. I did work for an intelligence agency—the business of parachuting into Italy was something too much, I admit. Of course, I don't tell tales only about myself. I am fully prepared to dose them with astounding fancies—or facts, for that matter—on many subjects. But my past, true or otherwise, does seem to fascinate them.

"I like to think I give them food for thought. They are accustomed to liars: they have parents, friends, and teachers; they read an occasional newspaper and listen to politicians. But a man who announces that he will lie to them is a phenomenon to which they must give a little consideration."

Shaw had become animated for the first time, but now he broke off and waved one hand dismissively. "Sorry. You aren't here to be entertained by my performance on a hobbyhorse.

"What can I say? A liar can't expect to be believed when he claims to be honest. However, for the record, I do so claim. I have not consciously invented or embellished anything in my tale tonight.

"What you make of it, or of me, is naturally—Great God in heaven!" Shaw sat bolt upright once more, an expression of horrified incredulity on his face. "Do you suspect *me* of this—of this—of that—?"

Mark Shaw at a loss for words was a notable event.

"Easy, easy," Adams said soothingly, if not quite in answer. "I did need to know about invention and embellishment.

"One more thing," he went on quickly, giving Shaw no time to consider the implications of his reply. "You said that when you entered the Feiths' house you saw 'what I took to be a library.' Did you mean that you had never been there before?"

"Oh, my," Shaw said ruefully. "In the context, this will sound bad. Well, there's no help for it.

"Feith and I were never friends," he said with a candid air. "For twenty years I have been, I suppose, his most outspoken opponent—politically, I mean. We weren't friends, but we weren't personal enemies. We had no trouble being civil to each other."

"I know that Mrs. Feith was a member of the local John Birch Society, but I don't remember ever hearing anything about Mr. Feith's politics," Adams said, inviting comment.

"Oh, Mrs. Feith," Shaw said scornfully. Then he looked chagrined. "When she was alive, I thought her empty-headed. But, poor thing, she never deserved to die that way. Nor did he."

Shaw shook his head.

"Well, let it go. They were both right-wingers by my standards, and I am left-wing by theirs. But I think I misled you. I should have said 'University politics,' not simply 'politics.' In brief, Feith, and Walter Nelson before him, were hell-bent on making the University bigger and bigger. To my mind, their policy was the opposite of making the University better and better. I wanted an academy. They created a degree mill.

"I did not," Shaw said with a sudden edge in his voice, "disapprove strongly enough to kill him."

"Did anyone?" Adams asked mildly. "Did Feith have enemies who hated him, rather than merely disapproving of his policies?"

"For God's sake," Shaw said irritably. "Am I supposed to suspect my friends, to repeat the heated but unconsidered remark of an acquaintance? You, of all policemen in the world," Shaw went on accusingly, "should know that everything in academic training and experience conditions us against violence. The pale cast of thought makes us at least slow to act."

"'Slow to act' is not 'never acting,'" said Adams.

Shaw made no answer.

"And what about students?"

"Students? Surely not."

Adams was surprised by the distress in Shaw's voice and expression.

"Why not? They have had much less of that academic

training and experience, and only a few weeks ago several thousand of them were involved in demonstrations of which Feith was the main target."

"I thought that had calmed down."

Shaw's voice had calmed, and Adams became more alert. "Did you have someone specific in mind?" he asked.

"God blast it!" Shaw cried furiously. "Get the sordid details from someone else— No. Wait." He took a deep breath and controlled his voice. "If I leave it at that, you will think I do have someone in mind. I don't.

"There have been rumors," he continued distastefully. "They say that Feith has been publishing, as his own, work that was actually done by graduate students."

Shaw leaned forward and spoke earnestly: "You must understand that this sort of rumor is not uncommon, particularly about men who have achieved high position or reputation. Such men have access to the research of large numbers of students, and what a student may see as theft, others may see as the application of the wide knowledge that only an experienced man is capable of."

"'Theft' is a strong word," Adams rejoined. "Have students felt they had been robbed? Have students *been* robbed?"

"By Feith? I have no way of knowing."

"By anyone? Do the rumors you called 'not uncommon' have a basis in fact?"

"Yes," Shaw conceded reluctantly. "Fewer have been robbed than believe they have. But . . . yes, to both questions."

"And one or more students believed they had been robbed by Feith?"

"Damn it, I don't know. How can I know how rumors start or how garbled they become by the time they reach me? I have admitted hearing rumors. I know no details and I want to know no details."

"All right," Adams said quietly. "I'm sorry I had to put you through this questioning. I'll come back tomorrow or the next day with a transcript of your statement for you to sign. I may have to ask more questions then, but I'll stop pestering you now."

Kovallo went ahead, but as Adams began to follow, Shaw laid a hand on his arm.

"Jeff."

So this was not to be business. Until now, they had studiously avoided calling each other anything at all.

"Must all my statement be made public? I haven't told Eleanor and Kate that I was shot at."

"I think you should, Mark. The news will get out, whatever I do."

"I suppose so," Shaw said tiredly. "Would you like . . . Shall I call Kate?"

"No. No, thanks."

"She thought you might not want to see her. I mean . . . you know what I mean. I was going to tell you that she will stay here tonight.

"Also," Shaw continued, "I owe you an apology—two, in fact."

"An apology? What for?"

"For flaring up at you—"

"Forget it, Mark."

"No. I was unfair. You have a job to do. It was just that I suddenly realized that we shall all have to answer embarrassing personal questions, bare our motives and prejudices, explain that cursing Feith over a drink really did not signify anything. It all seemed so grimy."

Some apology, Adams thought. If Kate felt the same way . . .

"The other is more serious," Shaw said. "It was unconscionable to call you. I tried your phone, then Kate's, without thought of—"

"As a practical matter," Adams interrupted brusquely, "the duty officer would have called me not more than five minutes after you did. For the rest, I don't see that it is reprehensible in an emergency to call the cop one knows, any more than to call the doctor one knows. Good night, Mark."

CHAPTER 6

Adams strode away quickly, but not too rapidly to note that from the porch and driveway, and as he crossed the street, he had, as Shaw had said, an unobstructed view of the Feiths' front door.

Kovallo was bursting with speech, but Adams forestalled him.

"Would you get a couple of flashlights from your patrol car, Kovallo? I want to see if we can find the spot where Shaw hit the dirt."

When the patrolman returned, Adams asked, "Did Shaw tell you any of his story before I came?"

"No, Inspector. He looked even sicker when I got there than when you came along, and he was drinking what looked like a good-sized shot of straight whiskey. There were a couple of women there, a Mrs. Shaw and a Miss Shaw— Is that your girl, Inspector?"

"Yes," Adams snapped. He regretted the apparent snub at once, but he welcomed the silence into which Kovallo relapsed.

They walked toward the Feiths' house, one on each side of the driveway, shining their lights on the ground. They had gone more than halfway when Kovallo, on the right, said quietly, "Here, Inspector."

A foot or so from the edge of the graveled drive, the

rain-softened earth showed two shallow but distinct dents. Three feet farther out were two sets of grooves, four to the left, three to the right. A crumpled leaf lay where the fourth finger of a right hand would have made its mark.

Adams raised his flashlight and turned slowly around in a complete circle. Somewhere among the trees on this side of the driveway, the sodden ground might hold the killer's tracks. Across the way, one of the big trees might contain a large-caliber bullet.

Adams looked up and saw that the clouds were gathering again. He must hurry.

"Kovallo, stand guard here. I'll send a technician to make casts as soon as possible."

"Sure, Inspector," Kovallo answered cheerfully.

Adams took a last look at the marks on the ground. With Shaw's story as a guide, they were readily interpreted as graphic evidence that he had flung himself down in fear, his knees leaving the two dents, his clawing fingers making the grooves.

Absence of the marks on the ground would have proved nothing. Their presence tended to confirm Shaw's story, *but the story was absurd.*

Swiftly Adams rehearsed the story in the skeptical manner he would have tried out on any potential suspect's report.

Shaw hears two pairs of gunshots in the night. Out he goes, heedless of danger, to investigate. He sees a brightly lighted house with a sinister open door, and heads straight for it. He never sees a person but does finally hear stealthy movement. Taking fright, he turns not away but toward the trees where a whole gang of killers might safely lie in ambush. Someone, who had presumably come out of Feith's study after sighting Shaw, shoots at him, misses, and runs away. Shaw, having heard footsteps departing, but no car, gets up and resumes his stroll. He discovers a horrible scene, retraces his steps, and, at last, thinks of calling a cop.

Forget the foolhardy professor; people do odd things. Pass over, for the moment, the careless killer loitering about until

Shaw nearly stumbles over him; killers have been known to do even odder things than other people. Never mind the phone call to Shaw's daughter's policeman friend; it might be as understandable as Adams had tactfully suggested when Shaw apologized.

Setting those matters aside left a remainder that strained credulity past the breaking point. That hadn't disturbed Adams much, at first. He had interviewed too many people whose capacity for belief far exceeded the White Queen's. Inaccuracy no longer surprised him; honesty sometimes did. Witnesses had things to hide; they tried to make themselves sound braver or quicker-witted than they had been; they became confused. Adams knew better than to place great reliance on the stories, particularly the first versions, that he heard.

When Shaw's story began to sound impossible, Adams suspected shock. Unfortunately, the answers to a few simple test questions had suggested that Shaw's mental equipment was functioning well enough.

For instance, Shaw had not pretended to remember how the Feiths' house had been lighted. Ordinarily, a witness's willingness to admit nonrecollection of a peripheral detail was reassuring. And Shaw had not sounded like a temporarily deranged man when he worked out that lights must have been on or else he would have noticed their absence.

Adams had retained a faint hope that, despite appearances, Shaw had been jarred sufficiently that his always active imagination had run riot, and that his story would evaporate.

The marks on the ground would not evaporate.

What then?

Shaw simply couldn't have heard what he claimed to have heard. And Adams didn't understand how he had avoided seeing the killer.

Shaw might yet prove to be inaccurate in some major respect that would make the rest comprehensible. Witnesses often were. Knowing that gave Adams no help sorting out what he had been told thus far.

Now at last Adams confronted the thought from which he had shied. Suppose that Shaw had not merely made mistakes. Suppose that he had lied.

Before a vision of arresting his prospective father-in-law had time to form, Adams redirected his thoughts to a related matter. Perhaps he should withdraw from this case. Other officers called him "Perfesser" and Adams wasn't sure if the jesting title expressed resentment or respect for the "eddicated cop" who had risen swiftly through the ranks. Would he be suspected of shielding the father of "his girl"? *Would* he shield Shaw? Adams shrugged. He didn't think he would, but the final decision would be up to Captain Vogel. Then Adams, who had never suffered from false modesty, tried to imagine another cop grappling with Shaw's explication of the pedagogical purposes of prevarication. He grinned and went back to work.

Why would Shaw lie? Had he killed the Feiths himself? Was he covering up for someone? Who? A radical student, or one whose work Feith had appropriated?

The Feiths' house loomed ahead, reminding him of heirs. They must be investigated promptly.

His thoughts returned to Shaw. What profit could there be for him in these murders? Adams wondered if he had handed Shaw an opportunity to misdirect him. Certainly his first question had allowed Shaw to emphasize that he himself had assets, while the Feiths' heirs would be much better off because of the murders.

But if Shaw was lying, why wasn't his tale more plausible? Adams felt sure that Shaw was capable of inventing a much more convincing story than the one he had told. On the other hand, Shaw might not care that his story was unbelievable if it created sufficient confusion to hide the truth.

"Hell," said Adams. It was disorienting to deal with a man who said, in effect, "It's true that I lie, but this time I'm truthful." Shaw belonged in a pataphysician's world, not a policeman's.

Adams opened the door and found Sergeant Crane and Dr. Waddell, the medical examiner, waiting for him. In answer to an inquiring eye, Crane said, "Nothing urgent," and Adams turned to the medical examiner.

"They were each shot twice with a damn big gun, as you may have noticed," Waddell began in characteristic style. "One of your men dug a bullet that looks like a forty-five out of the wall. I don't know if anything else was done to them. They may have been dead a couple of hours. Probably less." (Adams was surprised to see that his watch showed only a few minutes after midnight.) "Not much more I can tell you till I cut them up."

"Okay. Thanks, Doc." Waddell hated to be called "Doc" and his tough-guy manner irritated Adams. "You can go, but let me have a report quickly, please."

Waddell went off huffily, and Crane opened his mouth to speak but Adams prevented him.

"Is there a phone in an undisturbed room?"

"Sure. They're all over the place. One in the kitchen, others upstairs."

"Good." Adams turned and called out, "Petersen, go to the phone in the kitchen and tell the station I want to know if the Feiths have any children or other relatives living in Thorpe or nearby.

"Now, Crane."

But the sergeant was stopped again. A patrolman appeared at the door, saying, "Inspector Adams?"

"Here, Martin," Adams said wearily. "What is it?"

"We found where a car was parked and—"

"You found what?" Adams exclaimed.

"Car tracks, sir," Officer Martin said apologetically. "Me and Bandini were sent around to look for another entrance. There isn't any curb on that side, and we saw these tracks in the dirt. We looked around and saw marks on the hillside, like where somebody on foot slipped on the wet ground. Then we saw the clouds and—"

"All right, Martin. Sorry I yelled at you. I was surprised, but you did exactly right."

Now Adams issued a spate of orders. The lab squad was to leave the house until later, lest important evidence be washed away if rain fell again. Warren was to go with Martin and another officer to make plaster casts of the tracks of tires and feet. Turner and two officers were to go to where Kovallo waited, record the traces there, and then work their way through the woods toward Martin's party coming uphill. The bullet Shaw claimed had been fired at him was supposed to be embedded in a tree where the rain wouldn't harm it. It could wait.

"Now, Crane, before anything else comes up."

"Except for the two rooms downstairs, I didn't see anything that needs immediate attention," Crane said rapidly. "No signs of robbery or a search. Mrs. Feith's purse is in a bedroom upstairs and it has about sixty dollars in it.

"I did see," Crane said emphatically, "signs that they had plenty of dough—expensive furniture, some paintings that look original, a couple of high-priced cars in the garage, things like that. And of course this house and the land cost more than you and I earn in several years."

Adams nodded.

"Like the Doc said," Crane continued, "we got a bullet out of the wall alongside the stairs. It's probably the one that went out of the woman's back. Looks to me like she was four or five steps from the bottom when she got it. I'd say she was running, because she fell on her face and that slug was big enough to stop her cold unless she was moving at a pretty good clip.

"Warren and Turner finished in the hall. 'Course, they don't know what they will see under the microscopes, but they didn't think they had found anything very useful for us."

"Very well," said Adams. He went on to outline quickly what Shaw had told him.

"Uh-oh," Crane said. "If I've got it right, there's a big hole in that story."

"You've got it right," Adams replied. "There are some small ones, too, and now these tracks Martin reports seem to make another—"

"Hey, Inspector!" came a shout. "Here's the gun."

Adams muttered, "The devil," stepped out the door, and bellowed, "Everybody stand still and don't muck up tracks. The man next to whoever yelled, turn your light on him."

"It's me, sir—Parker," a subdued voice called.

Adams ran across the lawn toward a spot among the trees where half a dozen flashlights shone on the embarrassed Parker. As he left the grass, Adams noticed that Turner had been thorough. To his left, dabs of white plaster marked Turner's path, and presumably the killer's. It ran parallel to the driveway for several yards, then turned left, and at the turn Adams saw a jumble of footprints that Turner had not bothered to plaster. The killer, it was to be supposed, had stood there, moving from foot to foot.

Ten or twelve feet to Adams's right was the place where Shaw had thrown himself on the ground. To the left, plaster ran straight for some distance and then curved toward where Martin and Bandini had found tire tracks.

Adams looked up and around, and his eyes were drawn to the house across the street. The downstairs windows of Shaw's house were hidden by bushes or low trees, although light showed through the foliage. But at an upstairs window Adams could see a woman's figure. Kate?

Adams dragged his eyes away. Parker was ahead and obliquely to the left, perhaps twenty feet from the gunman's line of flight. Adams moved forward slowly, shining his light on the ground.

"Tracks?" he asked tersely as he neared Parker.

"Don't seem to be any here, sir. Looks like he heaved the gun away when he started to run."

It was, as Waddell had said, a damn big gun, bigger in every dimension than, say, a policeman's service pistol. The barrel was at least ten inches long and about the right size for a .45-caliber bullet.

The most remarkable aspect of the revolver was not its size, but its adornment. The barrel was completely covered with engraving and polished so that it glittered under the flashlights. The butt was even more eye-catching. No plain wood there. The handles were of ivory and intricately carved.

Adams threw his hands up and said, "Crane, you look for Wild Bill Hickok and I'll see if I can find Calamity Jane."

"Inspector," called another voice. Petersen was hurrying toward them. "I got the addresses, and Captain Vogel wants you on the phone."

Adams grunted irritably. He was beginning to feel baited. He had wanted to hurry, but events were moving altogether too fast for comfort. He might overlook something crucial in the rush. On the other hand, Vogel was his boss. More than that, the Captain was clearly showing his concern over the case, both by going to headquarters on this holiday eve and by calling Adams to the phone.

Adams looked at his watch and saw that it was just 12:30, and reached a decision. All the evidence and all the puzzles here needed attention, but so did the heirs.

"Crane, take charge. And, Turner, fingerprint that cannon as carefully as you know how."

As he trotted toward the house, Adams saw that the paper Petersen had handed him bore two addresses, one for "Feith, Karl (son)," and one for "Evans, Mrs. Margaret Feith (daughter)," and "Evans, John William." Both addresses were in Thorpe.

CHAPTER 7

Captain Vogel listened without interrupting to Adams's swift summary of findings and questions. At the end, he said slowly, "It sounds, um, elaborate."

Adams breathed easier. Vogel seldom missed much, but this case was out of the ordinary, even without counting Shaw's strange story.

"Right, Captain."

"You take my point, then?"

"Yes, sir. It makes me think of a very nasty Halloween trick."

"Good. What can I do to help?"

Vogel seemed to assume that Adams would stay on the case, Adams noted.

"Well, sir, I think the heirs ought to be interviewed right away. If one of them did do it, I hate to give him time to calm down and get his story pat. I can't see them both at once, and there is no one here who can take charge if both Crane and I leave."

"You want me to come up there?"

"Oh, no, sir. Crane knows what to do, and he'll do it right. I thought maybe you would—"

"All right. Which one?"

"Well, sir—"

"Never mind. I'll take the daughter. Meet me at the station afterwards, unless something comes up."

"Yes, sir. Thanks."

Adams leaned against the wall, closed his eyes, and thought hard for thirty seconds. He ran down a mental checklist, trying to be sure he had left nothing major undone. Only one task remained before he could leave, he decided. He pushed himself upright and went into the hall to search the bodies.

The woman—he wasn't very doubtful that she was Mrs. Feith, but he would be cautious until he had positive identification—wore pajamas and a dressing gown, but no shoes or slippers. Her only jewelry was a wedding ring. Her pockets contained a single, balled-up tissue paper.

The man wore jacket, slacks, and shoes, but no tie. His wallet contained a driver's license, several credit cards and a University library card, all in the name of Ernst Feith, and forty-three dollars in cash. Handkerchief and loose change were in one pants pocket, keys and a cigarette lighter in another. One side pocket of the jacket held a pipe and a pouch of tobacco; the other held a postcard from the University library informing "Prof. E. Feith" that a book was being held for him. The breast pockets of jacket and shirt held a total of four ballpoint pens and one mechanical pencil. The inside pocket of the jacket held an appointment book.

Adams lifted the book out carefully and used his pen to open it. It was a leather-bound, loose-leaf holder approximately four inches by five inches, with dividers labeled "Diary," "Months," "Cash," "Alphabet," and "Notes." The first divider announced that this was a Seven Star Diary. "Ernst Feith" was written in the space provided for the owner's name, and the same or similar handwriting filled many other pages, especially in the alphabet section, where names and addresses were listed.

The diary section contained a page for each day of the month. There were no entries for November 27th and 28th. The entry for November 29th was "Mrs. Brown."

"Swell," Adams said.

He turned to the alphabet section again, and found a Mrs. Brown listed with an address in Thorpe.

Most of the pages in the diary held writing: "Eric—lunch,"

"Dr. Vance—2:15"—that sort of thing. All of the pages, Adams noticed, had printed at the bottom what he supposed was meant as an inspiring motto. "No day is wasted if something is learned," said one. "Deep knowledge listens, slight knowledge talks," declared another.

"Oh, boy," said Adams.

He put all his findings into the plastic evidence bags that the technical squad had left beside the bodies, and took them out to Turner for examination in the lab.

"What can you tell me about the gun?" he asked.

"It's a Colt—a forty-four, not a forty-five. It's an oldie, from the serial number, but not so old that it is single-action. One of the first double-action ones, I'd say."

A single-action gun must be cocked and fired in separate operations. A double-action gun is cocked and fired by one pull of the trigger.

"Too old to stand up to modern gunpowder?" Adams asked.

Turner scratched his head. "Hard to say, sir. It was built to be rugged, and it's in good condition. But it's seventy, eighty years old, so black powder is what it was meant for. I don't know what would happen with modern gunpowder."

"All right. Go on."

"There were five expended cartridges in the chamber. The last one was under the hammer, so the killer must have carried the gun with an empty cylinder under the hammer, so it couldn't go off accidentally."

"He seems to know something about guns," Crane interjected.

Adams shrugged. "Fingerprints?"

"Only a couple, and they were smeared," Turner answered. "He probably wore gloves."

"Had the gun been wiped off?"

"Yeah, sure. This gun is for show, sir. The owner would have dusted it off regularly."

"No doubt. Anything else?"

"No, sir."

"Crane?"

"I phoned in the serial number, to start tracing the gun."

"Good."

"And I think we are getting some pretty good casts of the footprints."

"Yes? That's good," Adams said in a tone implying distrust of such apparently straightforward evidence.

Adams issued instructions to Crane, selected Kovallo to drive him in a radio car to Karl Feith's address, and finished, as usual, with "Any questions?"

"One, sir. Is this case screwy for a reason?" Crane asked.

"It's the right question," Adams said. "I don't know the answer yet. Maybe some things were arranged to catch our attention. Maybe the killer is just stupid. When we know who owned that gun, we may have a better idea of what we are up against."

Kovallo's car was still parked on the road facing uphill.

"Drive to the end, Kovallo. We'll check the park."

A couple of hundred feet beyond the Feiths' and Shaws' driveways, the tarred road ended at the entrance to Hilltop State Park. Kovallo halted short of the dirt road that began there, and Adams got out. The gate was shut and locked, and no fresh automobile tracks went past it. However, the track of a single tire looped onto the dirt and back to the tar, as if a car had made a U-turn. The mark had been made since the rain stopped, but it might signify no more than the presence of a courting couple. Nevertheless, Adams got on the radio to direct that a plaster cast be made.

"Okay, Kovallo. We'll go down and stop at Martin and Bandini's car, and look at the tracks they found."

With the park closed, the only way to drive down from the summit was on Lakeview Drive. No other road came all the way up The Hill. Kovallo reversed, drove past the driveways and around a curve of perhaps 150 degrees, and stopped behind a parked police car.

Adams got out again and went to examine the freshly plastered tire tracks that curved onto the shoulder and back to the road. Three of the tires had been very worn, almost bald. The fourth tire had hardly been worn at all, and its tread looked to Adams identical to the one he had seen at the entrance to the park.

Adams moved slowly along the track. A car had parked here; Adams could make out the spots where the four wheels had sunk slightly into the soft earth. He could also see the narrow but distinct V-shape of the edge of each tire track which showed that the car had been going downhill when it pulled in and when it departed. What he could not find was the spatter of dirt that should have been thrown back when power was exerted through the driving wheels.

Adams turned to look up the hillside. No stairway or path led up the moderately steep slope, but Adams's flashlight showed two white lines. The lines were plaster, one in long streaks, one in footstep-size dabs.

Adams looked about. At the very top of the slope, the Feiths' house was visible. The nearest house on this side was three hundred feet or more from where Adams stood, while the Shaws', the only one on the other side, was perhaps four hundred feet from the Feiths'. The dead couple had had privacy, and an isolated location where a murderer could expect to shoot a noisy gun without attracting attention.

Adams returned his gaze to the tire tracks. They might yet signify a courting couple but the footprints suggested a different explanation. They indicated that the killer had driven to the end of the road, turned around, and come back to park where he need not start the engine but only release the brake to roll away. Then he had walked uphill, but had run and skidded on the way back.

Crane had said "screwy," and he didn't know the half of it.

The killer carefully prepared his escape, and used a gun and powder that ought to be traceable within a day or two. He committed a ruthless murder that left him so unmoved he calmly stayed to ransack Feith's study. Yet when Shaw appeared he became so addled that he headed north, away from his getaway car. Hiding among the trees where he couldn't be seen, he gave away his position by firing one useless shot at Shaw. Then he left the gun to be found almost at once, but remembered to let his car roll silently so as not to call attention immediately to the manner of his departure.

So much nonsense had to mean something, Adams thought. Then he chuckled. The students in Logic I would rip that idea to shreds. It was true, nonetheless, he was sure.

And three bald tires? What did they mean?

Adams shrugged and turned.

"Let's go see young Mr. Feith, Kovallo."

CHAPTER

8

Karl Feith lived on Washington Street near the center of town, two short blocks east of University Avenue and two longer blocks north of the campus, in the area where students congregated. Two- and three-story apartment buildings filled the quarter now, but 310 Washington was one of the few remaining brown shingled houses.

Under a carport alongside were a battered VW and an old but well-maintained MG. The tires of the VW were worn, but only a little, and the MG's were in good condition. Both cars were dry; their engine covers and exhaust pipes were cool.

There were four nameplates beside the house door. Two bore two males' names each; one bore the names of a married couple; the last bore Karl Feith's name alone. Two upstairs windows showed lights. The rest of the house was dark.

Adams rang Feith's bell, waited a few seconds, and rang again. A window opened above and an irritable voice called, "Who is it? What do you want at this hour of the night?"

Adams stepped back, saw a man leaning out of one of the lighted windows, and gestured to Kovallo to move into the light so that his uniform could be seen.

"We are police officers. Are you Karl Feith?"

"Yes. What's the matter?"

"May we come in and talk to you?"

"Oh, all right," Feith said pettishly. "I'll be down in a minute."

The window closed with a slam.

Kovallo took off his cap and rubbed the top of his head. "Everybody loves a cop," he said reflectively.

This, from solid, stolid Kovallo, startled Adams into laughter.

"Ssh," he said. "It's a secret."

"Yeah." Kovallo replaced his cap. "Yeah, I know."

A light went on and a moment later a shadowy form appeared in the glass panel of the front door. A man opened the door and said shortly, "Well, what is it?"

"Mr. Feith?" The man nodded. "Could we come in? I think it would be better than standing out here."

"I suppose so," Feith said grudgingly, and led the way upstairs.

The very first sight to greet Adams as he entered Feith's apartment was Kate Shaw. *Desperate Gullibility* lay face down on a coffee table in the middle of the room. The photograph on the book jacket, as Adams had noticed before, was remarkably good.

Adams took a deep breath and forced himself to make a slow survey, just as the police manual prescribed.

First on his left was a closed door, possibly to a closet, then a narrow wall and an open door through which Adams saw a rumpled bed. Feith moved abruptly to that door and shut it. An odd gesture, Adams thought, but he made no comment.

Beyond the bedroom were low shelves containing books and a stereo set. On the wall above were photographs of Feith holding a gun and standing beside a dead deer in one, a dead bear in the other. Through another open door at the opposite end of the room Adams saw a kitchen sink. Next came a desk constructed of cement blocks and a board and bearing an electric typewriter holding a piece of paper. Before the desk was a typing chair. Beside it was an easy chair, and then another low bookcase between the two windows in the front wall. Over the bookcase was a rack for guns. It had spaces for three guns but only held two, a rifle and a double-barreled shotgun.

Another armchair and more bookshelves completed the circuit.

In the center of the room a couch faced the windows and coffee table. On the table, in addition to Kate's book, were a text called *An Introduction to Modern Physics*, an ashtray containing four cigarette butts, and a glass with a small amount of what looked like flat beer in it.

Feith sat in the chair beside the desk and said, "What do you want?" He did not invite the policemen to sit down.

Adams examined the son and heir with interest. Feith was about thirty, heavyset, jowled, and balding. His thin lips turned down at the corners, giving him an ill-tempered expression that accorded well with his speech so far. He was wearing a pajama shirt, pants, and shoes without socks.

"I'm afraid I have bad news, Mr. Feith. Your parents are dead."

Feith stared. "Dead?" He cleared his throat. "Both of them?"

Adams nodded.

Feith pressed his eyes with the thumb and forefinger of one hand. When he let his hand drop, his eyes were a little red and damp, and the wrinkles around them showed up strongly.

That, Adams thought cynically, is the way to make yourself look shocked and saddened. But he realized that he had taken an instant dislike to Feith, so he kept silent and expressionless.

"Was it a wreck?" Feith asked. Then he frowned and his voice took on a puzzled note. "But they were going to stay here."

"Stay here?" Adams inquired.

"Yes. Usually they go to the cabin in the mountains at Thanksgiving for a last weekend before the heavy snow falls. But this year Dad said the trip was becoming too hard, and they would stay home until summer.

"But what is all this? Why don't you just tell me what happened? I'm not going to faint, if that's what you're waiting for."

"It is not only a matter of breaking the news gently, Mr. Feith. We came to ask some questions. You see, your parents were killed."

"Killed?" Feith said doubtfully. "You mean somebody killed them?"

"That's right. Could you tell us what you did this evening from, let's say, six o'clock on?"

Feith sat up with a jerk. "What are you implying?" he barked.

"Nothing, Mr. Feith," Adams said in his flat, official voice. "Your parents were murdered. We have to ask all the obvious people all the obvious questions."

By the set of his mouth and the tone of his voice, Feith was not mollified. But he did answer.

"I spent the evening here, alone," Feith began confidently. Then he faltered. "Uh, I mean, alone except for a little while. My brother-in-law dropped in—oh, and I went for a walk at, I don't know, eleven or eleven-thirty," he ended with renewed assurance.

Adams made no comment, but he took himself to the other armchair, signed to Kivallo to sit on the couch, and settled in for a long session.

"What's your brother-in-law's name?"

"Evans. John Evans."

"You have only one sister."

"Yes."

"What time did Evans get here?"

Feith squirmed. "Oh, I don't know. About eight, I guess."

"How long did he stay?"

"An hour, maybe."

"No one else came to visit, and you visited no one?"

"Uh, yes. That's right."

Adams waited, staring at Feith. Feith looked away.

"Did you meet anyone while you were out walking?"

"No."

"You said you were here all evening. Starting when?"

Feith seemed surprised, but he answered, "Five, five-fifteen, I suppose."

"What about dinner?"

"Dinner? What about it?"

"Did you eat here?"

"I did," Feith said belligerently. "I made myself a grilled cheese- and-bacon sandwich. I ate a carrot with it. I also drank a glass of beer. Afterwards I had exactly one piece of chocolate candy and one cup of coffee with milk, not cream, and sugar. Satisfied?"

"What time did you eat?" Adams asked with no change in tone.

"Oh, for—!" Feith began. Then he took a deep breath and went on with exaggerated patience: "The six-o'clock news began a minute or two before I began cooking my sandwich and ended while I was making coffee. Is that precise enough for you?"

"What time did you take your walk? How long were you out?"

"Strange as it may seem," Feith said sarcastically, "I did not time myself."

"Could you give me an estimate?" Adams asked imperturbably.

"About eleven," Feith snapped.

"How long were you out?"

"Twenty, twenty-five minutes."

"And Evans arrived about what time?"

Feith fidgeted again, then adopted a candid air.

"I'm afraid I just didn't notice. After eight, I think. And he was gone before nine-thirty."

"So you did notice the time that he left."

"Well, uh, I went into the bedroom not long after he left and saw the clock."

"You are sure he was here for approximately an hour?"

Feith's discomfort was growing. He looked at the wall,

crossed his legs, looked at Adams, pulled at his earlobe.

"Uh, I think so."

"Longer than half an hour?"

"Yes, yes, yes. I suppose so."

"Less than an hour and fifteen minutes?"

"How many times do I have to say I don't know?" Feith demanded heatedly. "I don't know. I do not know. I do not know. Got it?"

"And no one else visited you?"

"No. No one. What does it matter anyway? If you are trying to show that I don't have an alibi, I can save you the trouble. I have no alibi—Oh. You mean the murders were committed around nine o'clock. Is that it?"

"Is someone here now?" Adams went on as if he had not heard Feith's outburst or question. "Is someone in the bedroom?"

"No," Feith snapped.

"Do you mind if I look around?"

Feith hesitated. "No. I mean, no, you can't look around." His voice became angry again. "Have you got a warrant? You can't just prowl through people's homes without cause, you know."

"We have cause," Adams said, "and we can get a warrant if we have to."

"Go get it, then."

"Mr. Feith, you're making things hard for yourself," Adams counseled. "If you try to prevent us from looking around, we will have to assume that there is something here that you're afraid to let us see."

"Draw any damn conclusion you like," Feith answered sulkily.

"Be sensible, Feith," Adams expostulated. "This is a murder case."

"Oh, you be sensible!" Feith rejoined. "I didn't murder my own mother and father, for heaven's sake!"

Adams stared in awe. Now it was his turn for exaggerated patience.

"Mr. Feith, we are policemen. We are working on a murder case. You must see that we cannot believe your unsupported assertion."

"I don't care what you believe."

The time had come, Adams decided, to lose his temper. He leaped from the chair, took a step toward Feith, then pulled up short, leaning forward slightly as if barely holding himself in check.

"Goddamn it, Feith!" He did not shout, but made his voice low, hard, and menacing. "Quit fooling around. I don't hunt for sport. I exterminate vermin. I'm after a murderer, and you are becoming suspect number one. If you didn't do it, get out of my way or I'll smash you like a cockroach."

It was a little melodramatic, Adams judged, but it seemed to work.

"Oh, all right," Feith muttered. "Rummage around if you want."

"Keep an eye on him, Kovallo," Adams said in the same hard tone, and flung away into a rapid tour of the apartment.

No one was in or under the bed, in the bathroom or in either the bedroom or living-room closet. All windows were locked on the inside, and there was no other exit except the door that led from the living room to the hall.

Adams went around again more slowly, searching thoroughly. He opened every drawer, pawed through clothing, examined bottles and boxes in the medicine chest and kitchen cabinets. He even took down books and thumbed through them. Feith's taste ran to adventure stories, guns and hunting—and France. He owned a large collection of guides, histories, and novels, some in English and some in French, which Feith said was his. Finding nothing, he returned to and a tape-recorded teach-yourself French course.

"Thinking of skipping to Europe?" Adams asked.

Feith adopted a long-suffering tone. "I spent the summer before last in France and I was planning to go again next summer, if you don't mind."

"I'll let you know."

The rifle in the rack was .30 caliber, the shotgun was 12 gauge. There were boxes of ammunition for both, and also a box of .22-caliber shells, but not a single .44-caliber bullet. There was no muddy or bloodstained clothing. If Feith had a cache of marijuana, Adams couldn't find it.

On the other hand, he did note a few matters of interest.

The double bed was more rumpled than seemed likely if Feith had been quietly reading the paperback science-fiction novel that lay open on the pillow. On each of the bedside tables was an empty glass smelling faintly of liquor. In the bathroom, two large towels were damp. In the kitchen, an almost full fifth of bourbon and an empty quart of beer stood on the counter beside the sink. Two of the cigarettes in the ashtray on the coffee table had filter tips and two did not.

Adams went to stand before Feith, hands on hips, and asked roughly, "Who's your bed partner, Feith?"

Feith turned his head away. "I don't have to answer questions like that."

"You may," Adams said stonily.

He remained standing over Feith and slammed questions at him.

Feith needed money, didn't he? What time had Evans arrived? Where was the third gun that belonged in the rack on the wall? How much did he expect to inherit from his parents? What did he do for a living? Was it usual for John Evans to drop in? How many guns did he own? Had he hated his parents? Who drank the second glass of whiskey and used the second damp towel?

After half an hour, Adams went out and searched the MG plant himself before Feith once more and to ask crudely, "Do you only screw in your double bed, or have you figured out how to do it in bucket seats?"

"You can't talk to me that way," Feith complained.

"No? Stop me," Adams challenged.

Feith looked away and said nothing.

The questions resumed. Adams asked everything he had asked before. Sometimes he pursued related topics: Feith's job, income, and prospective inheritance. Sometimes he changed subjects rapidly: Feith's guns, Evans's taste in drinks, the time of Feith's evening stroll.

None of Feith's answers changed; none contradicted any other. Only his manner changed. His confidence grew. He no longer fidgeted when Adams asked about Evans's visit.

At the end of another half hour, Adams gave up. He did run through the whole set of questions once more, but merely to put Feith's statement into coherent order. He paid minimal attention to Feith's answers, only noting that they remained the same as before. He thought back over Feith's complete performance, trying to ferret out what he had missed. He had missed something, he was sure, or Feith wouldn't have relaxed.

Feith was twenty-eight and had never married. He held a master's degree and taught science at Thorpe High School, earning $9,600 a year. He claimed not to know how much wealth his parents had possessed, how much he would inherit, or even if his parents had made wills. He admitted without apparent reluctance that relations with his father had not been warm, but asserted that he and his mother had been close.

With no greater reluctance, Feith admitted that he would welcome any money he inherited. He was part owner of a bookstore specializing in scientific texts, and the store, he volunteered, was losing money. He named one Thomas Fredericks as his partner.

Feith stated that he owned four guns. The two on view in the apartment he used for hunting. Missing from the rack was a .22-caliber rifle which he said he kept at the Rifle Club's shooting range, along with a .22 target pistol. He did not own and never had owned a .44-caliber handgun or rifle. After some argument, he handed over the key to his locker at the shooting range.

Feith continued to deny having had any visitors except John Evans. He asserted that he himself had drunk from both glasses in the bedroom. "I forgot I had a glass," he said, "and got a second one when I wanted a refill." He remained vague about the times of John Evans's visit and of his evening walk. He said that he had worked on preparing an examination—the page in the typewriter was half-filled with questions about physics—and had devoted the rest of the evening to light reading.

Feith declared that he had not killed his parents. He said he did not know who had. He said that, so far as he knew, he and his sister were the only ones who would inherit from his parents. He said that he knew of no one, including himself and his sister, who had hated his parents enough to kill them.

Adams made something of a production out of gathering glasses from the bedroom, bottles from the kitchen, and the ashtray from the living room. They would all be fingerprinted, he announced. Feith did not appear concerned.

"There had better not be prints on these from anyone but you and Evans," Adams said threateningly.

"There won't be, unless you plant some," Feith said nastily.

Adams marched out with firm tread and stern mien, but in the patrol car he slumped back and closed his eyes.

"All I needed to make this case interesting," he said tiredly, "was a suspect who goes out of his way to make sure he doesn't have an alibi."

"Yeah," Kovallo said sympathetically.

"Comments, Kovallo? Did you notice anything that I missed?"

"No, sir. Except I wonder if part of Feith's trouble is that he doesn't have a girlfriend, but a boyfriend."

Adams sat up. "Very good, Kovallo. That would explain . . . or would it? Is it really worth being suspected of murder in order to keep homosexuality secret, even from a couple of cops?"

"He's a teacher," Kovallo said.

"Yes," Adams said dubiously. "But what is the school going to do to him, as long as he keeps his hands off the kids? Besides, simply saying that a male friend visited him is hardly grounds for dismissal.

"Maybe he made his denial before he realized that he needed an alibi," Adams went on, thinking aloud. "Then he might have stuck to it, fearing that changing his story would make us wonder just what kind of friendship he was talking about.

"No. It won't do. The questions that really bothered him were the ones about Evans's visit, and that doesn't fit at all."

"Maybe he's sleeping with his sister's husband," Kovallo suggested.

Adams half turned and stared. "I don't think I would ever have thought of that," he said respectfully. "Are you on the promotion list, Kovallo?"

"No, sir. I failed the sergeants' test."

"Take it again, Kovallo. Take it again. The way the times they are a-changing, we are going to need you in the Inspectors' Bureau."

Kovallo looked at him suspiciously, but Adams had intended no sarcasm.

"Let's go, Kovallo. Captain Vogel's waiting."

CHAPTER 9

Vogel was sitting in Adams's chair glowering at papers spread on the top of the desk.

"Sorry to keep you waiting, Captain."

"I haven't been here long," Vogel said, "and I had plenty to do."

Adams leaned over and saw that the papers were the large sheets on which Thorpe Police Department schedules were made up.

"We were just getting caught up on the overtime from the demonstrations," Vogel said mournfully. "Now these murders of yours have racked up some more. I had to call in two extra men tonight, and," he finished accusingly, "you're sure to need help tomorrow."

"I'd offer to help out," Adams said with a grin, "but I have the feeling I'm going to be busy for the next couple of days."

"I make the jokes around here, when there are any to be made, which there aren't," Vogel grumbled. He pushed the papers into a stack and continued with no change of tone, "The Evanses told a pack of lies."

"Great," Adams said dryly. "So did Feith."

"He did, did he?" Vogel said thoughtfully. "Maybe that will be a break for us."

Adams said, "Maybe." He didn't sound hopeful.

Vogel tipped back the chair and put his feet on the desk. "I didn't press the Evanses very hard, for a couple of reasons. We don't have enough trustworthy facts yet to be sure, if they change their story, that they haven't told more lies."

Adams nodded. He also preferred to know most of the answers before asking questions. He had gone after Karl Feith strenuously only because Feith appeared so nervous that Adams thought—wrongly, as it turned out—that he might break down quickly.

"The other reason is also the reason I stayed around," Vogel continued. "Price is typing a report for you, but I wanted to give you my impressions in unofficial language. The Evanses' stories aren't quite the same, and they are kind of strange."

"Strange," Adams repeated hollowly. He sat heavily on the edge of the desk. "Strange, you say?"

"Yeah. You'll see. I'll tell it from the beginning.

"The Evanses live at 3963 Walnut, in that tract that was built up in the early fifties. All the houses looked the same then, but most have a different porch, or a dormer, or something distinctive now. The Evanses' doesn't have any additions, though, and it could use a coat of paint.

"Remember those public-service ads we put out a few years ago? The ones that said, 'Don't leave your house like this. It's an open invitation to a burglar,' or something of the sort?"

Adams remembered.

"Their house looked like the illustration. There was one light in the living room. One was on over the front door, and one on the garage showed plainly that the garage doors were open and one of the two stalls was empty.

"We checked out the car that was there. Top and sides were dry and underneath was wet, like the car had been out after the rain stopped but before the pavement dried. The exhaust pipe and oil pan were a little warm, like the engine had been running a couple of hours earlier. Since we got there just at one, that would be around eleven. An interesting time, no?"

"Yes," Adams said. "Were the tires in good condition?"

"They looked okay to me. Why?"

Adams described the tracks that had been found near the murder site.

"That is kind of weird, but the tires I saw weren't bald."

Adams shrugged.

"After we finished with the car, we went and rang the bell and found out somebody was home, after all. When she saw Price's uniform, she turned white and kind of moaned, 'John. Is John hurt?'

"Well, that's a pretty common reaction when cops arrive at the door in the middle of the night, so I went into my routine of soothing noises and emphatically repeated a few times that it was her mother and father I was there to talk about.

"After a while, she let us in and answered some questions without seeming to notice them. She allowed as how she was Mrs. Evans and that the 'John' she referred to was her husband. She said that he wasn't home and that she didn't know where he was. She also said that John was driving his own car, that the one in the garage was hers, and that she had stayed home the whole night with her kids, aged six and four.

"Only then—you understand, these were my impressions at the time—only then did she seem to absorb what I had said earlier.

"'My mother and father?' she said. 'What happened to them?'

"I told her they were dead. She mumbled, 'Oh, God,' and things like that. I heard the word 'accident' and then something that sounded like 'They were not going to go.'

"'Go where?' I said.

"'It's so sad,' she said, giving me a real tragic look. 'Mom told me they wouldn't go up to the cabin this year. She said Dad was getting too old to make the drive at this time of year.'"

"Karl Feith told me the same thing," said Adams.

"Make anything of it?"

"No."

Vogel shrugged and continued, "I started to ask another

question about the cabin, but she interrupted, 'Please tell me what happened? Are they both dead?'

"I said, 'Yes, ma'am.'

"She got pinch-faced, but she didn't look near as much like she was going to faint as she did when she first saw us at the door, so I went on and said they had been killed.

"'Killed?' she said, like the word didn't tell her anything. 'What do you mean?'

"'They were shot,' I said.

"She gave us some more oh-gods, and then a car drove into the garage. A minute later, John Evans walked in. It was twenty-four minutes past one by my watch."

The two men silently compared timepieces. Both showed 3:17.

"Well, when Evans walked in, Mrs. Evans jumped up, threw her arms around him, and said, 'John, John. Mother and Father are dead. Somebody shot them.' She said 'shot' like she couldn't believe it.

"Things got a little confused then, with them and me all talking at once. Price took down most of the words, but I wanted to tell you about what I saw.

"The first thing was that Mr. and Mrs. Evans were hanging on to each other like . . . I don't know what, but *not* like an old married couple. Which isn't such a hot description, but keep it in mind for what follows.

"I cut through the babble by saying Evans's name loudly, and they both shut up. And then Mrs. Evans let go of him like she was dropping him. She looked like she had made a mistake."

Adams frowned and began to ask a question, but Vogel went on.

"I once saw a girl run up to a soldier in a railroad station, grab him, start to kiss him, and then realize he wasn't her guy. Mrs. Evans looked like that.

"The next thing," Vogel said, "was even more striking. I asked Evans where he had been. He said he visited his brother-in-law Karl Feith around eight o'clock. He was getting set to say more, but he stopped. Mrs. Evans was giving him a look that said, plain as day, 'Liar.' He saw it, and he got a look on his face like—well, like somebody who had just been caught in a lie— What's the matter with you?"

Adams had hit the desk with his fist and muttered something under his breath.

"Feith told me exactly the same thing," he said bitterly, "and he looked like a liar, too. Now what in hell are they playing at?"

"Got me," said Vogel. "Evans said he saw Feith from about eight to nine. What did Feith say?"

"The same. It's lunatic. Feith hemmed and hawed and fidgeted and scratched, and none of it makes any difference since they are talking about a time a couple of hours before the Feiths were shot."

Adams paced rapidly away from the desk and then back. "Do you know what time the rain stopped?"

"Not exactly. Around eight-thirty."

"So all the tracks up at the Feiths' could have been made any time after that," Adams said thoughtfully. "Dr. Waddell guessed that they were killed around eleven, and Shaw said he heard the shots a little before eleven. I'll have to pin Waddell down about time, but if his first guess was wrong, I can see a way to make sense of Shaw's story."

"You think the time of the murders was faked?"

"It's possible, at least."

"Maybe so. Do you think the Evanses and young Feith worked together?"

"That's possible, too."

"Yeah." Vogel sounded unconvinced. "But why fake the time, and then give themselves alibis for a different time?"

"Reasonable doubt," Adams said. As Vogel's eyebrows rose, Adams went on, "A jury would have to vote for acquittal if it was simply baffled. I've already wondered if Mark Shaw's story was intended to create so much confusion no one would be able to tell what was true and what was false. Maybe these alibis that aren't alibis are supposed to do the same thing."

"Give it a rest," Vogel advised. "It sounds too complicated to me. Anyway, let me tell the remainder of my story. As you will see, Evans at least may have an alibi."

Adams grinned. "Which simply has to mean that he did it—right?"

"It has started sounding like that kind of story," Vogel agreed. "According to Evans, he left Feith about nine and went to the bar of the Lakeshore Restaurant for a beer."

"Oh, no," said Adams. "It will be too much of a muchness if I have to give him an alibi myself. Kate and I left the restaurant about that time, and I may have seen him."

"He isn't going to need you as a witness, if his story is true, because he will have half a dozen people to call on. He claims he was at the bar when he heard about the mud slide— I guess," Vogel interrupted himself as Adams's expression changed, "that you haven't heard about it."

"No," Adams said, "but if it was full of bodies and Billy the Kid-type guns, I'll quit and become a garbage man or something."

"I think," Vogel said pacifically, "that this really is just a coincidence. Because of all the rain we have had, the embankment along Lakeshore Drive began to slip. The worst of it crossed the road and sloshed into the Yacht Club's grounds right where a lot of boats are up in cradles for the winter. A patrol car and a couple of fire trucks were there for a while.

"Anyway, Evans says he was at the bar when somebody came in asking people for help, and he was one of the ones who went to the rescue. He gave me the names of some people who saw him."

"What time was that?"

"Around ten. I don't know exactly, but our log or the Fire Department's will tell you what time the first report was phoned in."

"So it does seem that Evans has an alibi," Adams ruminated. "Does he own a boat?"

"No. He says his father-in-law did, and so do some friends of his."

"Um," said Adams, still thinking about times. "Does Evans claim he stayed at the Yacht Club the whole time, from around ten until one in the morning?"

"That's what he says. And I can tell you this. He couldn't have driven out of the parking lot for most of that time. The mud partially blocked the entrance, and the patrol car I mentioned blocked the road. That was meant to keep traffic out, but it kept cars in at the same time.

"Speaking of cars," Vogel added, "I looked over Evans's on my way out. His tires aren't badly worn, either."

"Three bald tires," Adams said, shaking his head. "They and that fantastic gun keep bothering me. It's as if the killer flaunted them in our faces." He shrugged. "Oh, well, it's early days still. Did you get anything else from the Evanses?"

"Routine stuff. He's twenty-nine, she's twenty-six. They have been married six or seven years. I didn't ask for precise dates, but I got the idea that she was pregnant when they got married.

"Evans works at Kruger's Ford dealership on Main Street. He says he makes about ten thousand a year. She doesn't have a job. They said they will be glad to inherit some money—they didn't put it that way, but it's what they meant—but they claimed they don't know how much her parents had or how much they left to anyone.

"Both of their cars, by the way, are Fords. His is last year's model and has only six thousand miles on the counter, which makes me think it was probably a demonstrator that he bought when this year's models came out. It's a green-and-white two-door hardtop.

"Hers is three or four years older and has been driven nearly sixty thousand miles. It's a blue four-door sedan in good condition except for a big dent in the left-rear— *Now* what's the matter?" Vogel exclaimed.

Adams's heart had suddenly started pounding and he had to take a deep shaky breath. "A blue four-door Ford sedan with a big dent in the left-rear fender," he said carefully.

"That's right. What about it?"

"Just this," Adams said through his teeth. "That car or its twin came within six inches of killing Kate and me tonight."

Tersely he described the too narrow escape from collision during the drive toward the Feiths' home a little after 11 P.M.

"Is Kate all right?"

"I guess so, except for having been scared out of about ten years of her life, as I was."

"I can imagine," Vogel said sympathetically. But he hadn't been there and his mind's eye didn't insist on seeing two speeding cars all but touching. Reassured about Kate, he went on in a satisfied tone: "Well, well, well. Our Mrs. Evans deposes that she was home the whole evening. Being a good mother, she couldn't leave two young children, she says. But you saw what sure sounds like her car, and at a place and time that are very, very interesting."

"Yes," said Adams.

"Meantime, Mr. Evans was jaunting around from before eight until after one. He and Karl Feith both say that they had a chummy little get-together from eight to nine. Then Evans went off to spend several hours under the eyes of a bartender and anybody else who happened to be frequenting a public place. And what does young Mr. Feith say he did for the next few hours?"

"Ahh," Adams said disgustedly. He outlined Feith's story, ending with Kovallo's suggestion about just how chummy Feith and Evans might be.

"Good Lord! What an imagination— Good Lord!" Vogel's eyes opened wide. "Is it possible that he's right?"

"Why not?" said Adams.

Vogel considered the question for a moment. "I guess I'm old-fashioned. It seems to me that there ought to be a reason. What's Feith like?" he asked with unprofessional curiosity in his voice.

"He doesn't lisp or wear sequins," Adams said. "He's close to six feet, weighs a hundred and seventy or eighty pounds. Getting flabby. Dark brown hair and eyes. Prominent chin and nose. He's nervous, irritable, given to petulance, and I know a lot of other men who aren't swish that I could say the same things about. What are the Evanses like?"

"He's close to my size. Six foot one or a little more and around two hundred and twenty pounds. He looks like an ex-athlete going to pot. Blond, blue-eyed, kind of a baby face. He doesn't have many wrinkles. He looks like he is generally pretty easygoing—placid, even—though he was pretty nervy when I saw him.

"Mrs. Evans has dark hair and eyes and a definite nose and chin. She looks older than her husband. She has deep lines beside her nose and mouth. I'd say she was generally pretty tense, although it's possible that she was wildly off-balance tonight. She's five foot five or thereabouts. I don't know what she weighs. She looks skinny to me."

Adams grinned. The conclusion was perfectly useless as description. Vogel's idea of a svelte woman was his own wife, athletic director at the Y.W.C.A., who was not fat, by any means, but a solid one hundred and sixty pounds.

"Lighter than Kate?" Adams asked.

Vogel thought Kate was skinny, and would think so until she gained at least thirty pounds. He had once said as much, and had been surprised when they laughed at him.

"Never mind. You can see for yourself soon enough," he said with a tolerant smile. "Anything else I can tell you?"

"No, sir. I think that will do for now. And thanks for the assistance."

"Don't thank me. I work here, too, you know. For tomorrow," he went on brusquely, "I have told Logan to be here at eight, but you'll be in charge. Crane is assigned to you for the duration, and you can have some men out of the morning shift if you need them."

"That should be enough, I think."

Vogel yawned hugely. "Whew. I'm too old for these hours. I'm going home to bed before I get any older."

CHAPTER 10

Captain Vogel's yawn had been contagious, and Adams would have been glad to be on his way to bed. Instead, having released Kovallo, Adams took the unmarked police car he used on business and drove uphill once more. The clouds had not yet produced the rain they promised, but they had settled well down on The Hill, making the roads slick and drastically limiting visibility. The mist was so thick that when Adams turned in at the Feiths' driveway, he couldn't see the house, only a ghostly glow of lights.

"Inspector!" Sergeant Crane said in surprise as Adams entered. "I didn't hear your car."

Crane was watching Turner and Warren slowly pack their equipment away. The faces of all three were gray with fatigue, their voices hoarse and flat.

"Have you taken any breaks?" Adams asked in concern.

"Yes, sir. Coffee was sent up, and we all had bag lunches tonight."

When the University was in session, two coffee shops remained open through the night. On holidays, they closed early and policemen had to carry sandwiches.

"I let most of the men go when the fog came down," Crane continued. "Turner and Warren had finished outside by then. They just finished here a few minutes ago."

"All right. Fill me in."

"Yes, sir. We made casts and photographs of the various tracks. As you thought, the tire that made the marks near the park entrance was the same as one of the ones that parked down below. One set of foot tracks came up from where the car parked and toward the back of the house but disappeared where the lawn begins. If the guy kept on the way he was going, he would have ended up at the corner over there, half a dozen steps from the front door.

"You have seen part of the other set—the running and slipping tracks—that start the other side of the lawn and go toward where we found the gun. They continue in a shallow arc around the house, along the edge of the lawn, and then down to the spot where the car parked."

"We think he was wearing oversize galoshes, Inspector," Warren interjected. "They were size fifteen, but it looks to us like they were too big for the shoes inside."

"How much too big? Can you tell?"

"Not really, sir. I guess they would have to be at least a couple of sizes too big to show at all, but the difference might be a lot more."

"What about the killer's weight?"

"Hard to tell in that muck, sir," said Turner. "We tried to make some tests, but about all we can say is that he weighed more than a hundred and fifty and probably less than two twenty, maybe a good deal less."

"All right," Adams said. Nothing was to be gained by regretting that the range was wide enough to include two-thirds of the adult population of Thorpe.

"Anything else?"

"Not outside," Crane said. "I looked through the paper on the floor in the study and found a few things. A carbon copy of Feith's will, for one."

"Good. What does it say?"

"Leaving aside small bequests to charities, everything goes to his wife if she survives him, and is split between the two children if she doesn't. I expect the lawyers will have fun fighting over who died first."

	a	b	c	d	e	f	g	h	i	j	k	l	m	n	o	p	q	r	s	t	u	v	w	x	y	z
A	A	B	C	D	E	F	G	H	I	J	K	L	M	N	O	P	Q	R	S	T	U	V	W	X	Y	Z
B	B	C	D	E	F	G	H	I	J	K	L	M	N	O	P	Q	R	S	T	U	V	W	X	Y	Z	A
C	C	D	E	F	G	H	I	J	K	L	M	N	O	P	Q	R	S	T	U	V	W	X	Y	Z	A	B
D	D	E	F	G	H	I	J	K	L	M	N	O	P	Q	R	S	T	U	V	W	X	Y	Z	A	B	C
E	E	F	G	H	I	J	K	L	M	N	O	P	Q	R	S	T	U	V	W	X	Y	Z	A	B	C	D
F	F	G	H	I	J	K	L	M	N	O	P	Q	R	S	T	U	V	W	X	Y	Z	A	B	C	D	E
G	G	H	I	J	K	L	M	N	O	P	Q	R	S	T	U	V	W	X	Y	Z	A	B	C	D	E	F
H	H	I	J	K	L	M	N	O	P	Q	R	S	T	U	V	W	X	Y	Z	A	B	C	D	E	F	G
I	I	J	K	L	M	N	O	P	Q	R	S	T	U	V	W	X	Y	Z	A	B	C	D	E	F	G	H
J	J	K	L	M	N	O	P	Q	R	S	T	U	V	W	X	Y	Z	A	B	C	D	E	F	G	H	I
K	K	L	M	N	O	P	Q	R	S	T	U	V	W	X	Y	Z	A	B	C	D	E	F	G	H	I	J
L	L	M	N	O	P	Q	R	S	T	U	V	W	X	Y	Z	A	B	C	D	E	F	G	H	I	J	K
M	M	N	O	P	Q	R	S	T	U	V	W	X	Y	Z	A	B	C	D	E	F	G	H	I	J	K	L
N	N	O	P	Q	R	S	T	U	V	W	X	Y	Z	A	B	C	D	E	F	G	H	I	J	K	L	M

O	O	P	Q	R	S	T	U	V	W	X	Y	Z	A	B	C	D	E	F	G	H	I	J	K	L	M	N
P	P	Q	R	S	T	U	V	W	X	Y	Z	A	B	C	D	E	F	G	H	I	J	K	L	M	N	O
Q	Q	R	S	T	U	V	W	X	Y	Z	A	B	C	D	E	F	G	H	I	J	K	L	M	N	O	P
R	R	S	T	U	V	W	X	Y	Z	A	B	C	D	E	F	G	H	I	J	K	L	M	N	O	P	Q
S	S	T	U	V	W	X	Y	Z	A	B	C	D	E	F	G	H	I	J	K	L	M	N	O	P	Q	R
T	T	U	V	W	X	Y	Z	A	B	C	D	E	F	G	H	I	J	K	L	M	N	O	P	Q	R	S
U	U	V	W	X	Y	Z	A	B	C	D	E	F	G	H	I	J	K	L	M	N	O	P	Q	R	S	T
V	V	W	X	Y	Z	A	B	C	D	E	F	G	H	I	J	K	L	M	N	O	P	Q	R	S	T	U
W	W	X	Y	Z	A	B	C	D	E	F	G	H	I	J	K	L	M	N	O	P	Q	R	S	T	U	V
X	X	Y	Z	A	B	C	D	E	F	G	H	I	J	K	L	M	N	O	P	Q	R	S	T	U	V	W
Y	Y	Z	A	B	C	D	E	F	G	H	I	J	K	L	M	N	O	P	Q	R	S	T	U	V	W	X
Z	Z	A	B	C	D	E	F	G	H	I	J	K	L	M	N	O	P	Q	R	S	T	U	V	W	X	Y
	A	B	C	D	E	F	G	H	I	J	K	L	M	N	O	P	Q	R	S	T	U	V	W	X	Y	Z
	25	24	23	22	21	20	19	18	17	16	15	14	13	12	11	10	09	08	07	06	05	04	03	02	01	00
	26	27	28	29	30	31	32	33	34	35	36	37	38	39	40	41	42	43	44	45	46	47	48	49	50	51
	77	76	75	74	73	72	71	70	69	68	67	66	65	64	63	62	61	60	59	58	57	56	55	54	53	52
	78	79	80	81	82	83	84	85	86	87	88	89	90	91	92	93	94	95	96	97	98	99				

"Um," Adams said. "You didn't find Mrs. Feith's will?"

"No, sir. The name of an attorney in Thorpe is on his. Maybe the same one drew up hers."

Adams nodded and added another item to the long list of questions still to be pursued.

"All right. Go on."

Crane held out a thick folder and said, "Income-tax returns. I haven't really studied them, but just glancing through I can see that they have been paying Uncle Sam more than I make. These are joint returns for the last six years, and they had an income of around a hundred thousand bucks in every one of them. He got a pretty hefty salary, and the rest of it came from stocks and bonds and rent. Then there are some insurance policies. It looks to me like the heirs will get a bundle.

"One last thing," Crane said in a tone that made Adams glance sharply at him. "More funny business, I guess."

Crane opened an envelope and drew out two pieces of paper which he handed to Adams.

"These were under the blotter on Feith's desk in the study. The big one had the dead man's fingerprints on the front, none on the back. The little one didn't have any prints on it at all."

The big one was an 8½-by-11-inch sheet of photocopy paper bearing the material reproduced on pages 76 and 77.

The little one was half the size of the larger, but was also a photocopy of typewritten matter. It looked like this:

```
22 Nov.

1 4/1 2/0
9/3 9/2 1
1 3/0 1/2
5/2 4/1 0
0 4/0 0/2
2/0 3/4 7
4 2/1 7/0
7/2 6/4 4
0 6/4 1/1
5/5 9/6 4
6 1/9 1/5
6/7 7/1 2
6 2/1 9/0
8/9 4/3 0
9 6/4 3/9
3/0 9/1 8
1 0/4 5/1
6/0 3/0 7
___________

8-7-8-3-6-3
```

The slashes between numbers and the line drawn through the sum had not been part of the original material, but had been added to the copy with a crayon or felt-tip pen.

"You know what they are, Inspector?"

"I know what this one is," Adams answered, tapping the larger sheet. "It's called a Vigenère tableau and it's a sort of super-duper Captain Marvel decoder ring. I don't remember just how it works, but the idea is that it gives you a lot of different letters to substitute for each letter in the message you want to encipher—'e' might come out 'z' one time, 'o' the next, 'f' the next, and so on.

"The block of letters and numbers is presumably for turning the letters of a cipher message into numbers. And this"—he tapped the smaller sheet—"appears to be a completed cipher message."

"Secret messages!" Crane exclaimed.

"I'm told," Adams said mildly, "that some people play with cryptograms the way others do crosswords and various kinds of puzzles."

But Crane was not to be diverted so easily as that.

"And some people aren't playing when they do then," he said. "Spies, for instance. Remember all the excitement there was at the research center Feith headed. Remember the stuff that was stolen, and that foreign student who killed himself. Remember—"

"Why would anyone steal from the center if a spy was already in charge of the place?" Adams interrupted.

"Well, uh, maybe there were two sets of spies."

"Sure. Or three, or four. It's the great game, after all."

"Sir?"

"That's what Kipling called spying."

"Oh. Yeah. Well, maybe the theft, and then the demonstrations and the publicity put Feith in danger of exposure, and maybe somebody was afraid he would talk if he was arrested."

Adams's reluctance to entertain the notion of espionage was as strong as Crane's enthusiasm, but he didn't wish to give the appearance of rejecting the idea out of hand.

"You could be right," he said, returning the papers. "We will have to find someone to decipher the message before we can say if it's something for us to worry about. Until then, there's plenty to keep us busy."

It sounded a lot like what it was, an unsuccessful effort to change the subject gracefully, but it was the best Adams could do at something after four in the morning. He rushed on to outline the results of his and Vogel's interviews with the Feiths' children, which served at least to occupy Crane's attention until Turner and Warren finished packing their equipment. Then Adams shooed them all out, with orders to go home and get what sleep they could. Adams stayed behind to make a quick tour of the house, paying particular attention to entrances and reading matter.

He tested all the windows and doors on the ground floor. Every window was locked from the inside. Every door, even the one between the kitchen and garage, had a bolt that could probably not be fiddled with from outside, certainly not quickly. Only the bolt of the front door was thrown back. It appeared that, as Adams had thought, the killer had been admitted by the front door and had let himself out the same way.

Adams also scanned bookcases. In his experience, hobbyists liked to read about their pastimes, and he hoped to find signs that Feith had been an amateur cryptanalyst.

Feith's study held mostly scientific publications, but one whole shelf was devoted to income-tax and investment guides and another was crammed with books on chess and bridge. Novels and magazines were in the living room. Upstairs, in a room that seemed to have been Mrs. Feith's retreat, were numerous political publications of a somewhat restricted range: reports of the House Committee on Un-American Activities, pamphlets from the John Birch Society and Christian Anti-Communist Crusade, such books as *The Capitalist Manifesto*, *None Dare Call It Treason*, and the works of Ayn Rand.

In no room was there a book on ciphers, codes, anagrams, or secret communications. There wasn't even a collection of crossword puzzles.

Perhaps Feith kept cryptographic material in his office on the campus. Adams added "F's off" to his notes.

That was for the future. One thing remained to be done now.

Adams drove slowly down into town and turned not left toward his apartment but right toward the lake. He passed Kate's cottage, looking determinedly straight ahead, went on a mile or so, and stopped near the entrance to the Yacht Club.

Ordinarily, Lakeshore Drive continued for another couple of hundred yards before dead-ending at an area which the

City Council kept talking about filling in to make a public beach, but which remained a marsh forty years after the dam downriver had created the lake. Now the bog seemed to have grown. The road disappeared under mud, and a long section of the Yacht Club's fence had been knocked down.

But Adams wasn't there to assess damage. He wanted to know if John Evans could have gone over or around the mud and up The Hill on foot. He saw at once that Evans, or anyone, could have done so easily.

The mud was nowhere more than a couple of feet deep. Moreover, the lower reaches of The Hill were only too steep for building, not for climbing, and the slope was covered with sturdy bushes that would have provided both handholds and effective cover. Evans need only have clambered up fifty or sixty yards and crossed the grounds of one house in order to reach Lakeview Drive. Or, if he were bold, he could have continued almost in a straight line toward the Feiths' house, cutting across yards and roads.

Adams was relieved, briefly, to see that Evans could have got along without a car. Those bald tires bothered him. It was easier to think of someone like a high-school student whose income from odd jobs was small, who replaced his tires no sooner than absolutely necessary, and who had taken his girlfriend out for a drive. A youngster who heard shots and then saw a man rushing down the hillside toward him might well release the brake and start rolling away without waiting to start an engine that was in little better condition than the tires.

Very inventive, thought Adams. He eliminated that troublesome car. He created the possibility of finding witnesses who might even be able to tell him something useful.

There was one small problem. Now he would have to imagine the murderer carting his big gun, carrying or wearing oversized galoshes, and tramping through yards reckless of wakeful householders and their watchful dogs.

He got in the car and drove back the way he had come. It

was nearly six in the morning. He would be lucky if he was able to get a full hour's sleep.

As he was repassing Kate's cottage, longing overwhelmed him. The night had promised joy and ended hellishly.

He forced his thoughts to return to the case: The first thing I need to do is to find out what game Feith and the Evanses are playing.

Mark Shaw's name came to mind unbidden. If he was playing a game. . . .

Some thoughts can't be faced in the hour before dawn. Adams concentrated on his driving.

CHAPTER 11

She held the big revolver in both hands and said, "Absurd it's true." She drove away in a blue car with a dented fender and treadless tires. He began to run. Somehow the gun had got into his hand. He ran and ran, but she was gone.

The clamor of the alarm clock woke him.

Adams stretched and yawned and grinned wryly. He didn't need an analyst's help to understand the main points of his dream.

"So much for putting Kate out of what passes for your mind— Blast!" They had made a date that he would certainly not be able to keep. He would have to call it off. "But not, you dope, at seven-fifteen in the morning," he reproved himself, pulling back his outstretched arm with a jerk.

He called her home a few minutes after nine, but got no answer. When he phoned her parents, he was told that she had left only moments before and she'd be home in a few minutes.

He couldn't wait. Business was demanding his attention. Despite his distracted state, he had set things moving with a rush as soon as he reached his desk at eight o'clock.

Inspector Logan had been detailed to take three men and look for footprints on the hillside above the Yacht Club. Sergeant Crane had been set to work making an appointment to go to the club with John Evans to "confirm," as it was tactfully put, his alibi.

When Crane reported Evans's sullen acquiescence, Adams said, "Make sure he sees Logan's squad. If he did climb The Hill, the sight may rattle him. For the rest, use your own judgment about the best approach to take. I don't object if you decide to lean on him pretty hard."

Meanwhile, Adams had read two reports he had been pleasantly surprised to find waiting on his desk. The first contained preliminary findings from autopsies. Dr. Waddell's mannerisms might be irritating but he had more than met Adams's request for speed. In other respects, his report was disappointing. It told him that the victims had died of gunshot wounds. Time of death had not been established exactly, but nothing about the corpses was inconsistent with the time of approximately 11 P.M. that could be inferred from Mark Shaw's story. Greater precision would be possible, Waddell added in a note, if Adams could determine when the victims had had dinner, for analysis of stomach contents showed that they had died three to four hours after eating a full meal.

Adams snorted. He was not about to count on finding a witness who just happened to know to the minute when the Feiths had dined—even assuming that the bodies were those of the Feiths.

Adams had been making that assumption, hoping that the F.B.I. or the State Criminal Records Office would soon provide positive identification from fingerprints. The second report did not eliminate the nagging doubt, but went far toward reducing it. Turner and Warren had evidently not gone straight home to bed, but had done some work in the police laboratory. The fingerprints they had taken from the man's body matched those on the Seven Star Diary Adams had found, those on the Vigenère tableau found in Feith's study, and most of those the technicians had taken from the books and papers in the study. The fingerprints of the woman matched those on the purse Crane had found, a few of those on books and papers in the study, and all of those picked up in the kitchen.

Adams was going to have to ride herd on those two and be sure they got some sleep, for they had stayed on in the lab long enough to receive the bullets Waddell had removed from the bodies. First tests indicated that the gun found on the Feiths' grounds was the one that had killed them. Although the fingerprints on the gun were smeared, they seemed to match none of the prints found in the house.

Adams became aware of a presence beside his desk and glanced up to find Officer Kovallo standing there in an attitude Adams could not interpret.

"Problems, Kovallo?"

"Uh, no, sir. I was wondering if you could use me."

"Sure." Adams frowned. "But you know, you can't work days and nights both."

Kovallo shifted his weight awkwardly. "Uh, I'm not scheduled to work tonight."

Adams almost laughed out loud. Poor Kovallo was struggling to find a way to volunteer without having to say so directly.

"Is this supposed to be a day off for you?"

Kovallo looked away. "Well, sir, you see, I'm not married."

"Well, I'll be—" Adams caught himself. "All right. But, Kovallo," he said in his superior-officer's voice, "on future days off you will study for the sergeants' test. Agreed?"

Kovallo settled his weight firmly on both feet and his expression became a trifle mutinous. "I'm not much of a student, Inspector."

"I'll help you, if you like."

"Oh. Okay, sir. Uh, thank you." He sounded as if he wasn't sure he was altogether grateful.

"See if you can track down the business partner Karl Feith mentioned," Adams said briskly. "Try to find somebody connected with the Boy Scouts who can let you in to look through Feith's locker at the shooting range. Find out if Evans is a member. Then get the name of Ernst Feith's lawyer from the will Crane found, and see if he drew up Mrs.

Feith's as well. If he did, ask him nicely to take time out from holiday activity to go to his office and get a copy for you."

Kovallo went to work cheerfully, leaving Adams smiling faintly. It was going to take some sweat to make Kovallo a sergeant, but a single man who volunteered to save a married one from working on a holiday was someone out of the ordinary.

Adams turned back to the job in hand. He phoned the weather bureau and learned that the rain had stopped at 8:36. The tire tracks near the Feiths' house could have been made at any time after that. Nevertheless, there wasn't much future for the notion that the time of the murders had been faked. Waddell's report made it clear that unless the Feiths had finished eating before six, they could not have been killed as early as nine o'clock.

Next, Adams went to the front desk, looked into the log, and found that the manager of the Yacht Club had reported the mud slide at 9:41. Evans could have started up The Hill before ten. Adams had already told the duty sergeant to instruct all officers to keep an eye out for a car with three severely worn tires. Now he asked for information, or mere rumors, about Karl Feith's sexual proclivities.

Returning to his desk, Adams typed a note asking the editor of the Thorpe *Gazette* to publish a request for anyone who had parked a car with bald tires on Lakeview Drive Wednesday night to inform the police—not that he expected results. The number of teenagers who would willingly tell the police about having parked anywhere to neck was probably less than one. But Adams would make all the routine motions.

At nine o'clock Adams called Captain Vogel, reported briefly on operations and plans, and sought advice on a question of protocol: How high-ranking need the Thorpe Police Department officer be who asked the Chief of the University Police Department for clearance to search Feith's office?

As Adams had hoped, Vogel said, "I'll call. Pete Love and I were lieutenants at the same time."

(Love and eight of the other ten campus cops were retired

T.P.D. officers. They had softer jobs, made more money through combining salaries and pensions, and maintained close relations with their former colleagues except when they felt taken for granted. Love had been a sergeant when Adams was a rookie and probably still thought of Adams as "Chief Adams's boy.")

"The people on overtime," Vogel said. "Let 'em go early if you can get along without them."

"Right."

After that, Adams felt free to take a moment to call Kate, with the results already reported. He made a mental note to try again, but he had no leisure to fret. Sergeant Olson came in to say, "Logan is in place, and Crane has just radioed that Evans has arrived at the Yacht Club."

"Okay, let's go."

Walking to the car, Adams examined his companion with interest, for he had not had occasion to work with "Babe" Olson before. Having a woman officer present for the interview with Mrs. Evans was good tactics. Juries had been swayed by dramatic depictions of hulking policemen browbeating a frail woman. And Sergeant Olson had a reputation as a good "nice" interrogator.

Not that she herself was frail. Far from it. She had earned her nickname with one awesome punch that kayoed a knife-wielding desperado. Men said she was as strong as an ox, and a Paul Bunyan fan bestowed the appropriate sobriquet.

Nor was she necessarily *nice*, but she knew how to put on a manner that soothed distraught witnesses and lulled unwary suspects. During interrogations in which Nasty, an antagonistic, aggressive questioner, alternated with Nice, a friendly, sympathetic one, Sergeant Olson played the latter role.

"Have you read the report on the Evanses?" Adams asked as they drove out of the parking lot.

"Yes, Inspector."

"Good. Crane has taken Evans away to work on him, leaving Mrs. Evans home alone for us to work on. Captain Vogel thought she was tense and nervous. Maybe she's always like that. Maybe something special was bothering her. For one, I think she lied about staying home all night.

"We'll play our approach by ear, but I wouldn't be surprised if I decide to be a tough guy. I owe her something if she was driving the car that nearly smacked me last night. You can be the good guy."

"All right," Olson said placidly.

"We'll take a look at her car first," Adams said as he parked. He could see from the curb all that he needed to see, but he went up close, walked all the way around the sedan, and stooped to peer at the dent in the rear fender.

"It's the same car."

"You're sure?"

Adams took a position within two feet of the damaged fender. "I'm not any closer now than I was last night. I'm sure, all right."

He felt a surge of anger, but quelled it immediately. On the job, the state of his temper was a matter of policy. He would rage, if he raged, for show and only after taking the measure of his subject.

CHAPTER 12

When she opened the door, Mrs. Evans was red-eyed, haggard, and hostile.

"Now what?" she demanded after a startled glance at the uniformed policewoman.

"Mrs. Evans, I'm Inspector Adams and this is Sergeant Olson. We would like to ask you a few questions."

"I answered questions last night. Did those other policemen take my husband away so you could get me alone?"

She's not so dumb, Adams thought.

"Why are you harassing us? You can't push us around."

She had been merely querulous at the start, but she ended on a shrill, nearly hysterical note. Adams opted for quiet reasonableness.

"Now, Mrs. Evans, we have a routine we have to follow. You stand to inherit a lot of money and naturally we have to investigate you pretty thoroughly. Then, too, if we are to catch the person who killed your parents, there are a great many things we need to know, things you may be able to help us with."

"What things?"

"Well, here's an example that may seem trivial to you, but is a troublesome loose end for us. Do you know a Mrs. Brown?"

"Do you mean the cleaning woman?"

"I don't know," Adams answered with an air of frankness. "Did a Mrs. Brown clean house for your parents?"

"Yes, she has for years. But it is simply ridiculous to suspect her of . . . of anything."

"I don't. Your father wrote her name in his diary and I didn't know why. That's the sort of problem that a member of the family can clear away at once."

"Oh, all right. Come in."

Mrs. Evans shared with her brother an ungracious manner, as well as a family likeness of nose, mouth, and chin, Adams thought.

She led the way to a neat, clean, characterless living room. "What else do you want to know?"

"To go back to Mrs. Brown, can you think of any reason why her name is in your father's appointment book?"

"No."

Adams let the abrupt monosyllable hang in the air and after a few seconds Mrs. Evans spoke again.

"Oh, well, maybe I do. I think she cleaned on Friday except at Thanksgiving, when my parents were away at the cabin. They may have arranged for her to come in this year, since they were staying home."

Having started her talking, Adams settled into a casually conversational tone. "It was unusual for them to stay home at this time of year, then?"

"Yes, they had gone up at Thanksgiving every year since they bought it."

"When was that?"

"It must have been twenty years ago, or more. I remember going there when I was very small."

"Was there a special reason why they didn't go this year?"

"I think they felt they were getting too old," she answered in a softened voice. "It's a three-hour trip each way to Crater Lake and I think that my father was becoming uncomfortable about long drives at night. My mother said last Sunday that the heavy rains had probably washed out the road—the last couple of miles are unpaved—so it was just as well they weren't going. I got the feeling she was trying to convince herself."

"So the decision wasn't final as late as last weekend?"

Mrs. Evans smiled a small, fond smile. "My mother may have thought it wasn't."

"I don't understand."

Adams understood perfectly, which was why he wanted her to stay on the subject. He could afford not to hear what she said about her father as a tyrant while he abstracted his attention to another problem.

Could it be that the murderer had not intended to murder? That he had been, say, a burglar who had not expected the Feiths to be home?

A burglar who carried that gun? Never.

Could the gun have been in the house? Adams would have to find out. But even if the . . . call him "intruder" . . . even if the intruder had thought the Feiths would be away, he would have seen the lights and discovered his error long before he entered the house. Besides, the evidence indicated that Ernst Feith had opened the front door for the killer—if the dead man was Ernst Feith.

Could it be that the Feiths had gone to their cabin after all? That some large-scale deception had been going on? That the features of the dead couple had been obliterated for a reason? Damn, thought Adams. He had been priding himself on omitting none of the routine, and he had overlooked the elementary precaution of having the cabin looked at.

". . . it was final," Mrs. Evans concluded.

Adams had no trouble reconstructing what he had not heard: Mother may have thought she was still making up her mind, but when Father made a decision . . . et cetera. He would remember that Ernst Feith had been bossy, but he was concerned now with Mrs. Evans. She had relaxed. His questions posed no threat. It was time to break the sequence, to shake her a little.

"Did your father own a gun?"

"Yes. A shotgun. It's at the cabin, I think."

"Had your mother made a will?"

The change of subject startled her, but she answered readily enough. "I think so. Mr. Brodsky, their lawyer, could tell you."

"What time did your parents usually eat dinner?"

"Dinner? What does dinner have to do with . . . with what happened?"

"It's just one of the things I need to know, ma'am."

With an air of humoring the simpleminded policeman, Mrs. Evans said, "My father generally got home about six. He would shower and they would have a cocktail before sitting down to eat about seven."

"Did your mother have a job?"

"No. Not for pay. But she was very active in . . . politics."

Adams picked up on the way she uttered the last word. "Not your sort of politics?"

"No, not really." She didn't elaborate, but she showed no sign of discomfort.

"Did you argue much?"

"We . . . differed about some things."

That was better. She didn't like that word "argue."

"What did you argue about?"

"We didn't argue," Mrs. Evans protested.

"Let's see," Adams said, pretending to consult his notes. "You're twenty-six. Married at twenty. I guess you were still in school then."

She nodded.

"Your parents disapproved, and you argued about that."

"No, no. They had wanted me to graduate, to marry a professor. It was the same year that Karl failed his orals. They were hurt. But we didn't argue. They didn't really disapprove. They were . . . disappointed, a little, that's all."

"Are you?"

"Am I what?"

"Disappointed."

She flinched. "No, no, of course not. Anyway, it's none of your business."

"Your husband doesn't make much money, does he?"

She gasped, but only in surprise. That was not the question she dreaded.

"He went out early last night and stayed out until after one in the morning. Where did he go?"

That was the right question. Mrs. Evans lowered her head and clutched the arms of her chair.

"I . . . oh . . . my husband earns enough for us to live on."

"Where did he go?" Adams insisted.

"He said . . . he said he went to Karl's, and then to the Yacht Club."

"I know what he said. I want to know what he did. Where did he go?" Adams rapped.

She buried her face in her hands. "I don't know," she moaned. "I don't know."

Adams frowned. He didn't understand her tone now. He changed tack.

"Well, then, perhaps you could tell us where *you* went."

She snapped erect and stared. Her mouth worked but no sound issued.

"You said you were here all evening." She nodded, never taking her eyes from his face. "But that wasn't true, was it?" She stared dumbly, and he said sarcastically, "You couldn't leave the children. That's what you told Captain Vogel. But that wasn't true, was it?"

"I didn't go out."

"Where did you go, Mrs. Evans?"

"I didn't go out. I didn't go out."

"What time did you go out, Mrs. Evans?"

"I didn't go out! I didn't! I didn't!" Her voice broke. "Oh, God! I didn't go out. You must believe me."

"The hell I must," Adams snapped. "I saw you."

She cringed back into the chair as if he had struck her. "No," she said. "No, you're lying!" she screamed. "If you had seen me, you would have done something last night."

"It was at the corner of University and Elm. Remember?"

She closed her eyes and turned her head away.

"I'm the guy you damned near smashed into. Remember that, Mrs. Evans?"

"I'm sorry."

Adams sat back. It was coming now.

"I—I did go out." He could see an idea coming to her. "Only for a few minutes. I was out of cigarettes."

"Oh, come on, Mrs. Evans," Adams said coldly. "You have lived in Thorpe too long to think there is any place you can get cigarettes up on Elm, or Hillside—"

Hillside. That bothered her. Hillside was one block up from the intersection of University and Elm.

"What is there on Hillside Avenue that is so important you had to leave your little children home alone at eleven o'clock?"

"Stop it!" she wailed. "Leave me alone. Go away. I don't have to answer your questions. It's nothing to do with you. My lawyer wouldn't let you treat me this way."

"Get your lawyer," Adams barked. "Go ahead, call him now. Then I'll get a warrant and lock you up as a material witness."

Her eyes opened wide. She knew as little about the actual likelihood of being imprisoned as Adams had hoped. "I'll take you away from the dear little kiddies you couldn't possibly leave alone, except at eleven o'clock at night."

Mrs. Evans dropped her head and sobbed. Adams looked at Sergeant Olson, nodded, stood up, and stamped toward the door.

"To hell with it," he flung over his shoulder. "I'll get that warrant now."

"Oh, no. Oh, please!" she cried.

Sergeant Olson moved to the arm of the chair and proffered a tissue. Adams stood near the door and watched with professional interest.

"There, there," Olson crooned. "There, there. I know it's hard, dear. He's a hard man."

Adams blinked. That was laying it on with a trowel.

Olson produced another tissue and said regretfully, "It would be terrible for the children. Policemen tramping through the house. Nightmares about prison. Fear for their mother." Her big hand patted the heaving shoulder, then gripped firmly. "You'll have to face it, dear. Chin up, now. Take it like medicine, there's a good girl."

Adams thought she had blown it. But no, she had judged accurately how much syrup Mrs. Evans could swallow.

Mrs. Evans nodded. She blew her nose. She gulped. "He's having an affair," she blurted.

"It's so awful, washing our dirty linen in public." She breathed noisily and unsteadily. "I've suspected . . . I've known for a long time. Last night was too much. The night before Thanksgiving. He said he was going to play pool—pool!"

She spat out the last word and, for the first time, raised her eyes from the floor. She looked at Adams with, he decided, contempt. He was a man, too.

"I put the children to bed. I fixed the ham. I made a pie. I came in here and sat down. I thought of all the things I should say to him when he came home." Tears flowed down her cheeks. "And then I thought I probably wouldn't say any of them because then he might leave me and— Oh, God, how I hated them!

"And then I was crying and at the same time I was thinking it would be terribly funny to go knock on her door and ask if I could play pool with them.

"And then, I don't know how, I was in the car. I really didn't want to go. I didn't want to make a scene. But I kept on driving.

"And then he wasn't there!" It was a cry of outrage. "The house was all dark and his car was nowhere around. I thought he had come home. He would find me gone and the children alone and—"

She turned to face Adams and said earnestly, "We do leave them sometimes. The dog is with them and they know that if they wake up they can call Mrs. Herbert next door. But not after midnight."

Adams couldn't decide which was stranger, her compulsion

to explain or the explanation she gave. His married friends kept telling him he would see many matters differently when he was a father. Maybe so.

"Uh-huh," he said.

Mrs. Evans wasn't listening. "He wasn't here," she said, sounding surprised even now. "I came home and he wasn't here. He didn't come and didn't come, and then the police came and, and . . . you know the rest."

Olson presented another tissue and said, "Who is she?"

"Carol Abbot. *Mrs.* Carol Abbot." She hissed the title viciously. "She's divorced but she has small children, too. You might ask her what she does about them when men come to visit her at night."

Olson let that pass. "Where does she live?"

"At 121 Hillside Avenue."

"Are you sure your husband went to see Mrs. Abbot, not your brother?"

Mrs. Evans looked up in surprise. "Why, I don't know. We—we haven't talked about last night. I assumed he made that up."

"Why?"

Mrs. Evans laughed humorlessly. "What could he say, in front of me, when a policeman asked him where he had been?"

Olson shrugged and looked at Adams.

"All right, Mrs. Evans. We will ask you to sign a formal statement another day."

Outside, Adams turned to Sergeant Olson and said appreciatively, "The Supreme Court will declare you unconstitutional one of these days, Babe."

"Well, now I know what a tough guy you can be," she rejoined with an edge to her voice that made him stare. She didn't return his gaze but strode away stiff-backed toward the car.

"Christ, I don't enjoy—umm."

Adams stopped and considered. He himself was able to play Nasty or Nice because he could, in some fashion he couldn't have explained, wall off his emotions. He wouldn't feel like a louse until later. It seemed that Olson, at least in the role of Nice, succeeded by engaging her emotions. To some degree, she had actually shared Mrs. Evan's anger, sorrow, and resentment of Adams, and she still did. It was an interesting difference in technique, and something to be borne in mind about Sergeant Olson.

He followed her slowly to the car and waited until she lit a cigarette before saying in a purely professional tone, "What did you think of her story?"

"It could be true."

"But you think not? Why?"

"I didn't say that. If she was trying to keep us from noticing that she doesn't have a shred of an alibi, her story was a pretty good effort."

Engaging her emotions didn't disengage her brain, Adams noted.

"But it could be true," Olson went on. "Sitting home alone, brooding about her husband and his floozy, getting madder and madder because he didn't come home and scareder and scareder that he wouldn't come home. Yes, she might have done just what she says she did."

"'Floozy.' What a word," Adams said lightly, and added quietly, "Don't take sides too strongly with the long-suffering wife against the abandoned divorcée, okay?"

"I wasn't," she answered indignantly. "I was only trying to put into one word what Mrs. Evans was feeling. What did *you* think of her story?"

"About what you did." He grinned tentatively at her. "Shall we see if we can get some confirmation from the floozy?"

"That's enough, now," Olson said warningly. Then she grinned in return. "You've paid me back for my 'tough guy' crack."

CHAPTER 13

Just down the street, within half a block of the Evanses' house, was a police call box where Adams phoned the station—T.P.D. policy was against discussing on radios subjects ham operators ought not overhear. He announced his new destination, requested that the state police visit the Feiths' cabin, and asked for news.

Neither Crane nor Logan had been heard from. Kovallo had gone to meet a lawyer named Brodsky and had not yet reported back. Captain Vogel had arranged that Adams could go to Ernst Feith's office whenever was convenient.

Not much titillation in that for an eavesdropper on the shortwave band, Adams thought. Nothing very useful for him, either.

Hillside Avenue comprised two short blocks running uphill from Elm Street across Hillside Terrace to Pleasant Hill Road. "On the flat," as Thorpe said, most streets were long and straight. On The Hill, they were short and curving.

When Adams had encountered Mrs. Evans the previous evening, she was on the simplest route from Hillside Avenue toward Walnut Street. But not the only route. She could have made her way eastward by zigzagging.

More to the point, she could instead have come from her parents' house, leaving Lakeview Drive about a third of the way down from the summit to follow a series of short streets that would have brought her to Elm and then to the point where Adams saw her car. The descent would have taken five to ten minutes longer that way, but would have avoided police patrols rushing to the murder site. And, of course, Mr. Evans could have gone up The Hill the same way from here.

Number 121 was a small house entirely surrounded by children. There must have been fifteen of them, all under the age of ten and all running at full tilt and yelling at full volume. The sudden stillness when Adams and Olson started along the footpath was palpable.

"The old lady who lived in a shoe," Adams murmured. "They can't all be hers, can they?"

"Not unless she pups every six months, or maybe quarterly," Olson said with a laugh.

The woman who opened the door said "Yes?" in the tone reserved for door-to-door salesmen and other nuisances. Then she caught sight of Sergeant Olson and her eyes opened wide.

"Mrs. Abbot?" She nodded and Adams displayed his badge. "I'm Inspector Adams, and this is Sergeant Olson. May we speak to you for a few minutes?"

"Why?"

"We would like to ask you a few questions."

"About what?" She wasn't hostile but she wasn't giving anything away.

"About John Evans."

Her eyes narrowed, and Adams realized she wasn't as young as he had first thought. Nearer thirty than twenty. She would turn few heads on the street, but close up those eyes might set a pulse racing.

"I don't think I—"

"Mrs. Abbot," Adams interrupted unceremoniously, "Mrs. Evans's parents were killed last night. We are trying to find out where Mr. Evans was."

"Oh!" she said. "Oh, come in."

She led them to a living room more cluttered than Mrs. Evans's had been. It wasn't littered, but a scatter of books and toys showed that it was used by some proportion of the children Adams had seen outdoors.

"Did he . . ." Mrs. Abbot let the question trail off. Adams waited politely, as if he did not know what she meant. She changed the subject. "What do you want to know?"

"Was John Evans here last night?"

"Yes."

"When?"

"I don't know exactly. From about eight to nine, I suppose."

Evans and Karl Feith said that they had been together from eight to nine. Mrs. Abbot said Evans had been with her from eight to nine. What *were* these people playing at?

Once again Adams settled himself for a long session.

"You are divorced?"

"Yes."

"Since when?"

"Last February."

"Have you been seeing Evans since then?"

Mrs. Abbot slowly shook her head. "I don't think I have to answer that."

"*Mrs.* Evans said she has suspected for a long time."

"Oh, dear." She wilted, but she rallied quickly. "I have told you about last night. I don't believe that anything else is your business."

She eyed him levelly, lips firmly together, on guard against a new low blow.

"Mrs. Abbot, this is a murder case. In a murder case, everything becomes my business."

He had trotted out the official phrase, a phrase many recalcitrant witnesses found terrible. It made her eyelids flicker, but it didn't overwhelm her. She looked at him thoughtfully—or was it calculatingly?—and said, "But—"

"Let's stick with last night." Adams wanted her talking, not arguing. "Could you be more precise about times?"

"I don't think so. The children were still up," she said as if trying to be helpful on this point at least. "They are supposed to be in bed by eight, but on holiday nights they get away with a little." She made an impatient gesture. "Sorry. That's why I know the time was around eight, but it doesn't give you any greater precision."

Adams was reminded of Mark Shaw. Big blue eyes *and* brains. Hell!

"What about the time that Evans left?"

Mrs. Abbot shrugged. "Again, I can't be exact. I do know that I got into bed within a minute of nine-thirty—I noticed that time because ordinarily I stay up a good deal later—and it took me no more than fifteen or twenty minutes to get ready for bed."

"What time does he usually come and go?"

"He . . . there was no usual time."

Adams considered her last statement. He could push her to be more explicit. Or he could take a chance, trusting his judgment that she was careful about tenses. He was in a hurry. He decided to risk it.

"And he won't be coming any more," he said flatly.

Mrs. Abbot looked away. "That's . . . clever of you."

Adams was becoming annoyed. If every question, except ones about eight-to-nine-o'clock, was to meet objections or to be answered only obliquely, this interview would take hours Adams wanted to spend elsewhere.

His efforts to hasten matters along had been remarkably unsuccessful. He had hit her with the reference to Mrs. Evans and with "murder case," and had shaken but not stunned her. He had played Sherlock Holmes, and had got away with it, but he hadn't awed her. She had understood immediately the clue that she herself had given him. His bag of tricks was nearly empty.

And yet, "was" had given him one opening. Had "clever" given him another? If she had decided he was as smart as she was, an appeal to reason might be effective.

"Mrs. Abbot," he said quietly. She looked at him attentively. "In a trial, everyone is presumed innocent. In an investigation, everyone is suspect. John Evans profits from murder. That makes him suspect.

"You give Evans an alibi. That makes *you* suspect." Her eyes went wide again. "Then you imply, but you don't say outright, that the night for which Evans needs an alibi is the last night he will be coming here."

She opened her mouth, but Adams gave her no time to argue.

"I have to ask about what would ordinarily be none of my business. I must know if you are telling the truth, or what you think is the truth. The only way I can find out is to pry."

"I. . . . all right."

She took a deep breath, turned her gaze to the space between the two police officers, and began to speak in a rapid monotone.

"I work half-time at the Ford agency, I met John, Mr.— Oh, well, I don't suppose it matters now. I met John there.

"Last spring, I broke my ankle. I couldn't drive my car. A neighbor took me to work and John brought me home sometimes.

"I was lonely. So was he."

She lifted one hand from her lap. "Oh, I know. I know. That's what all the loose women say, isn't it?" The hand dropped.

"At first, he drove me home just now and then. Later, even after my ankle healed, he would come for lunch three or four times a week. Andrea, my daughter, would be here. She only went to school in the morning last year. The children liked him. They miss . . . a father.

"Last night—" Her voice suddenly began to shake. "Last night, Philip asked me if John was going to be his new . . . his da . . . his daddy—I'm sorry!"

She clamped her eyes and jaws closed. Then her back straightened and she breathed once, tremblingly, and again, more steadily. Olson, Adams noticed, made no move to dig into her supply of tissues.

"I hadn't really thought about marrying John. I didn't want

to have to think about it. Philip . . . I had to think, then. As soon as I did, I knew I wasn't going to marry him, and when I realized that, I knew I had to . . . end it.

"It's really very ironic." Her voice, which had been almost under control, took on a forced, false brightness. "I fumbled for words to tell him gently. He was fumbling, too. We talked at cross-purposes for a while, until it finally dawned on me that we were trying to tell each other the same thing. He had to think of his own children. His wife . . .

"Well, we talked a little, and cried a little, and he went home. It's like something out of a bad movie, isn't it?" She repeated her small gesture, lifting her hand a few inches and dropping it again. "'We hadn't thought,'" she said harshly. "The saddest words, the most shameful words, that I know."

Adams could play various roles, but not minister.

"What made you decide not to marry Evans?" he asked dryly.

"I don't have reasons. The point is that I didn't have reasons *for* marrying him."

Adams returned to the question of times. She could not or would not be specific. Evans had arrived probably shortly after eight and had left somewhat after nine. Yes, he might have left at 9:10, possibly 9:05. Not earlier, she thought. She hadn't spent a full thirty minutes preparing for bed.

"You owned a car last spring, you said. Do you still own one?"

"Yes, the little red Fiat parked out front."

"Did Evans drive his own car here last night?"

"I suppose so. I didn't look."

"Which way did he go when he left, uphill or downhill?"

"I have no idea, I didn't follow him."

"You didn't watch him leave?"

"No. I didn't go to the door with him. Not last night."

Adams started over, but he was learning nothing new. When two children thundered in through the back door and demanded lunch—Mrs. Abbot called them Philip and

Andrea, and they had their mother's eyes—Adams decided to go.

"We won't take up any more of your time now, Mrs. Abbot. Thank you for your help."

Mrs. Abbot saw them to the door, politely. If she was angry at having been maneuvered into telling her story, she didn't show it.

When the door closed, Adams headed for the little red Fiat parked at the curb, although he could see at a glance that it was too small to have left the tracks near the Feiths' house. But he would go through the motions. He read the registration form on the steering column and crouched down to measure the distance between the wheels with his eye. It was her car. It was too narrow by a foot or more.

"What a day," Olson said. "Two tearjerkers before lunch are hard on my plumbing."

"Tearjerker?" Adams said. "I didn't think Mrs. Abbot was terribly brokenhearted. The dampness seemed to me to be more for her son's innocence or neediness or whatever than for the hail-and-farewell with Evans. By the way, why didn't you offer her one of your trusty tissues?"

"She wouldn't have taken it."

"No?"

"No. She wasn't going to cry in front of the cops." Olson paused. "Or any strangers." Another pause. "Or anybody, maybe."

"I take it that she wasn't quite what you expected, and that she didn't strike you as plain phony."

"I didn't expect anything in particular," Olson said without emphasis. "But if she's phony, she hides it well. What did you think of her story?"

Adams arched his eyebrow. "It could be true."

Olson made a face. "But?"

Adams went to the unmarked police car and leaned against it.

"The autopsy and Mark Shaw's evidence indicate that the

Feiths were killed shortly before eleven," he said slowly. "I have four people who are suspect in varying degrees, who have no alibis, and who keep telling mutually exclusive stories that require us to chase around trying to find out what happened between eight and nine o'clock. It's worrying."

Adams walked around the car and got into the driver's seat.

"That one is clever," he said with a nod toward Mrs. Abbot's house. "She said I was, but I wonder if I would have got heavier-handed clues to help me along if I had been dumber.

"She bowed to my powers of persuasion—or would she have found some other way, sooner or later, to give away her rights, tell me the same things, and bravely fight back the same tears?

"As for her story, it's a good one. Both women have stories that are simply grand. Can't you see a jury going absolutely catatonic over those plausible and oh-so-moving tales?"

Adams held up a finger. "One possibility is that they are all together in a plot, a carefully orchestrated mix of reasonable but uncheckable motives and actions, spiced with nonsensical conflicts for the befuddlement of investigators and jurors."

A second finger was raised. "Or somebody may have seen the advantages to be gained by befogging an already confusing family drama. Evans might have fiddled a clock here or at Karl Feith's—that isn't very likely, but you see the sort of thing I mean."

Adams made a fist and pounded softly on the steering wheel. "The third and most delightful possibility is that the stories *are* true. Not in every detail, of course. Evans can't have been in two places at once unless my high-school physics teacher was conning me. But if that foolishness can be cleared up, and if the rest is true—"

Adams was reminded again of Mark Shaw. If *his* story was true . . . Adams had passed over that possibility last night, in part because he couldn't conceive of what would follow from the premise.

"If the rest is true—what?" Olson said.

Adams grimaced. "Why, then, the whole miserable mess is pure coincidence that just happens to be helping the killer by wasting our time and distracting our attention."

CHAPTER 14

This time when Adams phoned, Crane was in.

"I suppose you have it all wrapped up for me by now," Adams said.

"No, not quite. There's still a loose end or two. For example, Evans may have an alibi. Then again, he may not."

"Crane, you forgot to turn the pages. That's where we were a couple of chapters ago. Didn't you get anything out of Evans?"

"Not much," Crane admitted. "Do you want a detailed report or just the high spots?"

"Are there any high spots? Never mind. An outline will do for now."

"Okay. We met Evans at the gate of the Yacht Club and started questioning him as soon as he got out of his car. At the same time, we kept sort of openly sneaking looks up the hillside toward Logan and his men.

"By the way, Inspector, Logan and company got all muddy, and that's about all they got. The slope has the consistency of Jell-o and it's still slipping, so footprints kind of ooze away in an hour or two. Besides, firemen and lots of other people are all over the place trying to figure out how to keep the houses up on Lakeview from sliding down to Lakeshore. There was a geologist or something from the University who gave Logan an earful about soil drainage and viscosity and like that."

"I'm glad somebody learned something today," Adams said. "According to Logan, the whole point of the lecture was that nobody has any idea how to stop The Hill from falling down, if that's what it's going to do."

Adams chuckled. He could imagine Andy Logan recording with glee that the egghead had a trunkful of big words and no notion how to solve the problem before him.

"Anyway," Crane continued, "Schmidt and I kept looking up The Hill, but we weren't having any effect on Evans that I could see. We leaned on him, like you said, but he didn't change his story. But I'll tell you this. If he had got any more nervous about the visit he claims he made to Karl Feith, he would have wet his pants."

"They are lousy liars," Adams said. "Or they want us to think they are."

"You think they are all in it together?" Crane said disbelievingly.

"We have to consider the possibility."

"Yeah. Jeez, what a case. Well, like I said, Evans got more and more antsy, but he didn't change anything he had said before. He claims he doesn't own a gun and never has. He says that he makes enough money to live on, that naturally he won't mind inheriting some, and that he didn't kill anybody to get more. He got all outraged that we would suspect him of killing his parents-in-law for money—which reminds me. I have a report from Kovallo on just how much money is involved."

"Finish Evans first."

"Right. We went round and round for a while and then went inside to the bar. You know about the public sections of the Yacht Club, Inspector?"

"I know. Members-only downstairs; bar and restaurant open to all upstairs." He and Kate had eaten their first and their latest dinners together in the Lakeshore Restaurant. It was the best one in town, a sad commentary on the others.

"Okay. Evans says he arrived around quarter past nine. The bartender agrees and so do a Mr. and Mrs. McConnell, who know Evans slightly. I talked to them on the phone a few minutes ago. They say Evans chucked down a beer practically in one gulp and ordered another, but then went out of the bar for a few minutes. When he returned, he sipped at his second beer and chatted with the McConnells until Fenley, the manager of the Yacht Club, came looking for helpers.

"Now, Fenley called us and the Fire Department before he asked for volunteers, so Evans was there at least until nine-forty-five. Fenley remembers seeing Evans then and also when people were leaving about one o'clock. He *may* have seen him other times, but he can't be sure."

"Wonderful," said Adams.

"Yeah, and that's what we are going to get from everybody. Evans gave me names of some people he saw, and when you called I had just finished talking to one of them, James Slade, who is secretary of the Yacht Club. He saw Evans all right, but he can't even make a guess at the time. He says, kind of snappishly, that he was 'too busy to look at the clock.'

"And that's how it's going to go," Crane said pessimistically. "These guys were worried about their precious boats. I guess they had some reason, since half a dozen were wrecked, but it means they weren't paying attention to who was where when."

"Probably so, but keep trying. You might strike it lucky. What happened to the McConnells?"

"He had a heart attack a couple of years ago, so they didn't volunteer to try to save anybody's boat. They left while it was still possible to drive out the gate."

"Is that all on Evans?"

"Yes. Kovallo has called in twice. He saw the lawyer, Brodsky, who was pretty helpful, for a lawyer. He gave Kovallo some interesting numbers. The Feiths owned stocks and bonds worth around a hundred thousand dollars and insurance totaling the same. The main thing is, they owned land and buildings with an *appraised* value for taxes of over three hundred thousand."

Adams whistled softly, appreciating Crane's point. In this state, appraised value was ordinarily half or less of current market value.

"So the whole estate amounts to more than eight hundred thousand dollars."

"Brodsky wouldn't say so. You know how lawyers are. Didn't want to be pinned down. Wouldn't estimate how much inheritance taxes will take. And so on. But it's a good chunk of money. Enough to kill for."

"Yes," said Adams. "What else did Kovallo get?"

"Let's see." Adams heard papers rattle. "Mrs. Feith's will is like her husband's. Except for small bequests, everything goes to her husband or, if he's dead, to the children in equal shares. Kovallo has a copy for us to look at.

"Then he went to the shooting range. Karl Feith's locker contained a twenty-two rifle and a twenty-two pistol, ammunition for both, and cleaning equipment. That's all. The guy who let Kovallo in said nobody is allowed to shoot anything bigger than a twenty-two on the range, so if Feith owns a forty-four, he had to practice someplace else. The guy also said that John and Margaret Evans aren't members and haven't been members during the four years he himself has belonged to the Rifle Club.

"Kovallo left word that he has an appointment with a guy named Fredericks but I don't know what that's about."

"Fredericks is the business partner Feith mentioned," Adams explained. "Has Logan gone up to finish searching around the Feiths' house?"

"He went, but he was moaning and groaning about how you sent him out to get covered with muck and kept the clean and easy jobs for yourself."

"When the rain returns, he can take a free shower," Adams said hardheartedly. "You go on phoning Evans's witnesses. Olson and I will go lean on him about his love life." He outlined what Mrs. Evans and Mrs. Abbot had told him.

Crane snorted. "He was a right busy boy last night."

"But not so busy that he was able to spend the same hour at Feith's apartment and Mrs. Abbot's house."

"And you don't think he visited Feith at all?"

"I know he didn't have time to visit Feith if he left Mrs. Abbot at nine and got to the Yacht Club at nine-fifteen. It would take him twenty minutes or more simply to drive from Mrs. Abbot's to Feith's and then to the club. Their times aren't precise, of course, but they still contradict Feith."

John Evans was washing his and his wife's cars outside the garage, and he was not pleased to see Adams and Olson.

"Keerist! Now what?" he exclaimed. "At this rate, I'm going to get to know the whole damn Police Department, two by two."

"You will see fewer of us if you stop telling lies," Adams replied bluntly.

"Now, hold on just a darned minute! I'm a citizen and a taxpayer—"

"What did you and Mrs. Abbot agree about last night?"

Evans recoiled visibly but made another effort. "I don't know what you're talking about," he blustered.

"You can tell us now," Adams said icily, "or you and Mrs. Abbot can come down to the station and discuss it there."

Evans's eyes slid away toward his house, then returned, then dropped.

"We agreed that, uh, it was all over between us," he said meekly.

"What was all over?"

"We had been, uh, seeing each other for a while."

"For how long?"

"Since last spring sometime. April or May."

"What time did you visit her last night?"

"I must have got there a little after eight. I left at five past nine."

"How do you know your departure time so precisely?"

"You know how it is. I mean, I was at loose ends, you know?" Adams made no response. "I mean, it had been kind of a strain, breaking up and all, and I was thinking about going home and wondering if I had time for a beer. So," Evans ended with the air of a boy who thinks he has found an unassailable excuse, "I looked at my watch."

"What made you decide to break it off last night?"

"Well, it was Thanksgiving, right? I got to thinking. The wife—well, she hasn't been happy. I was thinking about the kids. And—well, I just did."

Adams was beginning to feel at home. Evans thought at the level of the majority of witnesses and criminals Adams had to deal with. Evans had had a fling. Something—his wife's behavior, a child's action, sheer sentimentality over the family holiday, or all of them—had made him fear discovery or feel guilty. Now he would be a good husband and father. Adams noticed with faint amusement that Evans did not mention that Mrs. Abbot had also decided the time had come to end the affair.

"Did you go to your brother-in-law's at all?"

"As a matter of fact, I didn't," Evans said with an air of boys-will-be-boys candor. "Gee, I didn't get Karl in trouble, did I?"

"You will get yourself in plenty of trouble telling lies in a murder case," Adams said severely. "How did you two arrange that lie?"

"Well, I figured I was going to have to tell the wife something. I didn't think she really believed me when I said I was going to play pool, and I thought it would be a good idea to tell her something she could check up on. So I called Karl from the Yacht Club and asked him to say I dropped in and had a beer with him."

"What explanation did you give him?"

"Oh, I just said I had got myself into a bit of a jam—Say, how did you get on to me and Carol anyhow?"

Adams ignored Evans's question, and asked a spate of his own, watching and listening with an appearance of suspicion that was not assumed but was allowed to show. It did not seem to make Evans any more nervous than he had been.

Evans was certainly putting on an act, but not necessarily for Adams's benefit. It might be a permanent mannerism. Evans was not the only man Adams had encountered who went in for the hail-fellow, all-boys-together, I'm-a-little-simple routine. He could easily imagine that the show was only exaggerated now, when Evans had been caught in a lie and an extramarital affair.

On the other hand, if Evans was even half as ingenuous—half as brainless, to be blunt—as he appeared, would Carol Abbot have put up with him at all? Yes, Adams conceded reluctantly, she might have. In the aftermath of divorce, someone uncomplicated might have been comfortable.

Nevertheless, the contrast between them was so great that Adams must wonder at it. He was far from believing in a conspiracy, but he could not dismiss the possibility from mind. Carol Abbot was smart. Karl Feith might be. Mrs. Evans had shown that her mind could work when she was not engrossed in her own troubles, or pretending to be. This overgrown juvenile before him might be smart enough to play a part someone else directed.

But if Evans was playing such a part, Adams was unable to force him into a false word or gesture. He confirmed Carol Abbot's account, and he changed nothing else that he had previously told the police.

Adams left him with vague threats of the dire consequences that would follow the uncovering of any other lies, and headed for Karl Feith.

"Why didn't you tell him you learned about his girlfriend from his wife?" Olson asked.

"I didn't need to smack him with that, so far as I could see."

"It might make a difference to them."

"Adams & Olson: murders solved and marriages saved," Adams said with a laugh. He continued more seriously, "But, listen, Olson. We're cops, that's all. We don't give out information and we don't intervene in people's lives except on business."

"Oh, sure," said Olson, which was, Adams admitted, an

appropriate response to his sermonette. "What did you think of his story?"

"Ah-one and ah-two and ah-three," said Adams, beating time with one hand.

"It could be true," they said in unison.

CHAPTER 15

Karl Feith was home, looking as if he had just got out of bed and was not overjoyed to have police officers visiting.

"What time did Evans call you up last night?" Adams said without preamble.

"I don't know what you're—"

Adams waved him down. "Come on," he said without heat.

Feith shrugged. "Well, if it's like that . . . He called about nine-thirty."

"You and Evans are pretty close, are you?"

"I guess so. We get along."

"So close that you would lie for him to the police in a murder case?"

"Aw, look, Inspector, I didn't have a chance to think. I mean, hell, we didn't kill my parents, and I wasn't thinking about things from that point of view. And then I was stuck with what I had said. You were acting so suspicious that I was afraid you would lock me up if I changed my story."

Feith had some grounds for his plaint, Adams conceded, but not out loud. His manner remained glacial.

"Have you rethought any other parts of your story?"

"No."

"You stayed home the entire evening?"

"Yes—I mean, no. I told you, I went for a walk."

"When?"

"I don't know. Eleven, eleven-thirty."

"How long were you out?"

"Twenty minutes. Half an hour. Something like that."

"Where did you go?"

Feith went into his exaggerated-patience number. "I went out the front door, turned left, and walked half a block to Main Street. I turned right and walked two blocks to University Avenue, turned right and walked four blocks to Roosevelt Street, turned right again and walked two blocks to Washington where—surprise—I turned right for the fourth time and came home."

"Otherwise you stayed home all evening?"

"Yes."

"You had no visitors?"

"That's right."

"Did you receive any phone calls, other than the one from John Evans?"

"No."

"Did you make any phone calls?"

"Hell, I don't know," Feith said irritably. "I don't keep a minute-by-minute journal. I don't remember any."

"Is there some reason you don't remember?"

"What's that supposed to mean?"

"Mr. Feith, a man might forget whether he had made ten calls or eleven calls in an evening. He wouldn't forget, in less than twenty-four hours, whether he made any calls or none. 'I don't remember' is the formula for people who want to avoid both an admission and a perjury charge."

"Oh, for Christ's sake," Feith complained. "I'm not under oath, but if it will make you happy— No, I didn't make any phone calls last night. Satisfied?"

"Did you see anyone you knew while you were walking?"

"No. And you know what? I didn't grab a single passing stranger and say, 'Hey! Remember me in case there is a crime going on someplace right now, and the cops try to pin it on me.'"

"Did you see your neighbors in this building at any time yesterday evening?"

"No. I don't think anyone is home downstairs. Anyway, the

important point seems to be whether anybody saw me. Why don't you try asking the Wests or whoever is home?"

"Oh, I will," said Adams, "but I have a few more questions for you first."

In fact, Adams asked every question that he had put to Feith during the previous interview. He received all the same answers, except about Evans's visit. The only other changes were that Feith showed no signs of nervousness and that he delivered himself of a few new sarcasms.

The door across the hall was opened by a woman—a girl, really, for she could not have been more than twenty—whose radiant smile went out like a light when she saw Sergeant Olson. The door slammed, the chain lock rattled, and the girl called out, "Dick. Cops."

Adams shoved Olson hard to the right and took a long, swift step to his left, pushing aside his topcoat, unbuttoning his jacket, and putting his hand on his gun.

"I didn't recognize her. Did you?" Olson said.

"No. Go partway down the stairs."

"But—"

"Don't play hero. If there's shooting, go all the way down and call for help."

Adams, having leaped left out of the line of potential fire, was in a cul-de-sac and could not return to the stairs without crossing in front of the door. His jump had been a reflex precaution, his orders to Olson a reasoned one. Now Adams found the closed door less menacing than annoying.

That they had not recognized the girl meant nothing. She might be traveling with a gangster whose face had appeared on a wanted poster. Only, it was hard to conceive of a moll dumb enough to make such a spectacularly suspicious scene at the very sight of police officers. Adams felt he had been dragged into a charade.

Footsteps sounded inside the apartment. The door opened as far as the chain allowed and a hostile male voice said, "What do you want?"

It was an unpleasant surprise to be confronted after all with a face he had seen in a picture, and disquieting to be unable to remember when or where.

"Mr. West?" Adams said calmly, while his mind tried urgently to decide if the boy—he was little, if any, older than the girl—had been photographed with shoulder-length hair and a frontier-style mustache or had assumed them for disguise.

"Yeah."

"Inspector Adams of the Thorpe Police Department." He displayed his badge in one hand, keeping the other under his jacket, on the butt of his gun. "May we ask you a few questions?"

"You got a warrant?"

"Of course not."

"Then scram. If you want to talk to me, make an appointment through my lawyer. If you have ideas of planting pot in my furniture, you can forget them, Mr. Red Squad or Dope Squad or whatever you are."

Adams had a sudden vision of a newspaper page. It was in the Thorpe *Gazette* that he had seen the picture. West had been a leader of the demonstrations at the University, and Adams was almost sure he had been arrested. Adams also remembered suggesting to Mark Shaw that the Feiths had been killed by a student. And Shaw had reacted obscurely but strenuously.

"I'm not from the Narcotics Squad, Mr. West. I'm from Homicide. Professor and Mrs. Ernst Feith were murdered last night."

"Jesus!" West breathed, but pugnaciousness returned quickly. "What's that got to do with me? I didn't kill them."

Adams was well aware that he would be investigating this young radical very closely, but he said blandly, "My questions are not about you, Mr. West. The Feiths' son lives across the hall from you, and I'm checking up on him."

"I don't know anything about him," West said shortly.

"Dick," the girl's voice said.

"Yeah, yeah," West said.

West didn't move, but after a moment the door swung almost shut, the chain rattled again, and the door opened wide. The girl and boy stood side by side, filling the doorway and making no move to admit the officers.

"Thank you, Mrs. West."

She remained motionless, expressionless, and silent.

They weren't married, of course. The fact was no concern of his, but Adams wanted to know if the girl was refusing his thanks or declining to imply acceptance of the title he had bestowed.

"You are Mrs. West?"

The boy's mouth tightened, but the girl answered directly: "No. I call myself that for convenience. I'm Pamela Black."

Another surprise. Her name was familiar. Adams hadn't been free to attend Mark Shaw's fall production of *The Merchant of Venice*, but Kate had seen and raved about one Pamela Black. There couldn't be two of them.

"You played Portia."

He won a gleam of the dazzling smile from her, and West looked startled before saying brusquely, "Get on with it."

"Were you at home yesterday evening from, say, eight to midnight?"

"I was. Dick came home about nine."

"Did either of you see or hear Karl Feith during the evening?"

"No. Dick?" West shook his head. Pamela Black filled an awkward silence. "I heard his stereo or radio, but I don't know when. I hear it most nights, so I don't really notice it any more."

"Did you hear him go in or out?"

"No."

"Did you notice if he had visitors? Did you hear the bell, the front door opening and closing, voices on the stairs—anything like that?"

"No."

"Mr. West?"

West gave another shake of his head. He looked bored.

"Look, I'm not just prying," Adams said patiently. "I'm trying to catch a murderer. As an heir, Feith is naturally a suspect, and he declines to claim an alibi. There is some evidence that he had a visitor last night, but he won't give us his or her name. Feith is a high-school teacher and may be worried about scandal, but if he did have a visitor, he may be in the clear. Anything you can tell us might help us and him."

West said nothing until Pamela Black touched his arm. Then he complained, "I can't tell what I don't know."

"Can you tell me if Feith was home when you came in at nine?"

"His light was on," West said carefully.

"Was his record player going?"

"I don't know."

Adams swore silently. What he did not need just then was an antagonistic, wary, laconic witness. He tried another approach.

"Did you have any visitors during the evening?"

Pamela Black nodded but looked at West, who shook his head. Adams understood his meaning but pretended not to.

"Your visitors left before nine, Miss Black?"

"Our visitors are none of your business," West said vehemently.

Adams thought he must have set a world record for the number of times he had been told what was not his business in the last twelve hours.

"Dick," Pamela Black said softly, then checked herself. She wasn't going to argue with him before the cops.

Anger would only make West more belligerent. He wasn't likely to respond to cajolery. Adams attempted a light, persuasive tone.

"This isn't a witch-hunt, Mr. West. Your friends' affiliations and ideologies don't interest me. I don't care if you were holding an orgy, discussing Heraclitus, or plotting revolution."

"Our plots aren't that dramatic," West said, smoothing his

mustache. Pamela Black looked at the floor. Adams sensed suppressed laughter. The joke escaped him, but he would not mind if it prompted them to talk.

West dropped his hand and resumed his truculent manner. He looked at Pamela Black. She made no sign, but he spoke.

"Joe and Tina Walsh, 210 Grove Street," he said abruptly. Walsh had also been prominent in the demonstrations. "But just so you don't get the wrong idea, all we were plotting was stage business for a playwriting course."

"Mark Shaw's?"

"Yeah."

Adams filed for future consideration the question of whether it was the thought of these two couples that had distressed Mark Shaw last night.

"The Walshes came in with you?" West nodded. "So you don't know if Feith's hi-fi was on because you were talking as you came up the stairs," Adams continued briskly.

West's eyebrows rose, but Adams wasn't showing off. He was only trying to hurry the pace.

"Neither of you heard Feith or other people go in or out. The question is would you have been likely to hear them? Do you usually hear doorbells, footsteps, voices, and so on?"

"I'm not sure," Pamela Black said slowly. "I have heard people on the stairs occasionally, but I really don't know if I have heard most or scarcely any of the people who have gone in and out."

"By 'occasionally' do you mean once or twice a week, or a month, or a year?"

"I mean a total of two or three times. We only moved here in September."

"Feith was already here?"

"Oh, yes. He has lived here for ages."

Adams repressed a smile. More than two years was probably an age to these children.

"Have you ever seen any of Feith's visitors?"

"I haven't." She did not look at West.

"Mr. West?"

"A couple," he answered reluctantly. "Both were men. One

was big, blond, balding, thirty or thereabouts. Looked like an ex-football player going soft." This was not a bad thumbnail sketch of John Evans. "The other was younger, smaller—brown-haired, I think."

"Can you describe the younger man in more detail?"

"I only saw him once. I can tell you this. He drives a racing-green TC in mint condition."

"A TC in mint condition?" Adams said enthusiastically. "I'll have to find the owner just to see it. I had to settle for a TD as second-best, but I came to love it."

"Oh, yeah? So did I." West gave Adams a suspicious look, then seemed to decide the topic was safe. "Mine had a tragic encounter with a tree and now I'm reduced to Pam's Beetle."

"You must cast covetous eyes at Feith's TD."

"Nah. He's got one of those late ones with a TF engine and it's full of carbon 'cause he never blows it out. The tappets don't clatter; they jangle. It'll explode if he ever takes it over three thousand on the tach."

"That's a waste," Adams said, "but may be useful to me. Since it's so noisy, perhaps you would have heard it start. I know the carport is on the other side of the house, but last night was unusually quiet."

"I guess so." West considered, conceded a point. "Yeah, I would have heard it. I hear it other times, when there's more noise."

"Would you have heard the TC if it had come to visit?"

"Maybe, if it started right in front of the house or was revved up pretty high in first. But it's in good shape and has a good muffler."

It was discouraging. Since they didn't know if they would ordinarily hear a person on the stairs or a car outside, not hearing either last night was without significance.

"What time did your friends leave?"

"About midnight," West said, with a return to his prickly manner.

"All right. Thank you. If you think of anything that might help, would you call me?"

She nodded. He shut the door.

Adams and Olson went down and knocked at the doors of the ground-floor apartments. No one answered. Outside, Adams set off to circle the building.

"Creeps!" Olson exploded. "They're going to get plugged someday if they go into that routine every time a cop comes to the door."

"You sound as if you would cheer."

Olson shrugged.

"They're kids," Adams protested absently. There were no outside stairs, but Feith's kitchen and bathroom windows overlooked the carport.

"You mean that girl is a doll. And she's not too young to be sleeping around," Olson said scornfully. "I was young once, but I got damned old damned fast standing outside of doors I didn't know if somebody was going to shoot at me through or not."

Adams began to try unscrambling this peroration, but Olson went straight on. "And what are TC and TD and TF, anyway? They sound like diseases."

Adams was fairly sure she knew, but if she had vented her feelings and now wanted to change the subject, he was amenable.

"They're cars. That's a TD. It belongs to Feith."

The roof of the carport was only a few inches above Adams's head. It was wet, he discovered with an oath as he hoisted himself up and put a knee in a puddle. Feith could have gone in and out this way, but there was nothing on the roof to indicate that he had. The windowsills were clean.

Feith was in the kitchen. He pursed his lips and turned away when he saw Adams at the window.

"You owned one of those little things?" Olson said as Adams returned to earth.

"Well, no," he said. "I owned, and still own, a Porsche, but West digs MGs, so I fibbed."

"MG!" Olson exclaimed. "You said TC and TD and TF."

"They are MGs," Adams said patiently.

Olson glared.

"MG is the maker. TC, TD, and TF are MGs, like

Corvette is a Chevrolet."

"It takes all kinds," Olson said.

Adams didn't think she meant automobiles.

"We'll drive over to Grove Street before we go to the station."

"If the Walshes slam their door on us, I'll kick it down," Olson responded ferociously.

The Walshes' door wasn't opened at all. They weren't home, or weren't answering the bell. A neighbor said he thought they had left early that morning to spend Thanksgiving with relatives.

Returning to the car, Olson said, "Do you think they were lying about being home from nine o'clock on?"

Adams shrugged. He wished her to comment freely.

"That girl," Olson said, and stopped.

Adams waited.

"She has a thing about telling the truth."

Again Adams waited, but Olson was done and he was content. He shared her view, and he was glad to know that, despite all, she could make herself say other than the worst about "that girl."

"What about West?"

"A wise guy. But he never said anything that made me sit up and think, That's a lie. But then, they are actors, I gather."

"Seems so," Adams said. An administrative matter came to mind. "Where do you live?"

"On Laurel, a couple of blocks from the Evanses. Why?"

"You don't need to return to the station. I'll drop you off at home."

"Oh, okay." After a moment, she said, "I talk too much, I guess."

"What on earth— Oh, I see." Adams was usually conscientious about explanations, and now he kicked himself mentally for his inattentiveness. "I'm sorry. I'm not getting rid of you. I think I'm finished with interviews for today. Vogel said the people on overtime could go home early."

"Oh. Okay, then."

CHAPTER

16

After leaving Sergeant Olson, Adams drove over to Walnut Street. John Evans had finished washing cars, and seemed to have become a football team. At any rate, he held a ball and was being tackled by four or five small boys as Adams passed unnoticed and stopped at the call box on the corner.

Sergeant Crane began his report with a question.

"You remember Peewee Rice?"

"Sure."

Rice had been a vociferous Dodger fan in a high school full of Cardinal, Cub, Pirate, and even Yankee supporters who thought it funny to call him after a now long-gone shortstop, and screamingly funny when Rice grew to be six feet four and more than two hundred pounds.

"He called and asked if you're going to get to Feith's office today."

"Does he consider it urgent?"

Crane laughed. "That was an excuse. He was really making an opportunity to let us know that the campus cops have made him a sergeant."

In twenty years with the Thorpe Police Department, Rice had never passed the sergeants' examination, never displayed the smallest talent for administration or detection, and never turned in a written report that made sense. Yet he had been a useful policeman. His size made him almost a crowd-control unit by himself, and he had one characteristic that would be even more valuable to the University police than to the city force: he was imperturbably cheerful. He could give directions to lost pedestrians while sorting out a post-football-game traffic jam, or help bewildered freshmen during registration week, and leave them thinking, Now, there's a friendly cop. Of course, Adams was a little biased; he was the other half of the Bums' contingent in Thorpe

"I'll go see him soon," Adams said, "unless you have done some work while I was out and have solved the case."

"Ha," said Crane. "I've been making phone calls and getting as little out of them as I expected. Everybody saw Evans. Nobody can say they saw him after ten—and you know who saw him then? Not a yachtsman, but a cop: George Miller, who was the one sent to direct traffic. He knows Evans because he bought a car from him in September. He saw Evans when he arrived, which was within seconds of ten o'clock, but he doesn't remember seeing him after that, either."

"We aren't exactly narrowing the choice of suspects, are we?"

"No. I have also been going through Feith's papers. Did you know he was a naturalized citizen?"

"Yes. I think he was a refugee from Germany in the thirties."

"I don't know about the refugee part, but he was from Germany. I found his naturalization certificate.

"The rest of the papers don't tell me much more than I saw at a glance last night. The Feiths have been making a lot of money. I can't find any sign of unusual income or expenses, but maybe the bank can tell us more tomorrow."

"Maybe. Did Kovallo learn anything useful?"

"Well, he thinks Fredericks is a queer."

"Kovallo is developing a fixation," Adams said. "You heard his idea about Evans and Karl Feith?"

Crane chuckled. "Yeah, but he says Fredericks is a regular three-dollar bill."

"Not to be confused with an irregular one," Adams said sourly. His faith in his fellow officers' ability to identify homosexuals was small.

"He says Fredericks is a pretty little fella who called him 'dear' and has a house full of dark red velvet and satin."

"Oh, come on," Adams expostulated.

"That's what he said."

Adams laughed in spite of himself. Then he had an inspiration. "Does Fredericks drive a green MG-TC?"

"Darned if I know."

"Where is Kovallo now?"

"I sent him home to get some lunch."

Adams was forcefully reminded that it had been a long time since breakfast, and there wasn't so much as a greasy spoon open in Thorpe today. And he hadn't called Kate yet.

"When he returns, have him find out what kind of car Fredericks owns. What did he learn about the bookstore?"

"It's kind of complicated."

"Oh, grand," said Adams.

"Yeah. Fredericks is sole owner of the big book, stationery, and greeting-card shop on Main Street, as well as half owner of the textbook store with Feith. He claims he makes good money from the first and writes off the losses from the second on his taxes. It must be nice to be in such a high bracket you can make money by losing it."

"You mean you aren't in that bracket yet?"

"Ho, ho," said Crane. "Anyway, the textbook store opened two years ago, and Fredericks says they didn't expect it to make a profit immediately, but that he is sure it will in the long run."

"Did he provide figures on the losses?"

"Yes and no."

Crane must have been able to feel Adams's glower through the phone, for he elaborated hurriedly: "He said their bookkeeping was fouled up for this year by the demonstrations, because sales were down at the start of the term and higher than normal later. Last year, according to him, they lost about twelve hundred dollars. I suppose that means he and Feith had to pony up six hundred bucks apiece, which ain't nickels and dimes, but doesn't sound like they are about to go bankrupt."

"No. We'll check it with the bank tomorrow," Adams said. "Has Logan reported yet?"

"He called around an hour ago to say he had worked uphill as far as the Feiths' house and was giving everybody an hour off for lunch."

Adams was becoming so hungry he felt ill, but he had to ask, "Have you eaten?"

"Sure. My wife made sandwiches for me this morning."

Mrs. Crane was an attractive, pleasant woman, and at that moment Adams disliked her intensely.

"Do you have any other news for me?"

"The state police went to the Feiths' cabin. Nobody was there and it looked as if nobody had been there recently. The lab tested the ashtrays and glasses you took from Karl Feith's apartment, and there were no prints but his on anything. No answers yet to the queries we sent about the dead couple's fingerprints, ownership of the gun, or Shaw's claim to have been in the O.S.S. No word on the car with bald tires. That's it."

"And a numbing recital of negatives it is," Adams said. "Maybe you can come up with something positive on four students." He gave Crane the names and addresses of West, Black, and the Walshes. "I think West and Walsh were busted during the protests, probably by the Sheriff's Department. See what you can learn, and I'll ask the campus police about them. I'll be at the University if you need me."

"Sergeant Rice, I believe," Adams said, holding out a hand. "Congratulations."

Rice heaved himself up from behind his desk, grinned hugely, and engulfed Adams's hand in an enormous paw.

"Three years I was a private. Twenty years I was a patrolman. But my teachers always said persistence pays, and now I'm getting up in the world."

"Not only up," Adams said. "You must be getting close to three hundred pounds."

"I don't get enough exercise these days," said Rice, sucking in his stomach, which made him a trifle less than twice as wide as Adams. "But I'm still under two ninety."

"By an ounce, at least. But I'm wasting away to nothing myself. Is there a machine where I can get a sandwich or even a candy bar?"

"No, but I got a peanut-butter sandwich you can have. My old lady is trying to put me on a diet. She knows that if she gives me two meat sandwiches, I'll eat them both whether I'm hungry or not. But I don't like peanut butter, especially with apricot jam, and I won't eat it unless I'm starving, so you can have it."

How could Adams refuse an offer like that?

"I got a little milk left in my thermos, if you want."

Adams was out of practice at peanut-butter eating. He had taken too large a bite and couldn't dislodge the lump from the roof of his mouth. He made an inarticulate noise and nodded.

"Thanks," he said some time later. "What do you know about a couple of students named Dick West and Joe Walsh?"

"Oh, them," said Rice. He went to a file and took out two folders. "Don't have much on Walsh. He's a senior who spent his first two years at a junior college. Was arrested during the sit-in in the Dean of Students' Office. He's an English major. He's twenty-three, so I guess he was in the service or working or something that kept him out of school. He's married to a girl who was named Christina Canata. She's also a senior and an English major and was arrested at the sit-in too. We don't have any record of political stuff by either of them before this year.

"West is something else. Came here as a freshman, and right off the bat he joined the Red Party—I think the name was picked to bug the fraternity boys and their parents. The Reds run candidates for student government, and they hold rallies for civil rights, against the war in Vietnam, and so on.

"Last spring, West was chairman of a McCarthy for President group, and he said in one of his speeches during the demonstrations later on that he'd been at the Democratic Convention in Chicago. I don't know how he was before, but this fall he went in for talking about 'pigs' and saying things like 'Chemical-biological warfare is genocide,' and 'Ernst Feith and his kind are the mad scientists of our times.' He got himself arrested the day the police car was wrecked, and charged with everything the Sheriff could think of. He was bailed out, and then arrested again a couple of weeks later."

"What's his major?"

"Major? Oh, same as the Walshes'—English. Got all A's too, at least before this year."

"Is he an actor?"

"Not that I know of." Rice turned pages. "Wait, it says here that he wrote a play that the Drama Department did last year."

"What do you know about one Pamela Black?"

"I've heard the name. Matter of fact, I saw it on a poster for one of Professor Shaw's plays." Rice went to the files again. "We don't have a folder for her. What's your interest in her?"

"She lives with West."

"Um." Rice made a note in West's file. "Anything else I can tell you?"

"Yes. What's the true story on the theft and the guards and all the rest of the fuss at U.R.C. last spring?"

Rice made a face. "Ahh, that was the dumbest business you ever heard about. Seems there was this student from the Middle East or someplace who was flunking out and was afraid his government wouldn't be too pleased with him. So he must have decided he would be better off if he took some secrets home.

"Well, that was pretty dumb to begin with, and then he kept the papers he swiped in his room where the F.B.I. found them first thing.

"Then, nobody seems to have paid him much mind. He wasn't going to be prosecuted, because he was going to be thrown out of the country anyway, so he wasn't being watched all that closely, and he tore up a shirt and hanged himself.

"If all that wasn't dumb enough, Feith and his assistant at the Research Center, a guy named Ashenden, went into conniptions about posting guards and changing locks. Somehow they managed to take out the old locks and only then they found out that the new ones wouldn't arrive for weeks.

"I mean, it was *dumb*."

"Sounds that way," Adams agreed. "What about the guards? Were they really from a private company, not federal agents under cover?"

"Hell, yes."

"How can you be sure?"

"Well, don't spread it around, but my brother-in-law owns the Atlas Security Agency, and when word came down that guards were wanted, I told him about it."

"Atlas? That's here in Thorpe, isn't it?"

"Right. It only got started six, seven years ago and it's still pretty small. I know all the guys who work there. They aren't bad guys as private guards go, but none of them was ever F.B.I. material."

"What do you know about Ernst Feith?"

"Not a lot more than what I've read in the papers. We aren't big on gathering intelligence, you know. Students and professors don't let cops buy them beers in exchange for rumors like petty crooks do. You probably learned more about Feith while you were taking classes than anybody in the campus force knows."

"I'm in the wrong field to hear gossip about scientists, unfortunately. Last night, for the first time, I heard a rumor that Feith had helped himself too freely to other people's research. Have you heard that one?"

"Not before this minute."

"Oh, well. What about Mark Shaw?"

"I like to listen to him talk," Rice said surprisingly. "Heard him speak at a couple of rallies this fall. I didn't understand half what he said, and neither did anybody else, but he has a great voice."

Kate would laugh. Lord only knew how Shaw himself would react.

"Did Shaw mention Feith in his speeches?"

"Yes, but it was kind of funny. The kids wanted to hear about germ warfare and the military-industrial-academic complex. Stuff like that. But Shaw kept talking about how Feith and Walter Nelson had ruined the University. He had a super word: brontosaurocracy, which turns out to mean something about a giant bureaucracy with a midget brain.

"I thought that was pretty good, and the students cheered the parts about ruin, but they looked kind of baffled by the other stuff. The last time Shaw spoke, he followed one of the kids who stirred everybody up with some of that 'Fascist scientist' stuff. Well, Shaw chewed 'em up one side and down the other. Things like 'indulging in sloganeering . . . latter-day Know-Nothingism'—he really laid into them. They didn't give him any cheers that time, and he didn't speak at any more rallies after that."

It was certainly in character for Shaw to turn his formidable scorn on protesters he favored but considered to be making little, or wrongful, use of their brains. As for his views of Feith, they were well known and shared by no small number of other faculty members, including at least a few in the physical sciences. There probably is no such thing as too small a motive for murder, but Adams had great difficulty taking seriously the possibility that Shaw or someone else had killed Feith because of a conflict over academic policy.

"Do you know anything interesting about this Ashenden you mentioned?"

"No. I don't know anything about him at all, except that he is assistant director of U.R.C." Rice opened the University directory. "It says here that he's a professor of biochemistry. You want his address?"

Adams wrote it down.

"You want to go to Feith's offices now?"

"Offices? How many did he have?"

"Two. One is number 405 in the Life Sciences Building. These keys will let you in. The other is number 22 in the U.R.C. building, and these keys will open the fancy new locks there."

Adams took the two sets of keys Rice held out. "The guards are gone, I take it."

"Yeah, and glad of it, so I hear. The protesters made them pretty nervous. Drop the keys off here before you go, okay?"

"Right. Thanks again, and thank Mrs. Rice, for the sandwich."

"Any time, but you can thank her yourself someday. She'll never believe me if I tell her I gave away a sandwich, even peanut butter."

CHAPTER 17

Adams spent no more than fifteen minutes in Feith's office in the Life Sciences Building, garnering little but an impression that Feith himself had not spent much time there. Bookshelves, while not bare, didn't have the jammed look that Adams expected in faculty members' offices, and not one volume concerned cryptography. The desk and cabinets contained only lecture notes, rosters of students, and other materials relating to courses and of no interest to Adams.

Examination of the office at the University Research Center took longer, for it was larger and fuller, but it wasn't much more interesting. There were numerous publications that were cryptic to Adams—the sort that open with a sentence and proceed for tens of pages with no more words, only formulas—but he didn't think they contained the kind of code he was after. Carbon copies of letters showed that Feith had sent and received a large amount of mail about academic conferences, applicants for positions at Thorpe State, and grants, notably government grants, for research.

Adams thumbed through the files of correspondence looking for gaps that might indicate that certain letters had been removed. He shuffled the stacks of mimeographed scientific papers, moved books and opened drawers, seeking signs of search or theft. Finally, having found nothing useful to a policeman, he sat at Feith's desk and stared blankly at the door.

The door opened.

Adams lunged sideways, tipping over the chair with a crash, and made a frantic grab for his gun.

"Boy! You're kind of jumpy, aren't you?" said a masculine voice in a tone appropriate for commenting on the weather. "Is Dr. Feith around?"

Adams took a deep breath. "No. Who—"

"It's okay. I'll just stick this in the file and be on my way."

He went unhesitatingly to a filing cabinet, drew out a thick folder, and inserted the paper he had shown to Adams.

Such a display of incuriousness about a jumpy stranger in a murdered man's office wasn't credible. But before Adams acted on his suspicions, he needed a moment to absorb the vision.

The nonchalant young man returning the folder he had withdrawn was astonishingly hirsute, possessing both a massive shock of hair on his head and the most impressive full beard Adams had ever seen outside of an old painting. He was also the most rumpled person Adams had ever encountered. No two of his innumerable hairs appeared to be parallel. His shirttail hung out below a jacket that must have been crushed into a ball for months before it was donned. What had been done to the pants was more than Adams could imagine. If Metternich had nightmares about bomb-throwing anarchists, they probably looked like this.

"Feith be back soon?" said the man over his shoulder.

"No. Who—"

"It's okay. I gotta get some sleep anyhow. So long."

"Stop!" Adams roared. "Who are you?"

"Huh? Al Morris. Feith is my adviser, you know?"

"I did not know. In any case, what do you think you are doing in here?"

"Huh? I told you. Feith is my adviser. My files are here."

"And that gives you the right to barge into his office?"

Morris said carefully, as if explaining something really quite simple to an imbecile, "He is my adviser. I finished a run in the laboratory. I saw the light in here. I tried the door and it was open. I came in to put a note in my file."

"You mean he *was* your doctoral adviser?"

"Huh? What do you mean, 'was'? Say, who are you and what are you doing here?"

"I am Inspector Adams of the Thorpe Police Department. Feith is dead and—"

"Dead?" Morris cried. "Oh, no. Oh, God. That's terrible. Oh, my God."

Morris staggered to a chair, looking as if he might actually cry. The Feiths' own children hadn't displayed half as much grief.

"Were you very close to him?" Adams asked gently.

"Huh?" For the first time, the monosyllable sounded like an expression of incomprehension, instead of a verbal tic. Morris seemed to return his attention from far away.

"Close? To him? Not likely. But he is—he was—my adviser. I'm hung, absolutely hung." Morris frowned. "An inspector, huh? Does that mean Feith was killed, or that he killed himself?"

"He seems to have been killed."

"Huh," Morris said. "I guess it does look a little funny, my busting in the way I did, but everybody walks into anybody's office unless the door is locked. I wouldn't have tried to come in, except that I saw the light and thought Feith was here. Otherwise I would have thought the door was locked."

"I should think that the security people would disapprove of that sort of thing."

"Jerks," Morris ejaculated. His beard twitched and Adams supposed that he was grimacing. "You know what they did?" Morris continued indignantly. "After that crazy Hassan ibn Sabah pulled his James Bond stunt last spring, the feebies locked me out for three days and ruined an experiment."

"Hassan ibn Sabah was the Arab who stole the classified papers?"

"He was an Iraqi, or Irani, I forget which. As for the papers, they were only classified because brainless bureaucrats get a charge out of stamping things. Hell, I've read them myself, and they weren't worth stealing."

"What was all the fuss about, then?"

"It was all a performance," Morris said with large contempt. "It was supposed to persuade the little men with the money and the 'Secret' stamps that U.R.C. was just as security-conscious as they were." Morris gave a snort of amusement. "The lock fiasco, and the protests later, helped make the image terrifically convincing—I don't think."

Adams considered Morris's statement with distaste. He could see himself interviewing officials who would tell him how important U.R.C.'s secrets were, and graduate students who would side with Morris. Adams was getting very tired of accounts that were both plausible and untestable.

"Let's talk about you for a minute. You're working on your doctorate in—what? Biochemistry?"

"Yeah." With an air of daring Adams to make anything of it, Morris added, "I'm the firefly man."

"The what?" Adams said in bafflement.

"Don't tell me I have encountered a resident of Thorpe who never heard about lightning bugs and cancer."

"Oh. All right. I feel like the stooge in a vaudeville show, but: What *is* the connection between cancer and the light in a firefly's tail?"

Morris grinned and opened his mouth, but then he seemed to decide that the occasion was not altogether suitable for witticisms about fundamental glows, broad beams, or whatever he had in mind.

"It's not as weird as it sounds," he said seriously. "You see, firefly extract can be used to test for living cells in solutions and, under some circumstances, to determine the health of the cells. If you take away the ATP, you can find some kinds of infections. If you—huh."

Morris had been waxing enthusiastic. Now he gave Adams a shrewd look.

"You understand any of that?"

"Not much."

"Two cultures," Morris said gloomily. "Look. Bioluminescence means the lightning bug's lightning, or phosphorescence in the ocean, or any of the other examples of light from plants and animals. It is produced chemically and the chemicals can be extracted and injected into other forms of life. It turns out that cancer dims the glow, which means that firefly extract can be used to test for cancer. That's what I'm working on.

"See? It's not so esoteric."

"Um," said Adams. Morris's research might be fascinating and useful, but it cast no light on Feith's murder. Unless . . .

"Was it data on firefly research that Hassan stole?"

"Huh? Lord, no. My research isn't classified."

"It's not? Why did the F.B.I. lock up your laboratory?"

"They didn't lock the lab. They wouldn't let me into the building at all, because I haven't been certified true-blue patriotic and pure in heart and mind by some cluck in Washington."

"You mean you don't have security clearance?"

"Right."

Adams shook his head in earnest. "Then what are you doing in U.R.C.?"

"Boy! You're as bad as the feebies. They couldn't get it through their thick—huh." Morris reconsidered and rephrased. Feebies and inspectors were both species of the genus cop, after all. "They couldn't seem to understand that there's nothing secret going on here."

Morris was full of surprises.

"I guess I am a little thick in the head," Adams said. "Could you explain your last remark in words of one syllable?"

"Huh? Look. U.R.C. is a paper organization. It has thirty-odd big shots who call themselves 'fellows' of the Center and use stationery with University Research Center on the letterhead when they apply for grants. When the money comes in, they hire some extra assistants and buy some equipment—and go right on working in the labs they already have in L.S.B. or the Chemistry Building. A lot of what they do is classified, of course, but that's mostly paranoia and a little self-aggrandizement, or maybe the other way around.

"The only labs here are four small and grubby ones in the

basement, and lowly grad students like me are consigned to them. Lowly and poor," Morris added resentfully. "Nobody is handing out pots of money for my project. But the nether regions were in Feith's little empire, and he assigned them to people like me."

"And reaped the benefits?"

"Huh? Well, sure. Each of us is working on a small piece of a large project that he directs. He gets the credit, but we have to get our doctorates somehow—Oh, God! What am I going to do now?"

"Will Feith's death prevent you from earning a doctorate?"

"Maybe not *a* doctorate, but maybe the one I was planning to get. Listen. You know the cliché about scientists who learn more and more about less and less? Well, graduate students know more about less than anybody. We get to be the world's greatest experts on subjects that sometimes nobody else knows anything at all about. Only our advisers have followed every step of our research. Only our advisers know that we even did any research.

"If an adviser dies—zap! You're up the creek. It happened to a friend of mine, and he had to start over from scratch. A year right down the drain. And I'm a lot farther along than he was.

"Up the creek! Boy! I haven't got a paddle or a canoe, and now the floods have started."

Commiseration was no use to Morris, and might be spurned if offered. Adams confined himself to letting sympathy appear in his tone as he asked, "Have you been working through the night?"

"Huh? Yeah."

"I won't keep you much longer, then. But if you aren't too tired, perhaps you would answer a few more questions." Sympathy wouldn't prevent him from pumping a witness whose exhaustion and distraction might permit unguarded words to escape. "You said it was 'not likely' you would have been close to Feith. Why was that?"

"Huh. That wasn't too bright, was it? *Nil nisi bonum*, especially to a policeman." Morris gazed at the ceiling meditatively. "And just what did you mean by that 'reaped the benefits' remark?"

Morris was only tired, not half-unconscious.

"I'm looking for motives, of course," Adams said. "I have heard a rumor that Feith helped himself to others' research. Have you heard that one?"

Morris burrowed into his beard with one hand while tugging at it with the other hand. The wonder, Adams saw, was not that the beard was disarranged, but that it flourished under such mayhem.

"Do I have to answer yes or no, or can I give you an explanation?" Morris said after a moment.

"I take what I can get," Adams replied.

"Okay. The first thing is, Feith was one cold fish. For instance, I call most of my professors by their first names and they call me Al, but not Feith. He was always Dr. Feith, and I was Mr. Morris, and that's how he was with everyone. I didn't go to his parties, or invite him to mine. We didn't hold bull sessions. He never said, 'Good work,' when you figured out how to solve some problem, and he never said, 'That's too bad,' when an experiment went wrong for mysterious reasons. The only halfway human emotion I ever saw him display was anger. He had a temper that went off like Krakatoa.

"On top of that he was the biggest big wheel at Thorpe State—not because he was necessarily the most hotshot scientist, but because he understood how to work the money machine. I don't mean he was a bad scientist. The point is that he was the most important scientist, but for nonscientific reasons.

"Controlling the money gave him power, but it made him enemies, too. I had, let's say, mixed feelings about being beholden to him for my lab, which you probably didn't miss when I was talking about being a poor grad-student peasant in his empire."

Adams nodded.

"Okay. He wasn't a friendly type, and he had power. The result was about what you might expect. Some people resented getting money from him; some resented not getting money from him. His motives were questioned, the quality of his research was denigrated. In short, people tried to find feet of clay, not to mention heart of ice and head of stone.

"It could get pretty silly, as I know from experience. Feith referred to me in a footnote as 'A. S. Morris' instead of 'Albert S. Morris,' which is the way I sign papers. With somebody else, I would have said something like, 'Hey, you bum, use my right name.' But you didn't say things like that to Feith, so I went around muttering under my breath—until Tom Barnes, another professor, pointed out that he had cited some work of mine in exactly the same way, and I never noticed."

"So it's only gossip?" Adams said. "Feith was not, to use the strongest word, stealing from students or other researchers?"

"That I can't tell you. There was gossip. But whether any of it was based on fact, I don't know."

Somewhere in the building a door closed.

"Hey, Mo!" a voice shouted.

Footsteps pounded along the corridor.

"Hey, Mo, where are you?"

"Here, Mike. In Feith's office," Morris called without getting up.

The door was flung open and slammed shut by a young man whose headlong rush ended in a sudden halt and a gape at Adams.

"Shees! Who are you?"

"He's a policeman," Morris said. "Feith is dead."

"I know. I heard about it on the radio and I was coming to tell you. That's why I was so shook to see somebody sitting in his chair."

"And who are you?" Adams asked.

"Me? I'm Mike Keefe."

"He's one of the cellar dwellers," Morris explained. He gave Keefe a teasing glance. "You think fireflies are funny?

Mike and Ashenden are breeding what you might call pre-plucked chickens."

"Aw, come on, Mo," Keefe complained. He turned to Adams with the same solemnity that Morris had adopted when trying to explain his work. "Look, it's really sensible. As much as twenty-five percent of the protein an ordinary chicken consumes goes into plumage. Eliminate the feathers and you get more meat for the same amount of food. That cuts costs, which is important everywhere, and it could revolutionize the nutritional situation in places like India and the Near East where shortages and religious factors limit meat consumption."

"If only they don't shiver themselves to death first," Morris said. "You may not know much about chickens, Inspector, but I can tell you that they are a little dim even by birdbrain standards. Mike's have the frustrating habit of taking one look at themselves and going right out of their tiny skulls."

Keefe was gathering himself for a retort, but Adams had had enough graduate-student humor for today.

"Was it your data that Hassan stole?"

Keefe shook his head, and Morris said, "Gawd! Not even in Washington are they dumb enough to turn any secrets over to him— What's the matter?"

"Keep talking," Adams said, waving Keefe aside and tiptoeing toward the door. He had heard a soft footfall.

"Holy cow," Morris said conversationally. "How am I supposed to think of anything to say when somebody says, 'Just say something'?"

"You're doing fine," Adams said.

He took a long stride and jerked the door open.

A man walking toward Adams jumped back.

"Good God! Who are you?"

"Shees! It's Dr. Ashenden."

Then the three civilians all talked at once, until Adams cut in sharply, "I am a police officer investigating the murders of Professor and Mrs. Feith—"

"*Mrs.* Feith, too?" Morris exclaimed.

Adams ignored him. "What are you doing here, Dr. Ashenden?"

"Why, I, you see—" Ashenden shook himself. "I'm sorry. It was a considerable shock to encounter a stranger here so soon after hearing news of the tragedy.

"I heard the news a short time ago. I was disturbed and distressed, and I went out to walk and to think. Without intending to do so, I followed familiar paths and found myself approaching this building. Then I saw the light burning in this office and came to investigate—rather absentmindedly, I fear, for I thought nothing more than that one of the graduate students was here. When you appeared . . . well, I thought I was confronting the killer."

"Does everyone in this high-security establishment have a key to everyone else's office?"

"No, of course not," Ashenden said defensively. "Each fellow, except me, has the key to his own office only."

"Do you mean that you don't have a key to your own office, or that you have keys to other offices?"

"I have a full set."

"Why?"

"I am assistant director of the Center. My duties are primarily administrative, and they include such housekeeping chores as unlocking the offices of fellows who forget their own keys."

"In short," said Adams, "you know better than anyone else that no graduate student could let himself into the office."

"I—yes, I see what you mean."

"So what made you think a student was in here?"

Ashenden threw up his hands. "Lord! How does one explain absence of mind?"

Adams offered no suggestions. Morris, who had been following the exchange with mounting glee, tugged fiercely at his beard.

"If I had thought it through," Ashenden said at last, "I would have realized that of course no graduate student could have got in. I suppose that what was in my mind was a vague notion that the door had been left unlocked. Some of the fellows are not as conscientious as they should be about locking up. But, there! If I had been thinking, I would have put that idea aside at once, for Dr. Feith was always careful, even before the, um, incident last spring.

"The truth is, I was not thinking ratiocinatively. I was incredulous and dismayed at the news of Dr. Feith's death—of his *murder!* Frankly, my thoughts were a jumble. Preoccupied as I was, I saw the light. I thought, A graduate student is in the office. And there I stopped."

Before Adams could comment, the radio receiver in his pocket began to buzz.

"Good heavens," said Ashenden.

"The man's wired for sound," said Keefe.

Damn, thought Adams, I still haven't called Kate.

Adams knew it was going to be bad as soon as he heard Crane say formally and expressionlessly, "Inspector Adams?"

"Yes."

"We have two more bodies, Inspector."

With three civilians ogling him across Feith's desk, Adams limited himself to a crisp "Who?"

"Don't know yet. A Mrs. Meadows of 219 Acacia Street called to report a killing at 220 Acacia. Officers Wilson and McClennan were sent. They reported finding the body of a man who looked like he had been shot with the same-size gun that was used on the Feiths. Wilson said he had been dead long enough that the blood had dried up hard.

"A few minutes later, Wilson called back and said there was a second body upstairs, also shot with a big gun. I thought you should know."

"Quite right. What has been done so far?"

"The M.E. and the lab squad have been called out. Captain Vogel is on his way to the station. He gave me orders for Logan to keep his crew standing by in case you need them. Logan was getting ready to pack up—but, geez, he's got a doozy, Inspector."

It must be extraordinary indeed if it could crack Crane's veneer of cool professionalism.

"Well?"

"He has four more of those diaries, like the one you found on Feith."

Adams forgot his audience momentarily and blurted, "Four?"

"Yes, sir. And that's not all. He also found three more of those what-do-you-call-'ems, the decoder gizmos, like the one I found under the blotter on Feith's desk."

"Tableaus," Adams said.

"Right. The whole mess was packed in a plastic bag that had really been given a heave. It was twenty, twenty-five feet from the killer's tracks. It had slid into a pile of dead leaves, which is why it wasn't found for so long."

"Fingerprints?"

"No, sir. I mean, we don't know yet. Logan called for the lab men, but then we had to send them to Acacia Street instead. Logan will bring the stuff down with him."

"Anything else?"

"Not about that, but Kovallo found out that Fredericks does drive a green MG. Is that important?"

"Probably not now," Adams said. "If Vogel takes charge there, you should join me at Acacia Street. Otherwise, send Kovallo. I'll be there in ten minutes."

CHAPTER

18

Adams shooed his rapt audience out of the building, answering no questions but issuing a pompous warning against a return to Feith's office before duly consituted authority gave permission.

He remembered to return keys to Sergeant Rice, and to phrase politely a request that both of Feith's offices be sealed by the campus police.

He even remembered to stop at the public telephone just outside the Administration Building and try to call Kate. He wasn't surprised when the machine swallowed two dimes and a quarter and refused to give him a dial tone. He didn't swear; he didn't kick the phone booth; but as he started to drive up The Hill once again, he did say bitterly, "Christ, I'm tired of things that might be true."

Which was not an example of pure sublimation, for that matter was on his mind, too.

It might be true that security at University Research Center was intended to build images more than to protect awesome secrets. It might be true that Feith was more fund-raiser than innovative scientist. And now there were four bodies, and Crane's suggestion of espionage no longer seemed so ridiculous.

Four bodies, four tableaus—and five diaries. The discrepancy was ominous, but numerological exercises held no appeal for Adams. Relations between bodies, bullets, diaries, and tableaus would emerge in the course of investigation—if they were related. Thus far Adams did not *know* that he was dealing with a single case.

It might seem overcautious to keep in mind the possibility that two murderers had been in action, with heavy-caliber guns, in the same night in Thorpe. But, until today, that any number of murderers would slay four people in one night in Thorpe would have seemed fantastic. In an improbable situation, Adams thought, he mustn't rule out anything as too improbable.

Eliminate the impossible, as Sherlock used to say, and what remains, however improbable, must be true—which was fine, except that Adams was having trouble with the eliminating.

Heirs. Radicals. Spies.

"Hell," said Adams.

Was it only accidental that the Feiths' heirs had no alibis? If not, had the additional victims been killed because of something they knew that endangered the killer? How did tableaus and diaries fit in?

As for radicals, two of them had given Adams and Olson some uncomfortable moments this morning, but—murderers? Thorpe State had lately gone far toward catching up with colleges that had previously experienced student protests, sometimes violent ones. Adams had recently seen a newspaper report about a bombing at a campus in California. Bombs there. Guns here. Why not?

Well, then, what about spies? Adams was no expert on espionage. He had just finished warning himself against dismissing anything from consideration. But he could not shake the conviction that, outside of thrillers, spies simply did not go around committing massacres. A rash of murders was almost guaranteed to draw the kind of attention that Adams supposed it was a spy's first concern to avoid.

Well, then, what circumstances could drive spies to violate the chief commandment of their calling? Crane had suggested an answer as soon as the first cipher message turned up.

Hassan ibn Sabah's apparently free-lance theft and the subsequent demonstrations had focused attention on U.R.C. If those events had threatened to uncover a spy ring, brutal elimination of the ring might have been chosen to preserve secrets in the long run.

Brutal elimination, yes. With a .44 and black-powder cartridges? Adams snorted.

Nevertheless, he considered Ashenden, one more in the parade of people whose accounts could be neither proved nor disproved. Had the man who possessed all the keys just happened to wander in the direction of the Center? Could news of Feith's death really have induced such remarkable absentmindedness in the man responsible for administrative matters?

It was too bad that Adams had been called away before he had time to form more of an impression of Feith's deputy. Even the time available had not been used to full advantage, for Adams acknowledged (with a sneering reproach for failing to live up to his own standard of professional conduct) that at the moment Ashenden arrived he had been distracted by those blasted chickens.

When Morris said, "shiver themselves to death," Adams envisioned bare-skinned hens doing precisely that. It was no use telling himself that his imagination was influenced by the fact that the only featherless chickens he had ever seen were dead. The image remained ugly. It was not natural—

Adams pulled himself up. "Natural" and "unnatural" were often slogans, not descriptive terms. The Hill that Adams was driving up once again was known as the city's natural northern boundary. The lake on the east was a natural boundary, too, although it existed because of a man-made dam. But Thorpe, in a jest that had turned sour since the explosion, the stench, and the demonstrations, called the campus to the south an unnatural boundary.

Thorpe State had once been an object of simple pride, and the citizens of Thorpe had rooted with the fervor of a pennant contender's fans for Walter Nelson's campaign to build the College into the University. Nelson himself was popular, and doubling the size of the school brought a boom to Thorpe.

In those days, Adams remembered, even Feith had been accepted, though he was a foreigner—not only from out of town but from out of the country. His alienness was reduced by marrying Nelson's daughter, and Nelson had often cited him as an invaluable assistant. Feith had always been good at extracting funds from Washington.

Attitudes had changed a good deal since those years. Perhaps Thorpe State had come to be resented by its dependents, as Feith was by his. Certainly the Chamber of Commerce put less emphasis these days on the fact that the University provided a full half of employment in the city. Then, too, Nelson's death had severed a tie. Town and gown were separated now by a gap that had been, or had seemed, smaller while he was alive. Indeed, the University had become rather foreign itself. The firefly episode had been a sign that while nuclear physics remained more glamorous, the other sciences were no less exotic as far as Thorpe was concerned.

Maybe they always had been, and Thorpe simply had not realized it. Thorpe State had seemed less unnatural when children went to its model farm to ride a pony or try to milk a cow. But Adams wondered if agronomists beefing up cattle had been more natural and more comprehensible, or only cruder, than genetic engineers stripping down chickens.

Again Adams checked himself. He was a cop, not a philosopher, and he had work to do. Turning off Lakeview, he noted that Acacia Street was no more than a few minutes' trip from the Feiths' house. He pulled into a space, and as he got out of his car, Sergeant Crane drove around the corner.

Officer James McClennan was a rookie whose fair hair and skin made him appear even younger than he was. Adams climbed two steps to the porch and looked closer. McClennan's lips were bloodless and his brow was beaded with sweat.

"Loosen your tie. Go around back and lie down for five minutes," Adams ordered.

McClennan swallowed noisily. "I'll be all—"

"When a superior officer gives you permission to lie down on the job, take advantage of it."

"He sick?" asked Crane, arriving as McClennan fled.

"He's new to this business," Adams said.

A label over the doorbell bore two names: M. Bauer and W. Overath. The front door stood ajar, and Adams pushed it open.

For the second time in less than twenty-four hours, Adams entered a house and confronted gore. Last night he had been caught off guard, and had nearly suffered McClennan's plight. Today, with the armor of professional experience in place, he looked on the scene with detachment.

The body of a man lay prone in a narrow hallway, feet toward the entrance. Adams didn't need to go closer to see that the dead man's head was wrecked, as the Feiths' had been.

On the stairs beyond the corpse, Turner of the lab squad was setting up photographic lights. Warren, camera in hand, stood in a doorway on the left beside the dead man's head and shoulders. On Adams's right was another door, and there Officer Wilson was standing.

"Got something interesting for you, Inspector," Wilson announced.

"Interesting?"

"Yes, sir. The room Warren is in is full of old guns, and a couple seem to be missing. If you come this way, you can circle around the house and get over there without going through the blood and, uh, stuff."

"You do have a way with words."

"Sir?"

"Nothing, nothing," Adams said absently, already scanning the room that had been disclosed as Wilson moved aside.

Here was another book-lined study, and another ransacked desk. Pigeonholes in the high, old-fashioned back had been emptied. The top drawer below the writing surface had been pulled right out and overturned, while the next drawer down had been opened and half-emptied. The lowest drawer was shut. Apparently the killer had sought something specific and had stopped searching when he found it.

"Start looking through those papers, will you, Crane?"

"Yes, sir."

Adams turned left and followed Wilson into the kitchen, which he surveyed as closely as the study. Three dinner dishes and three sets of silverware lay in the sink. Three wineglasses, a highball glass, an empty beer bottle, and a nearly full bottle of Scotch stood on the counter. On a table was a large, covered roasting pan which held, Adams found when he lifted the top, a steaming turkey. The back door was wide open.

"Was this door open when you got here, Wilson?"

"Yes, sir. It was just the way it is now. The front door was locked. I opened it from the inside."

Adams moved on, idly touching the side of the stove as he passed. Then he stopped, opened the oven, and felt inside. It was cold. Adams looked back at the roasting pan. Small, probably irrelevant puzzles like that were the bane of a policeman's life.

He went on to enter a room that ran the length of the house. Immediately before him was a round dining table covered with a green felt cloth. On it were two decks of cards, two glasses, an ashtray, and an earthenware bowl half-full of money, mostly small change. Beside the bowl lay a scorepad to which Adams gave thoughtful scrutiny.

"MB" and "WO" were presumably M. Bauer and W. Overath. Was "EF" Ernst Feith? And who was "GR"?

The case of the bridge-playing spies? Adams shrugged and turned away.

Guns dominated the half of the room toward which Adams now faced. Over the fireplace hung three muskets with powder horns and cases for balls. In the space between the hearth and the corner beyond were three rifles of various types and ages: one with a revolving cartridge cylinder, one

PLAYERS	MB	WO	EF	GR
1ST RUBBER	+ 50	− 50	+ 50	−150
2ND RUBBER	−1140	−1140	+1140	+1140
3RD RUBBER	−1200	+1200	+1200	−1200
TOTALS	−2190	− 90	+2490	− 210

WE	THEY	WE	THEY	WE	THEY
(50)			(1140)		(1200)
	50			100	
	200		700	100	
	50		300	50	700
	100		50	50	500
500	50		30	100	30
50	50	50			
30	60	30	80		30
90		30	60		60
					180
	70	20	120		60
	60	70			40
100	30	200	1340	400	1600
770	720				

lever-operated repeating rifle, and one that looked to Adams like a bolt-action Springfield of World War I vintage.

Handguns covered the walls around the window facing the street. Although Adams gave them only a cursory glance, he couldn't help noticing a few oddities. One pistol had six barrels in a revolving cylinder. Another had four barrels side by side and a single flintlock to fire them simultaneously. Adams thought that the kick must be phenomenal.

But it was a pair of holsters to the left of the window that caught his eye and drew him closer. Made of dark brown leather and decorated identically, the holsters looked to be the right size for a pair of .44s, and fancy enough to belong with the gun that had been found on the Feiths' property.

Both holsters were empty.

Below the display of handguns was a low chest of wide,

shallow drawers. Two had been pulled out. One held gun-cleaning equipment, none of which seemed to have been disturbed. The other contained a large loose-leaf binder labeled "Guns," and a wooden case. Adams lifted the lid of the case with one finger and disclosed twin flintlock dueling pistols with ramrod, bullet-mold, and other paraphernalia he did not know the purpose of.

On the floor beneath this second drawer lay a cardboard box that had once contained, so the printing on it declared, fifty .44-caliber black-powder cartridges. The manufacturer's address was in Southport, a town less than one hundred miles from Thorpe. The box was empty.

Two pistols. Fifty cartridges. Four bodies. Four—no, five diaries. The excesses in this case were so damned excessive.

"We're done with this one, Inspector," Warren called, "unless you want something special in the way of pictures."

"I don't think so." Adams turned to Wilson. "Where's the second body?"

"Upstairs. First bedroom on the right."

"Go ahead, Warren. I'll be along in a minute."

Warren leaped over the mess around the dead man's head to the stairs, and Adams took his place in the doorway.

The corpse was clad in a long-sleeved shirt, sleeveless sweater, pants, socks, and slippers. Adams saw no trace of the second wound he anticipated. Yet the man had certainly been forced down on the floor before being shot in the back of the head. The pattern of bloodstains showed that.

"Hang on to me for a sec, will you, Wilson?"

With Wilson gripping his arm to keep him from toppling, Adams leaned far forward and removed a wallet from the dead man's back pocket.

"Thanks."

A driver's license, a University library card, and four credit cards all bore the name Walter Overath. A grocery list had been jotted on the back of a notice, addressed to "Faculty," which announced one of the special meetings the Academic Senate had held during the demonstrations. "Turkey" headed the list.

Adams put the wallet aside, left Wilson to guard the front door, and went upstairs.

The bedroom was less of a shambles than the hallway below, because the victim had been shot while on a bed which had absorbed much of the blood. Yet the scene here was in a way more shocking, for this corpse had only one leg.

There were other, smaller shocks. Adams had unconsciously expected to find a woman's body, not that of another man. Adams had also begun to think that the killer's *modus operandi* was limited to shooting people in the back of the head, but the man before him had been shot in the forehead.

He had also been slugged. Near his left temple was a large, discolored indentation. Adams touched the spot lightly and felt bone move mushily under his fingertips.

All that was somewhat surprising, but it was to the stump of the man's right leg, and to the artificial limb laid neatly on the floor beside the bed, that Adams's eyes kept returning.

The man had been preparing for bed. He wore nothing but underwear. Pajamas lay beside him. A shirt was draped over the back of a chair and pants hung from a bureau drawer, both within easy reach of the bed. On top of the bureau, along with a handkerchief, keys, and small change, was a wallet in which Adams found cash, a social-security card in the name of Martin Bauer, and a Medic Alert card announcing that Martin Bauer had type-A blood and was allergic to penicillin.

"Hey, Inspector," Wilson shouted from downstairs. "Dr. Waddell is here and wants to know if he can start."

"Yes," Adams called back. "Ask him to see if the man down there was hit on the head before he was shot.

"It's all yours," Adams continued more quietly to Turner and Warren. "As soon as you're done with the bodies, one of you go back to the lab and fingerprint some material Inspector Logan brought in. The other should work downstairs, beginning with the cards and glasses on the dining table."

Adams toured the other rooms on the second floor rapidly. Two were bedrooms, one presumably Overath's, the other evidently not in use, for the mattresses on the twin beds were bare. The last room was another study with another rifled desk. A single drawer stood open and a folder had been emptied on top of the desk and onto the floor. Again, the implication seemed to be that the searcher had sought and found a particular object. On several of the spilled papers Adams saw Walter Overath's name.

The medical examiner was coming up the stairs as Adams started down.

"Can't tell you much," Waddell said. "Call it eighteen hours—which translates to mean that I don't think he's been dead more than twenty-four hours or less than twelve." He looked at his watch. "And eighteen hours is pretty close to the time of the other murders."

"Uh-huh. Was he hit?"

"Sure was. On the right side, toward the back of his head. My guess is a hammer, a heavy one, with a face about an inch in diameter. I would also guess that the blow was fatal. The skull was fractured, no doubt about it. Of course, the shot made damn sure he was dead."

"Yeah," Adams said. "The one upstairs seems to be named Martin Bauer, the one downstairs, Walter Overath. You can take them away when you're ready."

Waddell looked at him curiously, and Adams realized he was being curt.

"Bauer had an artificial leg. That makes it worse, somehow." He went on quickly, "Will you make an extra effort to pinpoint times of death?"

"Sure, but it isn't easy unless I have something to work from, like the time of a meal."

"I know. Do what you can, please. It may be important."

"Okay."

Adams descended and retraced his path through the living room and kitchen to the study where Crane was working. The sergeant reported that he had found papers bearing Bauer's name, and an address book that was not a Seven Star Diary. Adams described his findings, put Crane in charge once again, and departed to interview the woman who had discovered the bodies.

CHAPTER 19

Mrs. Meadows was short, plump, white-haired, and wearing bifocals—Central Casting's ideal jolly grandmother.

So much for typecasting.

Adams had never known her name, but her face and voice took him back to a day nearly nine years ago. On that day, a certain Officer Adams, so youthful that Inspector Adams could remember him with tolerant amusement, had been called upon to assist a woman give birth. Mother and child were fine as they left the squad car. Adams had fainted. Later a female pediatrician dosed him with coffee and a brisk lecture on midwifery. The lesson had served him well since, but at the time, hearing that his contribution had merely been to demonstrate anew that infants of the species are tougher than they look, he had felt he was being hit while he was down.

Dr. Meadows looked shaken, but not in immediate need of smelling salts, and she responded to Adams's apologetic preamble in a firm voice.

"Of course you must ask questions. I want to help, if I can." Then she faltered. "Are they both . . ."

"Yes, ma'am," Adams replied gently. "They are both dead."

She had expected the answer, but it was a blow nonetheless. For a moment she looked away.

"All right," she said, lifting her head. "I'm ready."

But doctors' armor is not impregnable. Adams's very first question nearly shattered her composure.

"Was there some special reason for you to go over there this afternoon?"

Her eyes filled suddenly, and she answered with an effort.

"I was taking the turkey. I . . . it's Thanksgiving, and we . . ."

She took a deep breath and began again. "I am retired, and a widow. My children have grown up and moved away. Martin was a widower, also retired, and his son works for a company in South America. Walter still teaches . . . taught at the University, but he was divorced long ago. After Mrs. Bauer died, Walter moved in with Martin. They were terrible cooks—maybe not quite as terrible as they pretended, but I was glad for the excuse to have something to do. I cooked dinners for all of us. We split the bills, and kept each other company.

"Today, I cooked the turkey. . . ."

Her voice faded away, and when she resumed her tone was sad. "They used to tease me. They said that sometime we ought to have an interesting fowl instead of just a dull turkey. I always said I could cook anything they would clean. Neither of them was about to take on that job, and every year they bought turkey and claimed it was the only kind of bird they could find already cleaned.

"They knew that I love turkey.

"And so I cooked it, and Walter was supposed to come and fetch it. But he didn't come, and I carried it over and went in the back door. I called. No one answered. I went to the front and saw . . ."

Adams pretended to consult his notes, giving her a few seconds of respite, but then he had to go on with the questioning.

Mrs. Bauer had died six years ago in an automobile accident. Mr. Bauer had not been in the car; he had lost his leg as a boy. He had been very distressed by his wife's death, and had retired from teaching soon after. Overath had moved into Bauer's house partly because he himself was lonely and partly to try to reduce Bauer's loneliness, not because Bauer's physical disability left him in need of a companion.

Dr. Meadows had known the Bauers and Overath for nearly thirty years—"My husband taught German at the University, and he helped them improve their English when they first arrived."

"They came from Germany?"

"Yes. They left to get away from Hitler. Walter was Jewish or part-Jewish. I think that had something to do with the trouble with his wife, too. He never talked about it, but I got the idea from something Martin said once."

"Did they emigrate at the same time as Ernst Feith?"

"A little later. Dr. Feith got out first, and he helped the others come to Thorpe."

Dr. Meadows seemed not to have heard that Feith, too, had been murdered. Adams hurried on.

Yes, Dr. Meadows had eaten dinner with Bauer and Overath last night. The dishes had been left unwashed because Wednesdays were bridge nights.

"They were very Teutonic about it," she said with a faint smile. "At eight o'clock, down they sat. Three rubbers, and by ten they were done. No chitchat, just concentrated bridge. They played like that nearly every Wednesday night for as long as I've known them, and I suppose they did the same in Germany. They were good. I sat in a few times when one of them was away, but I'm not in their class and playing that way wasn't much fun for me."

"Did they play for money?"

"Yes, but in a nice way. They played for a tenth of a cent a point, and normally no one lost more than a dollar. The losers put their money into a pot, and when a large enough amount had been amassed, they took it all and went out to dinner. Martin used to laugh about the reactions of waiters when they were paid forty or fifty dollars in nickels and dimes."

"Who were the others?"

"Why, Dr. Feith and Gunther Ritter."

Adams nodded, as if she had only confirmed what he had known all along.

"Had they arrived when you left last night?"

"Dr. Feith had. Gunther hadn't."

"What time was that?"

"Oh, five minutes to eight, maybe."

"You had started eating dinner around seven o'clock, then?"

"Yes, almost to the minute. We were always very prompt on Wednesdays."

Waddell would be proud of him.

"Do you happen to know Gunther Ritter's address?"

"Yes, of course. 1612 Beech Street. Apartment 5-A."

"One last question. Did you see or hear any disturbance during the night, or anything at all that you think might be relevant?"

"No, I'm afraid not. I draw my curtains at night and—well, I've grown a little deaf in the last few years."

"All right, Dr. Meadows. Thank you. If you think of anything I ought to know, you can leave a message for me at police headquarters."

With Gunther Ritter occupying his thoughts, Adams started away in a rush, but halfway across the street he turned back and went to the house next to the one he had just left. He showed his badge to the woman who answered the bell.

"This is not a business call, exactly. I'm trying to find someone who is a friend of Dr. Meadows."

"We're friendly," the woman said uncertainly.

"The two men across the street are dead. Dr. Meadows found their bodies. Someone ought to be with her."

"Oh, dear. Of course. I think Mrs. Draper is a close friend." She saw that Adams did not know Mrs. Draper. "I could call her, if you like."

"Yes, please," said Adams, and went away feeling a little better.

CHAPTER 20

Captain Vogel listened to Adams's report without interrupting, and at the end he said calmly, "Very well. I'll start putting men into position." But then he gave vent to his feelings. "Christ on a crutch! Did this Ritter knock them all off?"

"If he's alive, he probably did."

"Only, you don't think he's alive."

"Hell, I don't know. At the rate bodies are turning up, nobody in town will be left alive by Christmas."

"Yes. Well, don't take any chances going in after him. He may have that other gun, so do it by the book, hear?"

Since Adams considered heroics a form of stupidity, he would never have done it any other way.

The building was surrounded. Occupants of all apartments but Ritter's, on the top floor, were telephoned and instructed to go quietly out into the charge of officers waiting in the halls to evacuate them. Two men went to the roof, while two others took station at the foot of the fire escape. Adams and Crane, wearing bulky, constricting flak vests (which made Adams, at least, terribly conscious of all the unprotected parts of his body), went to Ritter's door with guns drawn.

They rang. They knocked. They called out. Finally, they kicked the door open.

Gunther Ritter was not the killer. He lay face down just inside his living room. He had been hit and shot in the head. A desk in the living room had obviously been searched.

Thereafter, many hours passed unnoticed. At some point, Adams became aware that night had fallen and that the day's scattered clouds had coalesced and produced a cold, persistent drizzle that was all too appropriate.

Turner and Warren came and took photographs and dusted for fingerprints. Dr. Waddell arrived, said he hoped that Adams would get out of this rut P.D.Q., opined that Ritter had been killed with the same weapons and in the same span of time as the others, and took himself and the body away.

Uniformed officers were detailed to interview neighbors, and reappeared at irregular intervals to report small profit from their labors. The only person who claimed to have heard a suspicious noise during the night was the man in the apartment directly below Ritter's. He said accusingly to his wife, "I told you that was no backfire." She remembered neither the noise nor his comment, and he had no idea what time he had heard whatever he heard.

Crane, who had remained in charge at Bauer and Overath's residence, phoned to say that Bauer had been the arms collector. In the loose-leaf binder Adams had seen, Bauer had kept a file on all the guns he owned. None had been manufactured after 1920; all had been made in the United States or the preceding Colonies. The missing weapons, described in such detail that there could be no mistake, were Colt New Navy Model double-action .44-caliber revolvers. They had been ordered specially in 1899 for presentation to an Army colonel upon his retirement. Their subsequent history was unknown until Bauer bought them at an auction in 1954, but Bauer had noted that the guns and their holsters were "filthy."

Later, the laboratory reported that the few fingerprints on the gun that had been found at the Feiths' were too smeared to be identified with confidence, but were probably Bauer's. There were fingerprints from two or three persons on the empty cartridge box, but they did not match any others the lab had, and they had probably been made by employees of the manufacturer.

Crane phoned again to say that the dead men's fingerprints had been identified on the glasses, cards, and scorepad at Bauer and Overath's house. The only other prints on crockery matched those on the roasting pan and had no doubt been made by Mrs. Meadows. Did Adams want to make sure by having Mrs. Meadows printed? Adams decided that could wait.

Captain Vogel phoned to say that the Seven Star Diaries found by Logan had been examined. Nothing was written in any of them. The cover of each diary carried prints from one of the dead men, but no other prints had been found on or in any of them. The front of each of the tableaus Logan had found also carried the prints of one man. The bullets, and the plastic bag in which all had been packed, were completely free of prints.

Then another cipher message turned up.

The top drawers of Ritter's desk had been ransacked, but the lower drawers had not. It seemed that the killer had stopped searching because he had found what he was after—presumably a Seven Star Diary and a tableau. Adams's men did not stop until they had searched everywhere. They opened every drawer and took out every item inside. In a double drawer filled with folders standing on edge, they found the message. It was down between two of the folders, where it might have fallen and lain unnoticed.

Like the cipher from Feith's desk, the one from Ritter's had been typed and photocopied. It had Ritter's prints on the front side. Unlike Feith's message, Ritter's had no lines drawn between numbers. Also, the dates and the numbers in the bodies of the two messages were different.

15 Nov.

```
   1 1 0 2 1
   8 0 4 1 6
   0 8 0 3 1
   5 2 5 0 0
   2 4 2 6 1
   4 3 3 0 7
   4 7 3 6 7
   0 8 5 0 6
   3 7 4 0 4
   4 0 9 1 0
   1 7 4 5 2
   3 1 2 5 8
   0 5 4 9 4
   6 5 9 4 2
   4 8 9 6 1
   9 5 6 9 7
 -----------
 6 1 8 5 1 7
```

At that point, Captain Vogel intervened, calling Adams away from Ritter's apartment to police headquarters. He had a Seven Star Diary, a tableau, and copies of the two cryptograms on his desk when Adams arrived.

Without preamble, Vogel said, "We have to decode these, Jeff."

"So decode 'em, then," Adams barked. "Sorry. I guess I'm getting tired." He rubbed his forehead. "But tired or not, I can't solve those things."

"Could Kate?"

Adams gaped. The thought of dragging Kate into this case appalled him.

Hard on the heels of that blow came another. The wall clock behind Vogel seemed to leap into sight to inform him that the time was well past ten.

"Good Lord!" said Vogel, following Adams's gaze. "Didn't you ever call her?"

Adams shook his head.

"Boy, are you going to get it. She must have tried to call you eight hours ago."

An old married man's jocular commiseration was not balm to Adams's soul at that moment.

"Take this stuff and get out of here," Vogel ordered brusquely. "The men are pretty near finished with the searches. Lieutenant Johnson has night duty, and he can supervise the last bits. Go on—git!"

Adams went to his desk with a condemned man's tread. There were three messages from Kate. She had called at two and at six, simply leaving her name. At ten she had left the message "Come when you can."

He imagined her waiting, becoming impatient, becoming anxious, finally rushing to make dinner in case he showed up at last. More waiting. She phoned, waited, phoned again. Turkey cooled. Gravy congealed.

Adams groaned.

CHAPTER 21

Kate must have been listening for him. As Adams stepped up on the porch, she flung open her door.

Woebegone though he was, he noticed that he might as well have saved his warnings against opening the door at night without first turning on the outside light. Besides, in the dark he wouldn't see her expression.

"Kate, I—"

"It's safe. I'm not mad."

"Ah, Kate. I don't have words to tell you—"

She silenced him with a kiss.

"Hush. Come in now."

He surrendered gratefully. He shed his coat and dropped his briefcase while she closed the door behind him. When she turned and saw him in the light, she exclaimed, "My poor dear. You're exhausted."

"I'm all right."

"Yes, of course," she said with gentle scorn, taking his hand and leading him to the sofa. "Your coloring is naturally purple under the eyes and ash gray everywhere else."

"That bad, is it?" He dropped onto the couch and discovered that a pillow at the small of the back was comforting. "I bow to a superior officer."

"Good. Do you want food straight away, or a drink first?"

"A drink would knock me cold. I'd love a sandwich."

Kate brought two, along with stuffing, cranberry sauce, and gravy that flowed smoothly after all.

"I expected crow," Adams said, "not this feast."

"The cook thanks you, but doubts that a starving man can tell turkey from buzzard. Have you eaten anything at all today?"

"Why, yes. I had a gourmet luncheon—a peanut-butter sandwich."

"Yuck," Kate said with feeling.

"It was a gift."

"And cheap at half the price." She surveyed him appraisingly. "Despite all, you begin to look as if you may survive. Coffee?"

"Yes, miss. I like this restaurant. I couldn't have bettered that stuffing myself."

"It was made with love," Kate said, as if naming an ingredient any sophisticated palate would recognize.

That shut him up.

They drank their coffee in silence. When the cups were empty, Kate said, "I won't be offended if you want to go right home and sleep—and that's not a sneaky way of throwing you out. I'll be glad to have you, if you want to stay."

"I would like to stay a little while."

"Do you want to talk?" She hesitated. "I would help, if I could."

"Is it so obvious that I need help?"

"I meant, you looked as if your thoughts were grim."

"I suppose they were. It's a grim business." He paused uncomfortably. "Oddly enough, I'm supposed to ask for your assistance."

"Says who?"

"Says Vogel. We have a couple of cryptograms, and we can't read them."

"Talk about the lame and the blind!" Kate ejaculated. "You really ought to ask someone else. I'm no expert."

"Kate Shaw! Come off it! You have written a thirty-page dissection of Ignatius Donnelly's crazy cryptogram. And now you go false-modest on me."

"I'm not, Jeff. Really, I'm not. I'm great at quoting other people's analyses, but I wouldn't know how to begin dismantling a cipher myself. My father is the person you should see. I understand ciphers when they are explained to me. He can explain them."

Adams squirmed. He would be more than pleased to go to someone else, but he was certainly not going to Mark Shaw.

"Well, at least take a look at my ciphers, okay?" He went to the hall and returned with his briefcase. "Amateur you may be, but you know a lot more than any cop in Thorpe seems to know."

He saw in her expression that his tone had rung false.

"Jeff, why do you refuse to go to my father?"

"He's a witness."

"And?"

"That's plenty. It's damned bad practice to introduce witnesses to evidence they haven't learned on their own. A defense attorney could create a distracting issue out of the use of a witness as an expert consultant."

"No doubt, but you protest too much. That's not the whole reason."

"Kate," he pleaded.

"Is it?"

Adams threw up his hands. "No. No, it's not," he admitted. "He told me a story that's full of holes."

"My God!" she whispered. "What are you saying?"

Stupid. So stupid. He ought to have been able to choose his words better than that.

"I don't mean that it's necessarily false, Kate. I mean that it doesn't make sense. Maybe it will after I have more chance to think about it, and maybe he can make it sensible in some simple, acceptable way. But so far, it's just screwball."

"And you suspect—"

"Kate! Don't read too much in. He may have made

mistakes. He may . . . oh, I don't know."

Again his tone betrayed him.

"He may . . . what?" Kate demanded. "Tell me, Jeff. I won't flare up at you again."

"All right," Adams said wearily. "Your father was obviously disturbed when I suggested that a radical student might have killed the Feiths. It made me wonder if he knew, or thought he knew, who did kill them, and if he was trying to cover up for the killer."

"Jeff, you can't seriously think— Blast! Yes, you can. I myself can almost believe he would do such a thing.

"What *is* his story, Jeff? All he told Mom and me was that he found the bodies and that someone fired a shot near or at him."

"Brother!" said Adams. "Is this ever against regulations! But here goes."

He told her a somewhat sanitized version of Mark Shaw's account, and she heard it through in attentive silence.

At the end, she said slowly, "It does seem strange that the killer hung about, instead of fleeing immediately. But that's his problem, not Dad's, so far as I can tell. And I don't see what else troubles you. Where are the holes you mentioned?"

"Wait," Adams said, and sat back thinking hard.

Certain difficulties had been obscured in his summary. But part of the story was so obviously impossible that Shaw's failure to see the anomaly had been baffling.

Kate, Adams was perfectly sure, was no less bright than her father, and she didn't notice it either.

Somehow that fact seemed important, but Adams couldn't work out why. It was as if he had caught just a glimpse of something he should recognize but could not quite name.

He realized that no matter how intelligent Kate and her father were, they might not see at all what his trained eye saw at once—and thinking that renewed his sense of almost understanding something crucial. But straining to clarify the vague perception only dimmed it.

"No," Adams said. "I have heard something significant, but

I can't make it come clear in my mind. I have already said too much—"

He had, indeed. The glance she gave him was like a blow.

"Kate. I didn't mean . . . You know I trust you."

"Yes. Exactly as far as Harry Hotspur's Kate."

Her contained fury shook him, and he was further discomforted because his memory was a perfect blank so far as Harry Hotspur's Kate was concerned.

She told him: "'Constant,' he called her, 'but yet a woman.' And what she did not know, she could not tell."

"All right, Kate. I am worried that you may tell what you do know. Not because you're a woman, but because you are your father's child. You'll be in his company. You have no skill as a liar—I can't be sorry about that. But please understand me, Kate, I mustn't let you give him a hint. I can't afford to have him setting his celebrated imagination to work prettying up his story for me."

She made no comment. Instead she seemed to change the subject abruptly.

"What stories do Karl and Margaret tell?"

"Karl and Margaret?" Adams said in surprise. "Do you know them?"

"Of course. They lived across the street from the time I was fourteen or fifteen, and Karl and I were in a few classes together."

"Were they your *friends?*"

"Not really. Not at all, to be frank. I was very earnest, rather puritanical, and I'm afraid I looked down my nose at Karl. He was the kind whose main effort went into trying to figure out what answer a teacher wanted to hear. I thought he was too smart for that, but maybe not. At any rate, he fizzled later."

"Could he say the same of you?"

"Perhaps, but there is a difference. I passed my orals, so I had a choice about going on for the Ph.D. He didn't."

"And Margaret?"

"Well, she was younger. Two years younger, I think, and

that's a lot at fifteen. After all, you are only two years older than I, yet our paths never crossed in high school."

Adams nodded.

"Besides, I was in my poetical phase then, while Margaret played softball and read comics— I was such a snob."

"But with age," Adams intoned, "you have achieved the wisdom to appreciate Baconians, Atlanteans, and, finally, softball players—is that about right?"

"Not quite right," Kate said with a grin. "I met Margaret and her husband in a store one day and couldn't resist the judgment that he was moderately handsome in a beefy sort of way, but, oh my, was he dumb—and, oh my, does that sound even cattier than I intended."

"Maybe you still need a little more aging before utter perfection will be attained," Adams said. "Me, too. I decided he was nearly brainless. But I couldn't figure out if they are well matched or not."

"Umm. I wonder. Margaret did get terrible grades, I remember, but she had an air of flaunting them. Every so often, she used to surprise me by understanding more than I expected. Age may not have brought great wisdom, but I can see now that she might have been rebelling, or simply opting out of competition with an older, and definitely favored brother. It would be interesting to know what she has become."

"You don't see them any more?"

"I see Karl occasionally. In fact, I saw him a month ago at a certain publication party of painful, if somewhat hazy, memory."

Adams winced.

"I think he had left before you arrived. A lot of people had."

She was really laying into him. And he had innocently supposed that her grievance had subsided. He would have to make it right, somehow. But now, to his relief, she seemed to decide she had taken enough revenge.

"Mom must have invited him. After all, she works with him." Mrs. Shaw, Adams knew, taught history at Thorpe

High School. "For all I know, she invited the whole family."

"Was she friends with the Feiths?"

"Not that I know of. She just doesn't like hostilities. She may have felt sorry for Mrs. Feith, too. She is inclined to pity a woman who doesn't have a career. According to Mom, women without careers adopt cats or causes."

"I take it that your mother didn't think highly of Mrs. Feith's choice of causes."

"My mom? Hoo, boy! She doesn't enjoy conflict, but if you want to hear fine-honed denunciation, you should get her started on book-banners sometime. Or the anti-fluoridation campaign. Are you aware that fluoride will make us stupid so the Reds can conquer us without a fight?"

"Aw, come on. You made that up."

"Never. Mrs. Feith put a pamphlet exposing the nefarious scheme in our mailbox."

"What did her husband—"

"Inspector Adams," Kate interrupted, frowning. "Are you interrogating me?"

He was, although he had not meant to. He sought refuge in a feeble joke.

"I only want the facts, ma'am."

"Scraps of gossip about family, friends, and acquaintances," Kate said with an edge to her voice. "I don't like it."

"No. No one does."

For a long moment she stared at him. "You have a rather terrible job."

More than the words, the distant tone shocked a protest from him.

"Kate, murder is terrible."

She turned her head and gazed into space with an expression he could not, dared not, interpret. He glanced down and discovered her hands clenched so tightly that her knuckles showed white. For a second, for an age, she was still and taut and infinitely far away. Then one hand opened and turned palm upward.

"Ask, then, if you must."

He breathed.

"I've asked too much of you already." He took her hand. "I ought to go. It's the only way to keep the question machine from starting up again."

"Ah, no. Not now. Not— What a big help I've been! I urge you to talk, and when you do, all you get from me is trouble."

"For God's sake, Kate. You don't owe me an apology. Don't be so hard on yourself."

"Just on you? Oh, no. I refuse to be the kind who demands that you keep half your life a secret." She produced a shaky smile. "Could we try again? You were going to tell me what Karl and Margaret had to say for themselves."

Adams could think of topics he would prefer, such as details of the halves she foresaw in his life. But if this was important to her, then it was important to him. Dutifully, he reported.

It wasn't easy to be brief describing the Feith children's behavior and explanations. In the end, Adams was glad, for Kate's tension eased as he talked. She did blanch, remembering fear, when he said that Mrs. Evans had been the driver of the car that nearly destroyed them. To the rest she listened in silence with no apparent reaction. Adams, too, began to relax.

When Adams finished with Karl Feith, Kate said, "Now, that's brass. Imagine denying he had had a visitor, with all those glasses and cigarette butts and things staring you in the face." She shook her head wonderingly. "But where does a cipher come in? Don't tell me the lovers send billets-doux in secret writing."

Her first remark gave Adams unexpected food for thought. Her conclusion triggered a horrifying suspicion.

"Don't you . . . Haven't you heard any news broadcasts?"

"No. Should I have?"

This was too much, Adams thought resentfully. This damned case had crashed into their lives at the worst possible moment. He had nearly killed her in a wreck. He had frightened her about her father, nagged her about childhood acquaintances, compelled her to offer excuses for feeling repugnance to which she had a right. And now he had to bear dreadful tidings.

"What is it, Jeff?"

No euphemisms came to mind.

"There have been other killings," he said. "Three men. All shot last night with the same gun that killed the Feiths, or its twin. All friends of the Feiths."

"Good God!" Kate cried. "It's horrible. It's mad."

"It's horrible. It may not be mad. All the men came from Germany in the late thirties, first Feith, then the others with Feith's help. They were all scientists. And they all had some connection with the cipher."

"I don't . . . I can't take it in. What does it matter that they came from Germany? That they were scientists? That they immigrated when they did?"

"In the years around World War Two, a lot of people claimed to be refugees. Some of them were agents for one government or another. The Nazi agents were caught, or closed up shop eventually. The others . . . who knows?"

"Do you mean that Feith and the others were spies?"

"I don't know. Not very many hours ago, I said blithely that some people work cryptograms for fun. That's hard to credit in this case."

"It's all hard to credit. It's all sickening." Kate's voice had gone shrill. She took a deep breath. "No wonder you said it was a grim business."

Adams shrugged helplessly.

Kate glanced sidelong at him. "And now you want me to work this cipher puzzle for you?"

"Kate! I don't want you anywhere near this business." Now his voice rose as self-control failed. "What am I supposed to do? Tell you sickening things? Keep secrets from you? Goddamn it! I don't do these things. When they happen, I have to ask questions, suspect people, do my terrible job."

She took his hand. "Jeff, oh, Jeff, I'm sorry. I didn't mean . . . what you heard. At least, I didn't want to mean it. I'm still kicking at the traces a little, I guess." She gave him a small, tentative smile. "And, after my fashion, I was trying to say that I will look at your puzzle, if you will show it to me."

He put both arms around her and clung. He was startled to hear Kate laugh after a few seconds. "Your damn job keeps coming between us." She moved away and tapped his brief-case. "This thing is demanding my attention by gouging a hole in my side. Shall I see what it has to offer?"

He let her take it.

"Don't look so solemn. I won't be scarred for life, by your briefcase or your murder case. I'm not fragile, only a little naive still. I can be tough, you know."

He forced himself to match her tone.

"I know, I know. You scare me to death."

"Um. That's good. Now, let's see." She was laying papers on the floor.

"Why, I thought there was nothing but an enciphered message. You have the whole shebang." She frowned and slid onto her knees amid the papers. "No, not quite. Let me see. Let me see."

Adams smiled fondly as she fidgeted and squirmed until she was prone, with one bare foot describing slow circles in the air and the other burrowing beneath a couch cushion. This wasn't the first time he had seen her work herself into something like a trance, focused completely on a problem. Already, he knew, she wouldn't hear him unless he shouted.

He yawned, and thought: What a night this has been. I think I must have blown a fuse at last.

His eyelids fell, and he jerked them up. "Kicking at the traces," she had said. And, "Half your life . . . half your life . . ."

He came awake with a jolt to find Kate leaning over him with a blanket.

"What time is it?"

"About three. You haven't slept long."

He sat up rubbing his eyes. "Poor Kate. I'm late. I dump my problems on you. I fall asleep and probably snore. All boor and a mile wide, that's me."

She folded her arms and looked stern. "If this is self-flagellation time, please go outside to bleed."

"Whew! You're tough, all right. But, Kate, I owe you some sort of apology."

"You don't," she said firmly. "Why don't you go back to

sleep? You can go to work as well from here as from your place."

"Temptress. But—well, I need to shave and change clothes, and I won't be surprised if Vogel calls. Which reminds me. Did you solve it?"

Kate shook her head. "No, I'm afraid not. It's too hard, or else it's missing a piece."

"God," Adams said gloomily. Every time he had found a new piece so far, he had found a body with it. "Well, tell me what you can, but slowly and simply, as if to one not very bright. My vital flame burns dim just now."

"Okay. First, I assumed you had reasons for dividing the November 22nd message into pairs as you did."

"*I* didn't. The lines between the numbers were there when we found it."

"Indeed? How very helpful."

"How so?"

"Without them, I would have no way of knowing if the numbers had been anagrammed or transposed."

"Let's try that one again," said Adams. "Words of one syllable, please."

"It's not so hard, actually. Let me give you a couple of examples. Decipherment might be supposed to start by pairing each digit in an odd-numbered row with the one directly below in an even-numbered row. Or by pairing the first and third, the second and fourth, the fifth and second digits from successive rows. Or by making a long string of the first column, followed by the second column, and so on. Or by—"

"All right. I follow you. But I thought you pretended not to know how to do this sort of thing."

"Now, don't start that again. It's a far cry from knowing that various methods can be used to knowing how to discover which method was used. As you will see, if you keep quiet for a while, I reach the limit of my knowledge in a hurry."

"Yes, ma'am. Go on."

"That's better. The first step is clear. I wrote down pairs of numbers and matched them with letters from the chart, producing this."

Kate handed Adams a sheet on which he read:

L	N	Q	N	E	M	Y	A	B	P	V	Z	D	W	V
14	12	09	39	21	13	01	25	24	10	04	00	22	03	47
Q	**I**	**S**	**A**	**S**	**T**	**P**	**K**	**S**	**N**	**Q**	**N**	**V**	**A**	**N**
42	17	07	26	44	06	41	15	59	64	61	91	56	77	12
P	**G**	**R**	**Q**	**E**	**S**	**R**	**P**	**Q**	**H**	**P**	**T**	**J**	**W**	**S**
62	19	08	94	30	96	43	93	09	18	10	45	16	03	07

"You will notice I left off the sum at the bottom of the column of figures. I assumed that because it was crossed out, it should be omitted."

"Okay, I'm still following. Now, these letters have to be matched with . . . well, with what?"

"Crash," said Kate. "We have run into my limit. I can't take the next step. I don't know the rules. I tried using the dates, because they stand out so obviously that they seem to demand to be used."

She rummaged among the papers.

"Here's one. I wrote out the date in words, and made that the key phrase. I paired letters from the date with those from the number-letter chart and used those pairs to give me coordinates in the tableau."

i j o a p m v w n y t w b q g
T W E N T Y T W O N O V E M B E R T W E N T Y
L N Q N E M Y A B P V Z D W V Q I S A S T P K

T W O N O V E M B E R T W E N T Y T W O N O
S N Q N V A N P G R Q E S R P Q H P T J W S

"As you can see, I quit because I was getting nonsense. I tried reversing pairs. I tried 'November twenty-two,' 'twenty-second November'— Nothing. I tried making combinations using 'D,' which goes with number 22 in the chart; I tried using 'V,' which is the twenty-second letter of the alphabet. All I got was gibberish.

"There's no end to possibilities, and I'm simply not enough of a cryptanalyst to figure out which ones are probabilities, much less to break the cipher without a key. I need some sort of key phrase."

"By God! I think she's got it!" Adams exclaimed.

"Jeff," Kate said reproachfully. "Don't make fun of me. I tried. I can't do it."

"My brainy beauty, I'm not fooling. I think you're right about what is missing. And I think—I hope—I have the missing piece."

Adams fumbled in the briefcase and drew out a Seven Star Diary.

"We found four of these memo books with no entries written in them, one for each male victim."

"Ugh! What a ghastly phrase."

"I've worn you out," Adams said contritely. "It's time to get some sleep. This can wait."

"You can't go now," Kate declared. "You got me into this project, and you aren't moving an inch until I see the end of it. Please."

Adams leaned over and gently ruffled her hair. "You are a glutton for punishment. But, okay.

"This is one of the books we found. Nothing written in it. But printed at the bottom of each page in the diary section is what I guess is meant as an inspirational motto."

"'A glass of truth with a drop of untruth in it makes the strongest poison,'" Kate read, from November 14th. And from November 10th, "'Your opinion of others shows what others think of you.'

"We are *not* inspired."

"Never mind. Call them what you like. The question is how would they serve as key phrases?"

"Very well. A different phrase for every date. It's elaborate, but clever." Kate held out a pad and pencil. "See if it works."

Adams copied the motto from November 22nd: "A big talent is like a kite; the higher it flies the more rascals there are who try to haul it down." Beneath it, he wrote the letters of the message dated '22 Nov.'

"The saying is longer than the message."

"No matter."

"Does it matter how I get letters from the tableau?"

"Yes, but there are only a few possibilities. You might as well start by assuming that the cipher-message letters are in the left column. Find your first letter, run across the row until you reach the first letter of the motto, then go up that column to the top. So, the 'L' matches with 'A' to give 'P.' If you read off the pairs, I'll operate the tableau for you."

It worked. In a short time, Adams had this before him:

p o s t p o n e m e n t i m p o s s i b l e x
A B I G T A L E N T I S L I K E A K I T E T H
L N Q N E M Y A B P V Z D W V Q I S A S T P K

m u s t m e e t n o v e m b e r x x v i i z
E H I G H E R I T F L I E S T H E M O R E R
S N Q N V A N P G R Q E S R P Q H P T J W S

The end of the deciphered message looked strange at first, but when the last "z" was seen to be a null which had been added to complete a five-digit line, and when normal spacing and punctuation were provided, the import was clear:

Postponement impossible. Must meet November XXVII.

"Do the other one," Kate said.

This time, Adams started from scratch, writing pairs of numbers, then letters above them. Kate read off the motto from November 15th: "A blow from a friend's hand is better than a caress from an enemy's." (She also muttered, "Muses and graces," but Adams left that out.) Soon his paper showed this:

m	e	e	t	n	o	v	e	m	b	e	r	x	x	v	i	i	a	t	u
A	B	L	O	W	F	R	O	M	A	F	R	I	E	N	D	S	H	A	N
O	X	H	V	J	R	W	K	A	Z	B	A	L	H	S	V	K	H	H	T
11	02	18	04	16	08	03	15	25	00	24	26	14	33	07	47	36	70	85	06

s	u	a	l	p	l	a	c	e	a	n	d	t	i	m	e	z	y	x	z
D	I	S	B	E	T	T	E	R	T	H	A	N	A	C	A	R	E	S	S
L	O	S	Q	P	I	T	C	N	T	U	X	U	S	Q	W	S	G	V	T
37	40	44	09	10	17	45	23	12	58	05	49	46	59	42	48	96	19	56	97

Adams could then write:

Meet November XXVII at usual place and time.

"So they were spies," Kate said. "And it looks as if one of them tried to put off the gathering."

"The Feiths have usually spent Thanksgiving at a cabin in the mountains," Adams said. "This year, they—or, rather, he—announced a couple of weeks ago that they would stay home for a change."

Abruptly, Kate began to shovel material into the briefcase. "I was wrong," she said shakily. "I didn't want to know the end. Keeping them from their holiday in order to kill them. That's especially nasty. I think you should go now."

But she let him hold her for a time, until she could say in her ordinary voice, "I guess I'm not so tough, after all. But I'll be all right now. And you must get some sleep. What time will you have to get up?"

"Around seven-thirty, I suppose."

"That's terrible. It's after four already. Come on. Now I am throwing you out."

"Oh, well. Parting is such sleepy sorrow."

"You're a dope. Good night, my dear."

"Good night, sweet Kate."

CHAPTER 22

Adams rarely dreamed, or rarely remembered dreaming, but for the second night (rather, the second scanty portion of a morning) in a row, his subconscious went into overdrive. Later, he remembered a chaos of scenes, as if he had been switching at irregular but frequent intervals from one TV program to another, and finding Kate in each and cars in both.

She sat frozen in terror beside him as a car hurtled toward them—it came head-on but he saw clearly the huge dent in its side. She opened his briefcase to disclose a copy of her own book, along with Karl Feith's glasses and ashtray, and hers were the only fingerprints on them. Mark Shaw drove an MG with treadless tires toward an open door, blind to the menacing gunman whose features Adams could not see. Kate clawed at the ground, angering Adams. He held out his arms, and she drew his hand toward her naked breast. Pamela Black slammed the car door and fired two pairs of shots through it; when Adams opened the door, a faceless man lay dead amid a litter of messages, and Kate said, "A piece is missing."

"Do what?" Adams mumbled.

"What?" said a woman's voice.

Adams leaped upright in panicky confusion. Why was he telephoning? Had he forgotten to call Kate yet? What was wrong? Had something happened to her?

"Who is this?"

"It's me, Inspector. Doris, the dispatcher. Are you all right?"

"Oh. Dodi."

Adams squinted and massaged his forehead with his free hand. His head ached savagely.

"Sorry, Dodi. I must have been sound asleep when I picked up the phone. Did I say something weird?"

"I think you said, 'No pieces are missing.'"

"I did?" Adams shifted his hand from forehead to the back of his neck. Then his eyes opened wide. "Did I, indeed? What a clever little devil the subconscious is."

"Inspector, are you all right?"

Adams grinned, headache half gone. "I'm fine, Dodi. And I owe you a box of candy for listening so carefully. I'm awake now, too. Go ahead with your news—bad news, no doubt.

"I have a message for you from Captain Vogel," Doris said in her dispatcher's voice with only a tinge of dubiousness. "He said that two F.B.I. agents will be here at nine, and could you arrange to meet with them?"

Adams had been braced for worse. "I'll be there," he said.

"And Sergeant Brenner—he's on the desk—says there's a pack of reporters out front and maybe you will want to come in by the back door."

"Already? What time is it?"

Adams had expected reporters, but not a pack first thing in the morning. He was afraid he must have overslept. But as Doris said, "Seven-thirty, Inspector," his alarm began to ring.

"When did Vogel get there?"

"He isn't here. He phoned at twelve-o-nine and left the message I gave you. Do you have any messages you want me to take?"

"No, except that if anyone wants me, I'll be in at eight. Thanks, Dodi. And thank Brenner for me, will you?"

Adams rolled out of bed intending to consider the intuition Dodi's sharp ear had preserved for him. But the riotous visions from his sleep intruded.

"Freud, Jung, and Adler protect us," he prayed.

He dropped his clothes on the floor and padded into the bathroon. Peering into the bloodshot, dark-circled eyes the mirror displayed, he decided Bogart was prettier.

"All the best columnists agree that the sexual revolution has come, and you—you've been bowdlerized. Something's going to burst if you don't get matters resolved in no time flat or a little less."

Captain Vogel was parking his car as Adams drove into the lot behind headquarters.

"Morning," Vogel said. "You get any sleep?"

"A little. Did you?"

"Not enough. I was on the phone with the feds till midnight. Did you get my message?"

"Uh-huh. Are they moving in on us?"

Adams might be provincial, or egotistical, but no federal agents were pushing him out of this case without a struggle.

Vogel grunted. "Yes and no."

"What's that supposed to mean?"

"Ahh," Vogel said disgustedly. "They say they only want to keep informed. I say the feds don't invite themselves to a conference unless they have something on their minds. And I'll tell you this. Whatever is on their minds was bothering them before they knew about the code messages."

"Cipher," Adams said automatically.

"Sure, sure. Hey, did Kate solve 'em?"

"'Meet November 27 at usual place and time,'" Adams recited. "That's the one dated November 15th. The other one says, 'Postponement impossible. Must meet November 27.'"

"Jesus P. Christmas! Our federal friends are going to love that."

If so, they hid their emotion well.

Agents McGuire and Tanner did pore over the cipher materials, and McGuire said "Thank you" politely when Vogel proffered copies. But their expressions never changed and they made no comment. Not a word of praise for the rapid solution, Adams noted with resentment on Kate's behalf (although, since he was determined to spare her further interrogation, he had not named her).

On the other hand, they offered none of the words of reproof Adams had been smarting under, in anticipation, for his unauthorized perusal in Feith's office of documents which might have been classified. Maybe they weren't such bad guys after all, even if McGuire did look like a graying Dick Tracy.

During his recital of events in Feith's office, Adams detected a stir of interest. Or, rather, not a stir. The agents became, if it was possible, more still and more blank-visaged, but their hands fairly flew as they made notes. Adams had tentatively assumed that U.R.C. was what was bothering them. He was mildly interested to have his guess confirmed. But Brer McGuire, he said nothin'.

Now and then, one or the other asked a question that provided no clue to their thoughts. For the rest, they listened and they seemed to record just about every word he and Vogel said, right down to his concluding "That's it."

McGuire nodded. "I have some fingerprints for you," he said crisply. "Feith's, Overath's, and Ritter's. The Bureau does not have Bauer's or Mrs. Feith's on file."

That was one way of indicating that three of the dead men had undergone security checks.

"Did Feith, Overath, and Ritter have current clearances?"

"Feith and Overath did. Ritter's was terminated in 1953 after his wife left him and took their two children to live in East Germany."

"East Germany, huh?"

McGuire was not to be drawn.

"I am authorized to say that Overath had not been engaged in classified research during the last year."

"Meaning that Feith was, or that you aren't saying?" Adams asked impatiently.

"He was."

That was all the yokels would get on that subject.

"You asked about Mark Shaw," McGuire said, turning to

Vogel. "He has never had a security clearance. He is not known to have joined the Party, but he was one of the people who went to Spain with the leftists during the Civil War. He never worked for the O.S.S."

"Holy cats!" said Vogel.

"However, he did do intelligence work during the war," McGuire continued, unperturbed. "He was with the Spanish Desk of Army Intelligence in Washington from April, 1942, through December, 1944. He was assigned to the staff of G-2 for the invasion of southern France, and served in Europe to the end of the war. He made lieutenant colonel, and retired in February, 1946."

"What in blazes did the Spanish Desk do?" Vogel demanded.

For the first time McGuire's façade slipped. "Uh, I don't exactly know. Gather information on Spain's intentions before the invasions of North Africa and southern Europe, I guess."

Adams was mildly amused. It was just like Shaw to present himself as a lone agent behind the lines, rather than a cog in an enormous bureaucracy. Still, his romancing hadn't been tailored from whole cloth. He would have received instruction in codes and ciphers from the Army.

"Has the Bureau kept track of Shaw since the war?"

"Not to my knowledge."

"What about Ritter? Was his wife left-wing? Was he?"

"I have no information on the Ritters' political opinions."

Not to give out, at any rate.

"What about Mrs. Feith? Her politics were public and far-right."

"I was never personally involved in security checks on the Feiths," McGuire said. "I know only that he had clearance."

"Well, what can you tell me about Ashenden?"

"He has clearance."

"But he and Feith between them managed to remove all the locks from the University Research Center."

McGuire shrugged.

Adams gave up.

"Fat lot of help they were," Vogel grumbled after the agents had gone. "The little bit of dope they had for us could have been Telexed cheaper, and would have taken up a lot less of our time."

"They're scouts," Adams said. "Somebody up there doesn't like what has been going on at U.R.C. 'Course, nobody likes the murders, but I think maybe the killings don't fit in with the lock fiasco. I expect they'll be back, and probably in force."

"You think they suspect Ashenden of something?"

"Hell, I don't know," Adams responded irritably. "You were here. You interpret Great Stone Face's silence."

"Now, now. I'll bet he shrugs mysteriously at all the cops."

Adams twisted his lips.

"Well, I guess while we're waiting for the gospel from Washington we could get Mark Shaw to spin fairy tales for us."

Adams snorted. He knew what Vogel was trying to do, and that irritated him, too.

"Or we could get Kovallo to spin tales about fairies."

Vogel looked so pleased with his last sally that Adams couldn't help smiling.

Vogel chuckled and, having jollied Adams out of his temper, returned to business. "What did you have in mind when you asked McGuire about Mrs. Feith's politics?"

"I was groping in the dark. I just wonder if there was some reason for Mrs. Feith to be so very outspoken, and so very far out, in her right-wing opinions."

"You mean, if her husband was a spy for Communists, she might have been covering up by acting anti-Communist."

"Something like that," Adams said. "I doubt it will get us anywhere, but I'll see what I can learn about the politics of all of them."

"Might as well," Vogel agreed. "Do you have anything planned that might be more profitable?"

"I don't know how profitable it will be, but I have plenty to do. The first thing is to see if these prints from Washington match up with any of our bodies."

They matched.

Adams must still confirm the identities of the others, but he felt that he could now safely assume that he knew who all the victims were. In fact, before the day was out, dental charts identified Mrs. Feith and Martin Bauer—which is briefly reported, but four hours of officers' time went into phoning and visiting local dentists.

Mrs. Brown occupied another hour. She confirmed that Mrs. Feith had asked her to clean house on Friday this week. That took a minute or two. Sergeant Olson devoted the remainder of the hour to questions which elicited exactly nothing of use to the police, although Mrs. Brown obviously wished to help.

The one advantage in having a massacre to investigate was that most people were more than commonly inclined to active assistance. Unfortunately, few of them had much to give that Adams could use.

Christmas decorations were going up on Main Street and shops were thronged, yet the owners of stationery stores left customers waiting and delved into their files and memories. Only, none remembered a purchase of four Seven Star Diaries at once, or purchases of individual diaries by any of those who had died or those who were suspects. It seemed that many owners of Seven Star Diaries bought refills annually from a mail-order distributor in California. Adams sent off a telegram to the police in Rosemead, California, asking for their assistance.

The manager of the weapons company in Southport had heard the news from Thorpe, and when Adams called he promptly agreed to hunt through his records. Within an hour, he phoned back to say that one box of .44-caliber black-powder cartridges had been sold to a man named Bauer. The order must have been telephoned, for there was no letter in the files. The order sheet was dated November 1st. The shells had been picked up, and paid for in cash, on November 16th.

"I'll send an officer down with photographs tomorrow," Adams said.

"Uh, okay. But the shells were picked up on a Saturday, and Saturdays are pretty busy," the manager said apologetically.

"Well, I'll send a man anyway."

CHAPTER 23

Most of Adams's time, and some of Vogel's, went into interviewing faculty members. Professors, too, were willing to cooperate. They even conceded the need for gossip. Results, however, were scanty.

Feith and Shaw were well known and controversial. Each had detractors and defenders, from whom Adams learned little he hadn't known. Feith had fewer friends but was more highly esteemed as a builder of the University. Shaw was better liked but was the object of some condescension as a mere gadfly. Several professors had heard it said that Feith had made use of students' work without proper credit. All took pains to point out that Feith was by no means the only faculty member subject to such allegations.

Bauer, Overath, and Ritter had been less famed but more popular than Feith. Nothing ill, nothing suspicious, was remembered of them.

Ashenden was considered a bright young man, a comer, one of the few who had earned Feith's respect and confidence. He had done, so it was said, some brilliant research. He was married, childless, and a flutist in the University Chamber Orchestra.

No one, living or dead, was known as a hobbyist, much less a serious student, of cryptography.

With the exception of Shaw, none of the men had espoused political views that had attracted attention. Shaw's views were judged vaguely leftist by some, vaguely anarchic by others.

Mention of Mrs. Feith brought constraint. Clearly, she had been an embarrassment. By dint of much probing, Adams extracted enough to form certain impressions. He was a little surprised to learn that Cornelia Nelson, as she then was, had been a highly regarded student whose doctoral thesis in plant genetics was still remembered. Upon marrying Feith, she had become the compleat housewife and mother. After the children reached an age to be away at school all day, she emerged as a political figure. Adams inferred, as much from awkward silences as from explicit statements, that in the eyes of her husband's colleagues, Mrs. Feith had evolved rapidly from mild eccentric to pure crank. What Mr. Feith had thought of his wife's views no one professed to know.

As for Karl Feith, memories had dimmed, or cooperativeness had limits. Eventually, Adams imposed on retired Dean of Students Alan Gage. (Gage had taken an interest in Adams, and bent a rule or two to enable the young policeman to pursue his part-time and somewhat erratic studies.)

Gage remembered that Karl Feith had failed his orals. He rather thought that Karl Feith had been pushed too hard, that something had snapped under parental pressure. Gage knew that Milligan, Feith's adviser, and Booth, then Dean of Graduate Studies, had made an effort to persuade Feith to delay the orals. He thought that they had tried to arrange for Feith to make up the failure. He knew nothing of Feith's response to their efforts, and Milligan and Booth were long dead.

Adams and Vogel posed questions about University Research Center, and elicited the full array of opinions Al Morris had led Adams to anticipate. Some people thought that U.R.C. existed solely for its image and as a conduit for funds; some thought U.R.C. was a major research establishment engaged in supersecret work; some thought U.R.C. was something of both.

Late in the afternoon, Inspector Logan returned from eight hours in banks. He had found, he announced, that bankers, too, were affected by multiple murder in their community. They not only gave him access to the victims' accounts, but they hardly demurred when he moved on to those of the living. Not that the records had told him much, he added morosely.

All of the dead had lived prosperously; none had lived extravagantly. Bauer's guns had been costly, but he had been collecting for many years, in no one of which had he spent as much as a thousand dollars on his hobby.

(The state police had gone into their records to find and transmit to Adams a report on Mrs. Bauer's accident. She had been alone in her car when she ran off the road at a curve on a foggy night. The autopsy found minute traces of alcohol in her bloodstream, but no sign of drugs or evidence of a heart attack or other organic failure that might have caused her to lose control of the car.)

Overath had sent substantial remittances each year to relatives still living in Germany.

Otherwise, there was no sign of unaccountable income or expenditures—"which," said Logan, "doesn't mean damn-all. If they had money to hide, they could have set up hundreds of small accounts under false names, and we would never find them."

The data on the living were no more illuminating.

The paychecks John Evans received varied by up to two hundred dollars from month to month. They had done so as long as he worked at the automobile agency, and the fluctuations probably marked changes in sales commissions. The Evanses were not in debt, except for a mortgage on which monthly payments had been made promptly. Their savings were small.

Karl Feith's income varied less, but his expenses had taken one sharp jump. Until two years ago, his savings had been growing steadily, but then they had evaporated within a few months. The bankers knew why. Feith's trip to Europe and investment in the bookstore he and Fredericks owned had occurred at that time. Feith's savings account now held less than five hundred dollars.

Fredericks made twice as much as Feith, lived well, saved consistently, and had good credit at the bank.

Ashenden and his wife had joint checking and savings accounts, neither of which showed remarkable deposits or withdrawals.

Last on Logan's list were the Shaws, and it appeared at first that his litany would remain monotonous to the end.

"They have two salaries, and they make a little from writing," Logan said. "Shaw has published three or four books in the last ten years, none of them best-sellers. Mrs. Shaw writes children's books under an alias."

Adams nodded, straight-faced. He knew about Mrs. Shaw's writing, and he suspected that Logan had thrown in "alias" to get a rise out of him.

"So much for records. I did pick up one interesting piece of gossip. The Shaws used to be rich."

"Rich! What do you mean, rich?"

"I don't have numbers, except that Tolman, the vice-president of First National, said that Shaw's grandfather used to own something like twenty square miles of prime farming land around here. By the way, he was married to a Vogel. Would that be a relative of yours, Captain?"

Vogel, who had been listening quietly, rolled his eyes. "Gawd! I hope not," he said. "It's not likely, though it's possible. Lots of Germans settled around here in the eighteen-fifties, and there was more than one Vogel among them."

Adams said, "Tell us about the money."

"Tolman isn't too clear what happened. He thinks Mark Shaw's father sold the land, invested in all the wrong things, and lost a bundle.

"He can't have been completely busted, though. He managed to hang on to his house on The Hill, and a piece of property by the lake. He gave the house to his son as a wedding present, moved himself into the place on the lake, and left that to his granddaughter.

"Tolman is about Mark Shaw's age, and he remembers that when they were kids the Shaws had money for cars and servants and trips abroad. Mark Shaw spent some time at school in Europe, Tolman says. But when it was time for college, the extra car and the servants were gone, and Mark Shaw came home and entered Thorpe State, where he didn't have to pay tuition."

"I see," said Adams.

Mark Shaw had been well-to-do. During adolescence, he had become poor, at least comparatively. He had been sent to school in Europe. Later he went to Spain as, he claimed now, a noncombatant. He was "not known" to have joined the Communist Party—and Adams didn't need to have it spelled out for him that those destined for undercover operations had never officially been Party members.

"Hell," Adams said. He would have preferred it if Logan's report had stayed dull. "All right. Thanks, Andy. That's all for today, I think, unless the Captain has questions or orders."

"No. Go on home, Andy." As Logan departed, Vogel said, "When are you going to knock off, Jeff? You won't be any good to me if you don't catch up on your sleep. And even a cop needs a little social life once in a while."

Adams grinned. Vogel's subtlety was of the massive sort.

"I'm meeting Kate for dinner at seven," he said. "Before I go, I need to read the latest autopsy reports."

"Okay. I got to shuffle schedules again. That fool Don Anderson slipped on his own cellar steps and broke an arm. But I'm coming back at six to chase you out."

Adams nodded assent. The morning's headache had decreased in intensity and increased in scope. He ached all over.

"I'll be ready."

But he wasn't.

The reports from Waddell and two surgeons he had conscripted to his aid from University Hospital told Adams only what he had expected. Bauer, Overath, and Ritter had died of a combination of blows and gunshot wounds. Assuming that the testimony Adams had gathered about mealtimes was accurate, the Feiths, Bauer, and Overath had been killed within a two-hour span centered on 10:30 P.M. If Ritter had eaten at about the same time as the others, then he had died at about the same time as the others.

Adams threw those papers aside and took up a report from the laboratory. The bullets recovered from the bodies of Bauer, Overath, and Ritter were .44-caliber, but they had not been fired from the gun that killed the Feiths.

Adams blinked and reread the lab report.

"No," said Adams. "There's a limit to how much I can swallow."

From his jacket pocket Adams took a ragged sheet of paper on which he had been making jottings during the day. Thus far, it read:

Why didn't M.S. see; why didn't Kate notice?
blam, blam, pause, blam, blam
Loitering killer
No pieces missing
Fingerprints—Diaries and Tableaus—Glasses
Bridge
Car with three bald tires

Now Adams inserted between the second and third items: "Two guns."

He stared at the list as if to bore a hole through it.

"Too elaborate," he said.

He drew a heavy line around the first two items, with an impatient slash of his pen.

"I can't get it clear. I just don't . . . Or maybe I do. . . ."

When he became aware of his surroundings again, Vogel was waving a hand before his eyes and saying, "Hey! Anybody home in there?"

"I want to re-enact it," Adams blurted. "I need times. I need to see."

"You're off your nut!" Vogel declared. "According to the lab, there may have been two killers. How are you going to time them?"

"There weren't two," Adams said. "All the diaries and tableaus were at the Feiths'."

Vogel thought it over.

"I'm getting slow. You're right," he said at last. "But you're still off your nut if you think I'm going to let you re-enact anything tonight. Half the cops in Thorpe, including you, are so tired they act like zombies. Besides, we got reporters coming out of the woodwork. If we start dashing around from Bauer's to Ritter's to Feith's, we'll be trampled to death in the rush."

"I suppose so," Adams conceded reluctantly. "Well, then, how would you like to play some bridge tonight? I need to time that, too."

Vogel laughed aloud. "You can't be for real! What do you think Kate is going to say to that idea?"

"Oog" was, more or less, what Adams said.

CHAPTER

24

"Sure," Kate said.

Dining on leftover turkey, Adams had resolutely presented a not so terrible picture of his job. Kate laughed at the story of Sergeant Olson and the floozy, smiled tolerantly at Dick West and Pamela Black, clucked sympathetically at the end of his recitation of profitless labors during the day.

"And now," she said finally, "what's really on your mind?"

"You're a witch! I keep saying that you can't keep a secret, but I might be made of glass, the way you see through me."

"Smoky glass, sometimes. Come on. Give."

Adams shifted uncomfortably. "I kind of hate to ask. You see, four of the, um . . ."

"Victims," Kate said. "I'm learning to bear your terminology, if not to love it."

"Well, then, four of the victims apparently played bridge Wednesday night. At least, we found a score sheet. They seem to have played a good many hands: a minimum of twenty-eight, even if some of the above-the-line scores are bonuses for honors, overtricks, and doubled contracts; and possibly as many as thirty-three.

"I have been told that they started at eight and finished by ten. I need to get an idea of whether they could have played so many hands in two hours."

"How?"

"By getting together with the Vogels and playing, say, thirty hands as fast as we can."

"You're basically an enthusiast, aren't you?" Kate said with an amused shake of her head. "But, sure. It's one way to be certain that you aren't out playing around with a floozy."

No retort springing to his lips, Adams went to the phone.

"Love a duck! You don't know when to quit, do you?" said Vogel. "Oh, well. I warned Mary about your scheme, so you might as well come on over."

The Vogels liked to study the dummy and ponder leads, to chat between hands, and to serve drinks or a snack between rubbers. This night, at Adams's behest, they played rapidly and without pause. Postmortems ended as the last card of the next deal went down. Whoever was dummy brought coffee.

Vogel griped continuously. He told Kate she must be out of her mind to put up with a cop who insisted on working twenty hours a day. "Doggone it," he grumbled when Adams spread his cards and claimed the last four tricks, "this big rush is just an excuse to con me." After bidding and making a small slam, he groaned. "Gee whiz, can't I have even a minute to savor my only triumph of the night?" When his wife said, "For heaven's sake, Bobby! Pipe down," he muttered, "Serpent in the nest."

But when thirty hands had been played and Adams had totted up scores, Vogel said immediately, "A hundred and thirty-two minutes. That's four minutes and twenty-four seconds per hand, and we aren't hotshots. Feith and the others would have had to be only a little better to play their three rubbers in two hours. What's important about it?"

"Just that. At least, it's not unimportant that they could have played three rubbers in two hours, but would have been pretty rushed to play them in much less time."

"So now you know. Do you want to run a reconstruction tomorrow night?"

"Yes. I would prefer to do it while most students are still out of town and conditions are similar to those of Wednesday night."

"Okay. Since you'll be working late, take the morning off, hear? Let other people do a little of the work."

Kate leaned over and kissed him on the cheek. "Gosh, I'm glad I don't have to work for such an ogre."

"Don't sass me, girl. Go on, you two. Scoot."

The weather had turned clear and cold again, as it had been after the rain on Wednesday night. Kate sat close beside him. Adams couldn't bring himself to make her move over and buckle on the seat belt.

As he drove the unmarked police car into the driveway, the headlights showed her old Buick convertible parked beside his even older Porsche coupé.

"The neighbors must think I'm living here."

"How tired are you, Jeff?" Kate said abruptly. "I mean, if you need to go home and sleep, it's all right."

"I would like to stay with you, if I may."

"Come in, then."

He followed her, took her coat, and hung it up.

"Do you want coffee, or a drink?"

"No, thanks, I—" He let his own coat fall in a heap and suddenly put his arms around her. "Kate, I want to make love to you. Now."

Her head tipped back. Her eyes closed—and then flew open again. "Wait. That phone's damned well going to be unplugged this time."

Adams woke up and smiled.

It was after ten according to the clock beside the bed. He hadn't exactly caught up on his sleep. But it was not his clock, not his bed.

He rolled over. Kate smiled back at him.

"Well, well. Fancy meeting you here."

"Who did you expect? A floozy?"

"A wench." He gathered her into his arms. "A wanton, wild, winsome, wonderful wench. My wench."

"You're delirious. I love you, too."

"Delirious, am I? And whose fault is that? Who sets my blood pounding and my mind reeling? Who makes my heart overflow? Who fills me with joy until I feel I must burst?"

"Mad. Quite mad." She laughed softly. "And overflowing again? So soon?"

"Wanton, wanton wench."

CHAPTER 25

Thus it was that Adams, bestowing cheerful greetings on all he met, arrived at his desk promptly at one in the afternoon.

Numerous messages awaited him.

Agent McGuire had formally notified the Thorpe Police Department that he and Agent Tanner would be staying at the Charlton Arms Hotel for an indefinite period. End of message.

"Huh," said Adams.

Officer Barlow had not yet returned from Southport, but he had telephoned. No employee of the arms and ammunition company had recognized a face among the photographs Barlow had displayed. However, fifty .44-caliber black-powder cartridges were not sold every day, and a clerk remembered the sale. He was fairly sure that the purchaser had been a man with one arm in a sling. More hesitantly he volunteered that the man might have limped.

Adams called Dr. Meadows and asked if Bauer had walked with a noticeable limp.

"Not ordinarily," she said. "Sometimes, if he was tired, he did."

"Did he break or sprain his arm a month or so ago?"

"Why, no. Whatever gave you that idea?"

"Something got garbled in transmission, I expect," Adams said. "Thank you, Dr. Meadows."

Who notices a face, in a busy store, especially if a bandaged arm and a game leg distract observers' eyes?

"Still, it was risky."

Then Adams remembered how his attention had been riveted by that fantastic gun, by the treadless tires, by apparently inescapable and inane inferences about the killer's behavior. He nodded his head slowly. Certain details, crucial ones at that, remained befogged, but the method was becoming clear.

"Maybe not so risky," he mused.

"You're in bad shape when you start talking to yourself," said Vogel, striding in and dropping onto a chair. "But you look rested."

Adams smiled broadly and involuntarily, but if Vogel noticed, he passed up the opportunity to make a crack.

"Did you see the message about our F.B.I. buddies?"

"Ashenden," said Adams.

"Huh?"

"I think they are after Ashenden."

Vogel thought it over. "Could be. What makes you think so?"

"He's too absentminded."

"Professors are supposed to be absentminded."

Adams grinned, but spoke seriously. "No. They concentrate. An astronomer may fall in a hole while stargazing, but he won't forget the phases of the moon or the position of Alpha Centauri. Ashenden isn't an administrator in the same sense that Tycho Brahe was an astronomer, so the analogy is far from exact. Still, he must have been competent or Feith, who had a good deal of experience with large-scale projects, wouldn't have kept him as deputy. Yet Ashenden managed to make a really monumental goof last spring, when the locks were removed from University Research Center. Then, first thing after hearing about Feith's murder, Ashenden shows up at the U.R.C. building and claims he was so shaken by the news that he simply forgot that no grad student could let himself into Feith's office.

"I don't believe it. I think he knew what he was doing—not that I know what that might be—and produced a damn good lie, a lie that would fit perfectly with the popular view of professors, when he found a cop there ahead of him."

"Hell," said Vogel. "Now I suppose we have to investigate him. Do you think he is a spy?"

"A secret agent? I have been feeling as if I had fallen into an E. Phillips Oppenheim opus. Why not Maugham?" Vogel glared in disapproval of allusions he didn't get. Adams continued more soberly, "Did you see Barlow's report on the ammunition?"

"Yeah. Not much help, is it? The rest of that junk is worse."

The "junk" consisted largely of citizens' responses to the plea for information that the *Gazette* had published in its Friday edition, boxed on page 1 beneath the row of pictures of the victims as they had looked in life. Above the photographs, the banner headline read, "HOLIDAY BLOODBATH."

The number of automobiles that had drawn suspicious attention Wednesday night was astonishing. But the proportion of them that could be found was small, and of those, all but one had been eliminated. The remaining one belonged to Mrs. Evans, and had been seen racing south on University Avenue, presumably after the brush with Adams.

The State Department of Motor Vehicles reported that no cars other than the ones Adams already knew about were registered in the names of any of the dead or living suspects.

No teenager had come forward to admit to parking high on Lakeview Drive.

No one had been found who had seen a car parked near the Feiths' house, or who had remarked a car or person near any of the murder sites.

Nor had anyone noticed gunshots. That was less surprising than it might appear at first, despite the unusual quiet of the holiday eve. Dr. Waddell had pointed out that Bauer, Overath, and Ritter had been slain by a gun pressed hard against their skin. The explosions would have been effectively muffled.

From Rosemead, California, came a telegram reporting that the distributor of Seven Star Diaries had no record of a single order for four diaries by an individual on the list Adams had sent.

The machine on which the cipher messages had been typed did not turn up.

Interviews with co-workers and colleagues confirmed that John and Margaret Evans had been something less than serenely happy of late, but if anyone had known of Evans's affair, he kept it to himself.

Karl Feith's colleagues proved to be more reluctant than University faculty to retail gossip. Many hours were required to learn little of use. Feith had tenure. He was considered an adequate, if uninspiring, teacher. No fellow teacher admitted to being a particular friend. None had traveled with him to France. He was thought to have been accompanied on the trip by a woman. He was believed to have had a number of affairs, all with women and all brief.

Fredericks made no secret of his homosexuality, but his manner had been considerably exaggerated by the time Kovallo's telephoned report had been retransmitted to Adams. Kovallo and Crane had quoted Fredericks exactly, but Kovallo granted that Fredericks might have been putting him on. As for the house full of velvet and satin, it dwindled in Kovallo's written report to a living room with, as Adams interpreted the description, wine-red drapes.

Ashenden had been a tenured associate professor for four years and Feith's deputy at U.R.C. for three years. "Brilliant" was the word most commonly applied to him, although little of his research for the last five or six years had been seen by his peers, since it was classified. He was not known to play bridge. His game was said to be poker.

Other, still less notable reports came in, were scanned, and went into the files. Adams and Vogel spent most of their time organizing the activities planned for after dark, but Adams also devoted an hour or so to trigonometry.

Adams had noticed, when he stood where the overlapping

footprints showed that the killer had waited for a time, that a straight line over the spot where Shaw had thrown himself down led to a tree on the other side of the driveway. He had instructed Inspector Logan to examine that tree for the bullet Shaw said had been fired at him, but Logan's search had been cut short by the need to deal with other findings on Thanksgiving Day. This morning, Sergeant Twining had been sent to renew the search, and he had found the bullet and made the precise measurements Adams had requested.

From the center of the trampled area to Shaw's knee marks was fourteen feet ten inches; from the same starting point to the rim of the tree trunk was forty-six feet and a fraction of an inch; from ground level to bullet hole was twenty-one feet eight inches.

With those numbers and a textbook borrowed from an officer's teenage child, Adams set about finding angles and deriving further distances. Since it was fifteen years or more since he had last had occasion to use sines, his initial effort was laughable. He managed to find that the gun should have been fired at an angle of less than one degree from the horizontal. When he checked the answer by working the problem backward, he found that the bullet should have been found approximately six hundred feet aboveground. Evidently, he had done something wrong.

His next effort was better, and eventually he determined that if the shot had been fired at ground level when Shaw was twelve feet away, the bullet would have passed within inches of his head. However, there was no sign that the killer had lain down, and it seemed likely that Shaw had been farther away, even assuming that the killer held the gun at arm's length. So Adams worked out a number of other possibilities, of which two may be recorded.

If the killer had squatted and fired from three feet above-ground when Shaw was fifteen feet away, the bullet would have missed Shaw by at least two feet.

If the killer had stood and fired from a shoulder height of, say, five feet, the bullet would have missed Shaw by at least four feet.

None of which was evidence, but at least none of it contradicted the notion that the shot had been aimed not to hit but to pass well over Shaw's head.

At seven, Adams went to Kate. Some time later, she drew away a little and said, "My love may feed on this"—she kissed him—"but my love must feed on more substantial stuff. May I give you something with proteins and calories in it?"

"That takes us from the sublime to the ridiculous in a hurry."

"Worse yet, to the reheated. Can you face turkey— Lord! Listen to me, fretting over meals. What a terrible effect you're having on me. I'm becoming domesticated."

Adams smiled. One thing that Kate had made unmistakably plain in the last couple of months was that she might someday become a wife, but never a housewife.

He said teasingly, "It must be love."

"I'm afraid you may be right." She stood up before he could reply. "Come on. Let's make sandwiches."

After they had eaten, as he prepared to leave, she said, "Will you come back to me tonight?"

"I may be very late."

"Ah, I almost forgot. Take this." She took a key from her pocket. "Let yourself in if I'm asleep. And wake me. I begrudge every hour— Oh, damn!"

"Kate, what's the matter?"

"I've done the stupidest thing, Jeff. I told the Laceys I would spend tomorrow afternoon with them. They are having people in for cocktails, and John wants me to come early and talk about a possible subject for my next book. When he phoned yesterday, I thought that because of the case you wouldn't be free, and—and . . ."

"Kate, darling, the sky won't fall. Some of the night and all of the morning I'll keep you to myself. In the afternoon I'll let you go, not gladly, but then how glad I'll be when you return."

"Heaven help us. I've turned fretful, and you talk foolishness. Do come back soon."

"I will, my very dear."

He kissed her, and left her. Backing out of the driveway, he noticed that the porch light was lit tonight. A light for him.

CHAPTER

26

By ten o'clock, the stage was set. Four uniformed officers under Captain Vogel's direction had parked two unmarked cars in the driveway and entered the Acacia Street house. Diagonally across the street, in another unmarked car, sat Adams, with a hammer in his lap, and Kovallo holding a stopwatch and a note pad. Adams had easily found a space out of the direct light from streetlamps and in a position where he could observe the house.

Action began precisely at ten.

The door of 220 Acacia opened and two men emerged. Calling "Good night" to two other men visible in the hall, they strolled to their cars and, after a moment's chat, drove away separately.

At ten past ten, Adams left his car. The hammer in his gloved hand was hidden by his topcoat from anyone directly in front of him. Neither hurrying nor dawdling, he walked to the house and rang the bell. Footsteps approached from the rear of the house, and the door opened.

"I'm sorry to bother you at this time of night, but may I come in for a minute?"

"Yeah, sure," said Officer Waite.

Waite turned away. Adams paused to push the door shut, took two long strides after Waite, swung the hammer, and said, "Now." Waite lay down.

Adams mounted the stairs two at a time. Officer Petersen, sitting on the edge of Bauer's bed, recoiled involuntarily as Adams rushed at him with the hammer raised. "Now," Adams said again, and Petersen fell back.

Returning to the ground floor, Adams went to the gun room. He took down the one big revolver that Vogel had restored to its holster and loaded it with bullets Barlow had brought from Southport. Adams pretended to take a gun from the second holster and load it as well.

A heavy box containing a thick block of wood covered by foam rubber had been placed in the hallway. Adams fired one shot into it. Upstairs, he fired a second shot into a similar box in Bauer's room. He made a show of searching Bauer's and Overath's desks, and departed.

"How long did it take, Kovallo?" Adams said as he slid into the driver's seat once again.

"Eight minutes and seventeen seconds."

"Even quicker than I expected."

Adams drove down The Hill, holding his speed exactly at the legal limit. He parked around the corner from the entrance to Ritter's apartment building. Hammer and gun in pockets, he proceeded without haste to the corner and half a block along Beech Street. The only passerby he saw, a man walking a dog, paid him no attention.

No one was in the lobby when Adams entered or appeared while he waited for the self-service elevator to descend from the third floor. There was no indoor stairway, and Adams assumed that the killer would not have risked being seen climbing the outside fire escape. Adams rode the elevator to the fifth floor and rang Ritter's bell.

"I'm sorry to bother you," Adams said again. "Could I come in for a minute?"

"Okay," said Officer Parker.

"Did you have any trouble parking in the garage or getting up here ahead of me?"

"No trouble at all. I've been here ten, twelve minutes."

Parker had stepped aside to admit Adams and close the door. Adams led the way along the short hall to the living-room door, where he stood aside to permit Parker to precede him. As Parker passed, Adams took the hammer from under his coat, raised it, and said, "Now." Down went Parker.

Adams drew the gun and fired once into another receptacle. Another show of searching followed. Then Adams returned the way he had come, seeing no one in the building or on the street.

"How long, Kovallo?"

"Five-o-nine for the drive. You were gone ten minutes and forty-seven seconds. That makes a total of, let's see, twenty-four thirteen so far."

Adams drove uphill at the authorized pace while Kovallo reloaded the gun, taking care to leave an empty cylinder under the firing hammer. (The killer, having loaded both guns at once, would not have needed to take time to reload.) At the top of The Hill, Adams made a U-turn and drove back down to park below the Feiths' house. This time, Kovallo got out when Adams did and followed a few steps behind up the slope and around the house to the front door.

Officer Petersen, emulating Lazarus, had revived. He opened the door with a self-conscious grin.

"Hello. May I come in?"

"Sure."

Adams went past, then waited for Petersen to shut the door and go ahead toward Feith's study. As soon as Petersen's back was fully turned, Adams pulled the gun and fired into yet another box. Petersen lay down, and Adams fired again.

As the sound of the explosion faded, a door opened on the second floor. Sergeant Olson, barefoot, appeared and dashed down the stairs. Adams waited until she was halfway down, then fired a third shot. She dropped the pillow she was carrying and after it hit the floor, he walked half the distance to it, returned to the box, and fired a fourth shot.

"You can get up, Pete," Adams said, heading for the study. "How long has it taken?"

"Thirty-four fifty-four," Vogel replied from his seat on a step of the second stairway.

"Uh, that's right," Kovallo agreed. "It took us six minutes

and twenty-eight seconds for the drive from Ritter's, two-o-five to climb up and get to the door, and two-o-eight from then until the last shot."

"And I haven't hurried at all."

Adams went to Feith's desk and looked out the window. Sergeant Crane, after driving up from Acacia Street, had taken position at the end of Shaw's driveway. He was under instruction to wait two minutes after hearing the fourth shot before walking at a moderate pace toward the Feiths' house.

Vogel stirred. "Aren't those two minutes up yet?"

"Nearly three," said Kovallo. After a pause, "Three minutes, now."

"Still no sign of him?" Vogel asked.

"No."

Vogel rose and moved slowly toward the door.

"Three and a half," Kovallo said.

"Christ! If something's happened to him . . ."

Vogel went out the door at a run, with Adams right behind him.

Near the end of the drive, Vogel shouted, "Crane! You there, Crane?"

The sergeant materialized instantly, as if by magic, in the circle of light under the streetlamp.

"What happened? Didn't you hear the shots?"

Crane stammered "Uh, no, sir. I'm sorry."

"Not your fault," Adams said. "It's mine. I should have realized that Crane wasn't likely to hear them."

"What are you talking about? Why couldn't he hear them? And how could you know he couldn't?"

"The first time I was in the Feiths' house, three or four cars pulled up in front. Men got out, slamming doors and talking. And I never heard a sound. Later that night, I drove up when Crane and the lab men were working quietly inside, and they didn't hear anything either. That place is built like a vault, and the tapestry in the hall muffles sound even more."

"You mean that Shaw didn't hear the shots he said he heard?" Vogel demanded.

"Maybe. I want to try it again, but with the front door open."

This time, after Adams loosed off four more shots and Kovallo announced, "Two minutes, Inspector," no more than half a dozen seconds elapsed before Crane appeared, crossing the street.

Adams raced out the door and across the lawn to the trees. Crane came on slowly until Adams shifted his feet and rustled underbrush. Crane halted for several seconds, went on again, stopped when he heard another sound, and turned toward Adams.

"Bang," Adams said.

Crane threw himself down and Adams fled through the trees and down the hillside to his car. Behind him, he knew, Crane would listen until the sound of flight could no longer be heard, would then count to ten and continue to the house.

When Adams climbed back up, he saw Crane starting back across Lakeview Drive with Kovallo close behind. The two men went on beyond the light, but soon reappeared. As they approached, Kovallo called, "Forty-four thirty-two, Inspector. Two minutes waiting, one fifty-two till you said, 'Bang,' and five forty-six for Sergeant Crane to go to the house and return to Shaw's."

"Inspector," Crane began excitedly.

"Wait. Let's do this in order. Call it fifty minutes. Add the ten I waited to make an hour. That would take us to eleven o'clock. We should add some time in case the bridge party didn't break up at exactly ten, but on the other hand, I could have moved a little faster. Shaw actually called me at about five past eleven. It's reasonable, I think."

Vogel nodded.

"But, Inspector," Crane burst out.

Adams held up a hand. "No. Let me tell you. You saw me when I ran out the door and across the lawn."

"I'd have had to be blind to miss you," Crane said. "You must have been in plain view for five or six seconds. I could hear you, too."

"Okay. We spotted that problem right off, and it took me until today to get a glimmer of an idea how to explain it.

"Here's a second problem. I never believed that the shots that killed the Feiths could have been fired in two pairs—blam, blam, pause, blam, blam. Tonight, the first time through, I shot Feith twice, then Mrs. Feith twice. The second time, I shot Feith once, then Mrs. Feith twice, then Feith again. The first time, I got one closely spaced pair, and two separated shots. The second time, I got four separated shots.

"I think the two problems are tied together. I—"

"But, Inspector, what I've been trying to tell you is, we got a third problem," Crane said. "I have good ears, and of course I was listening for shots. But I don't think that I would have recognized that the sounds I heard were shots unless I had been expecting them. In fact," Crane added, looking startled as a new idea came to mind, "I don't think I would have heard them at all if I had been inside Shaw's house."

"Are you sure, Crane?" Vogel demanded.

"Not positive, no. But pretty sure."

Both men turned to Adams.

"I suppose you should have realized that, too," Vogel said in an aggrieved tone.

"Maybe so, but I didn't," Adams admitted. "It makes . . . it almost makes sense. I still can't quite get it all into focus. Something is out of place or skewed."

Frowning in thought, he gazed at Shaw's house. "All right, then. We will just have to do it again, with a few changes, and get Shaw to take his own part."

"It's after eleven-thirty, Jeff. He may have gone to bed."

"I doubt it. I warned him there would be activity over here tonight. And his lights are on."

"Well, okay, if he'll play."

Shaw was not eager to play, but he did agree. And, after Adams claimed that his main concern was with establishing the timing of events of Wednesday night, Shaw's thespian instincts took over.

"I should be in the hall, just outside the door." He left the study and took his place between the study and the kitchen. "Ah, and the front-room lights should be off, as they were then."

"Oh, were they? I'll get them, and I'll stay by the door and fall in behind you when you go out."

They waited in silence for what felt a long time. The shots finally came, as Adams had arranged—blam, blam, pause, blam, blam. And they were loud.

Shaw twitched and exhaled audibly. He looked up consideringly, and started along the hall, slowly at first, then more quickly. On the porch, he stopped to peer around. He looked toward the Feiths' house, stared, took a hesitant step, then set off fairly briskly. At the very edge of the Feiths' property, he hesitated. It was no more than a catch in his stride, and he plunged on into the dark tunnel. He forged ahead steadily, but somewhat more slowly than he had proceeded down his own driveway and across the street.

About two-thirds of the way to the house, he halted abruptly.

"Must I go the whole distance?"

He was pale and his voice was hoarse. The play had become too real.

"No, Mark. This was a rough business to put you through. I'm sorry. I'll walk back with you."

Shaw turned about immediately and set off much more quickly than he had come.

Recrossing the street, Adams said, "Mark, were all the lights off in the front of your house, upstairs and down, on Wednesday?"

"Why, yes." Shaw produced a strained smile. "Is that a critical clue, Sergeant Cuff?"

"It helps," Adams said. "It completes the picture."

"Does it, indeed. That's interesting." Shaw did not sound overwhelmingly interested. "Good night, Jeff," he said, and was gone.

"You heard those all right, I take it," Vogel said as Adams

joined him amid the trees. "I let 'em off right here, the way you said."

"Loud and clear. How long did it take him?"

"Not as long as it took Crane. He showed in the light after forty-eight seconds, and only took another minute and ten seconds to get to where he stopped—and that was only a couple of steps short of where he claims he hit the dirt after being shot at."

Adams turned around. They were standing at the spot where the laboratory squad had found overlapping footprints that appeared to show that a man in overshoes had stood there for some time, shifting his weight from foot to foot. Adams could barely make out the darkened front of Shaw's house. Too bad he had not seen the house as it now was, and as Shaw said it had been when the murders were committed, rather than with lights in the front as there were by the time he arrived Wednesday night. Then Adams shook his head. No, he probably wouldn't have understood any sooner; there had been too many other tangles to clear away. Now, as he had told Shaw, the picture was complete.

Adams turned to look at the Feiths' house. "Cold-blooded bastard," he said in a hard voice. "But I'm damned if I can see how to prove it. The trial will be a circus if we don't have something solid to pin him to."

Crane said, "I don't understand, Inspector. I mean, if they were spies, why weren't the diaries and things destroyed?"

"Destroyed? Oh, no. All the pieces had to be here." Adams pounded fist into palm. "Except the car, maybe. Hm . . . Yes. Except the car. We have got to find that car."

"Okay, Sherlock, I give up," Vogel said. "Spell it out for us Watsons."

CHAPTER 27

The officer-actors having been released with the warning "We'll call you," Vogel, Adams, and Crane reviewed the performance. Plot analysis took little time. Neither Vogel nor Crane was a Watson, and both followed with ease the themes and motives Adams developed. But catharsis was denied them; the final scenes remained unwritten.

"Cold-blooded is right," Vogel said into the gloomy silence after Adams completed his exposition. "Right, too, that a trial would become a circus. I'm convinced. Crane's convinced. Maybe the prosecutor can be convinced. But what a good defense attorney will do to us— Hell, he won't need to be good. We haven't got a single piece of solid evidence."

"I know. Believe me, I know."

Crane said, "What about the car, Inspector? What you said at the Feiths' sounded like you think it's important."

"It's our only hope, as far as I can see. The one source of cheer now is that I think it's a real hope. The second gun, the hammer, the galoshes, the typewriter—all of them may have been disposed of. The car is a different matter.

"I'm speculating now, but I think the plot was designed to eliminate the need to get rid of the car, at least immediately. The tire tracks were a mistake, something we were not meant to observe. If I'm right, then not only would the car give us the evidence we lack, but we can realistically expect to discover that evidence."

Vogel looked dubious. "I don't follow you, Jeff. I mean, I understand all right that the tires would identify the car and the car, if it's his, would probably give us proof. What I don't get is why, mistake or no mistake about tracks, you think the car is sitting around someplace, waiting for us to stumble over it. Why wouldn't the killer have hid it where we would never find it? For that matter, why wouldn't he destroy it first thing—set it on fire, or dismantle it and chuck the pieces in the lake?"

"No doubt he does plan to do some such thing eventually. But he couldn't plan on having the time he would need until after the heat was off. He knew he would have to rush to get home before the cops came Wednesday night. He also had to guard against the possibility that after Wednesday we might set a watch on him and that an attempt to remove the car would simply lead us to it."

Adams frowned. "You know, the more I consider it, the more I think he may have decided against trying to get rid of the other evidence as well. If he could hide the car quickly and securely, it would serve as a cache for gun, hammer, and what-have-you.

"Well, be that as it may, I'm certain that we weren't supposed to know that there was a car. That's why he rolled downhill without starting the engine."

"Hold on, Jeff. You're getting way out on a limb. How can you be sure that those tracks weren't made by somebody else? By neckers, for instance? You used a car in the reconstruction, but for all we actually know, the murderer might have used a bicycle."

"Ride up and down The Hill on a bike, carting guns, hammer, and cipher materials, wearing overshoes or putting them on and off? Never.

"As for neckers, it's true I can't rule them out absolutely. But look at the problems involved. We know that the killer can't have reached the Feiths' before ten-thirty, and that he was gone before five past eleven. We also know that the killer's footprints started from the spot where the car parked, and returned to the same spot. If the killer didn't use that car, then it must have come along just in time to miss him going up The Hill, which is too pat for me. On top of that, you have to assume that lovers, or whoever, heard the shots or saw the killer coming back, or both, and rolled silently away just in time. And then you have to assume that the hypothetical lovers are so loath to have anything to do with cops that not even five murders jolted them into coming forward.

"No. He needed a car for speed and for carrying his paraphernalia. Somehow he acquired one without registering it, or was able to register it under a phony name. He kept three bald tires on it, perhaps because he didn't want to risk being recognized as the purchaser of new tires. And he planned that we would have no idea what to look for so that he could stash it in a hurry—maybe right out in the open, maybe under as much cover as would be provided by a garage rented under a false name."

Vogel didn't appear entirely convinced, but he said, "Supposing you're right, how are you going to find it?"

"It shouldn't be difficult, although it will take man power and time. First, establish round-the-clock surveillance. Then, search systematically, block by block, garage by garage, car by car, through the whole town if necessary, until it turns up. I could do the searching alone, but I would prefer to send out several details." Vogel was shaking his head. "I know, I know. It will play hob with schedules, but the fewer the men, the longer the time it will take."

Vogel erupted. "Time! Christ, we don't have any kind of time. You're forgetting what the Regents have done."

"The Regents?" Adams said in bewilderment. "I don't know what you're talking about."

"It was on the news tonight. The Regents held a special meeting yesterday and today. They hid themselves in a room in the Governor's offices, instead of meeting on campus as usual. And they voted against every damn thing the demonstrators wanted. There will be no review of policy on classified research. No investigation of University Research Center. And no request for dropping or reducing charges against students who were arrested."

Proclamation of an outbreak of plague might have been more disheartening. Adams's shoulders sagged. In his imagination he saw picket lines, tear gas, buses carrying protesters to the county jail. He heard chants of "Pig" and mutterings of "Commie punks" and, worst of all, the buzzer in his pocket summoning him to duty as often in December as in October.

"As if we didn't have enough troubles," Vogel rumbled on. "They might as well have told the students to go— Well, never mind. The point is that no later than Monday noon, the well-known substance is going to hit the fan. Once demonstrations start again, we won't have a prayer of maintaining twenty-four-hour-a-day surveillance, much less of conducting a methodical hunt through the city. If we can't find that car tomorrow, we may never find it."

Tomorrow? It was impossible. If he put every officer in Thorpe to beating the bushes, he still couldn't expect to find in one day a car about which he knew nothing except that its tires were worn. There was just no way. . . .

"If we could stir him up," Adams said slowly.

"Yes? Go on," Vogel responded encouragingly.

"Suppose we send him a message in cipher. A blackmail message. Something along these lines: 'I will tell the cops about the car with bald tires unless you meet me at such-and-such a place and time.'"

"Aw, come on," Vogel groaned. "Who would fall for a stunt like that?"

"Our murderer might," Adams said, firmly repressing doubts. "We know that he does make errors under pressure. He improvised wildly Wednesday night, and one of his spur-of-the-moment actions—the shot into the tree—was a tremendous error.

"He has had a few days to stew over the mistakes he knows he made, and to wonder frantically what mistakes he overlooked. Whether he has realized yet that he left tire tracks, he may be waking in the middle of the night—sweating, yet cold to the marrow—for fear that somehow or other we will stumble on that car.

"Now he receives a message referring to the tires. Suddenly he's faced with a mortal threat. He has no plan ready for this contingency. What can he do? Maybe he'll panic. Even if he doesn't, can he merely sit back and do nothing? Not unless he's superhuman, he can't."

"You're nuts," Vogel said.

"Maybe so, but the Regents seem to have deprived us of sane options. You know as well as I do that if we have another day like the one at the end of October when the tear gas blew into a school and the bank was robbed, he could drive a pink-striped tank down Main Street and nobody would notice. All he needs is a few hours when our attention is distracted, and that car will go into the lake, or to a used-car lot in another state, and then he's safe."

Vogel grimaced. He pulled his ear, shuffled papers on his desk. He swiveled his chair and stared at the wall.

"I must be nuts, too," he said at last. "Go ahead."

CHAPTER

28

The message Adams drafted was blunt. It said:

30 Nov.

1 9 0 9 0
1 1 6 1 4
3 7 2 4 2
1 1 1 0 3
4 8 1 8 2
5 5 0 5 3
4 0 0 7 3
0 2 3 0 4
6 3 6 6 2
6 0 5 0 0
5 1 1 5 5
2 8 9 2 8
4 6 5 5 0
0 1 0 1 3
5 7 2 2 1
4 5 1 9 8
2 9 7 5 7
3 3 5 0 5
7 7 7 8 4
4 0 8 4 6
0 1 5 9 4

  1 7 4 1 2
  0 3 5 0 5
  2 0 6 0 2
  4 2 3 6 3
  2 3 9 9 2
  4 7 4 8 2
  0 4 3 6 2

———————

9 2 2 0 9 2

(In plain English: "Meet three P.M. December 1 at Student Union or I tell police about three bald tires." The key was provided by the November 30th motto: "Success is like a cat—it doesn't come when called for.")

Now the message had to be delivered. Post and telegraph were out of the question. An envelope simply stuffed into the killer's mailbox might not be noticed until Monday. Hiring a messenger was too risky—if the murderer was already on the edge of panic, he might take a messenger hostage. That would break the case, but in a way Adams was not prepared to accept.

Adams considered the problem with care. He had recognized its existence at the moment he conceived the notion of a cipher message. At the same time, he had seen a possible solution, which he put aside with the feeling that one stunt was plenty. Now he re-examined the idea.

It was straight out of melodrama, and that was not necessarily a disadvantage. The killer might suspect that the cops were trying to goad him into rash action with a cipher message. Who would ever imagine that sober, responsible officers of the law would indulge in such a prank as Adams had in mind?

Captain Vogel certainly had trouble imagining it when Adams put the proposal before him.

"Don't fool around, Jeff," he said grumpily. "I'm too tired for jokes."

"Who's joking?"

"If you aren't, then you're . . . you're . . . I already said you were nuts. I don't know what to call it when a nut loses his mind."

There's a pataphysical question, Adams decided, but he kept the thought to himself. He set about persuading the captain that precisely because the plan was super-nutty, it just might work.

In the end, Vogel threw up his hands and said, "If this ever gets out, Chief Baker will personally escort the two of us to the funny farm."

Interpreting the remark as permission, Adams departed before Vogel could change his mind.

He went first to the lakeside, found a suitable rock, and taped the message to it. Soon he was sneaking through the night, straining eyes and ears for the smallest indication that he had been observed. He felt like a refugee from a Hardy boys' adventure, but the impulse to laugh ebbed when he reminded himself that the dark and silent house ahead sheltered a nonfictional killer. If the killer lay uneasily awake, the danger here was all too real.

Adams took a final look around, hurled the missive-wrapped missile through a window, and ran like hell.

Adams was halfway to his car when he realized the implications and began to swear. He consigned murderer and Regents together to the nethermost circle of the Inferno. Thanks to them, he must spend the rest of the night on duty. He would have to waken Kate only to take leave of her.

Kate made no reproach. She silenced with kisses his incoherent explanation, and sent him off in such emotional chaos that he was sure he would get no sleep at all.

In that he was wrong, but not by much.

Surveillance began seconds after a crash told Adams his rock had been well aimed. No further action was likely to occur for many hours, but Adams had to be at headquarters in case of need.

The cot in Vogel's office was narrow, uncomfortable, and lonely. Each time Adams drifted into unconsciousness, he was jolted awake again by barely audible sounds—the soft but heavy tread of large policemen, quiet voices reporting laconically, occasional bursts of static from transceivers installed in a makeshift command post in the office next door.

When he finally gave up the struggle to sleep, Adams felt as stiff and grubby as if he had sat up all night in a bus. He wanted a long hot shower, but had to settle for a quick shave. Then there was nothing to do but wait.

Crane came in at nine to take charge of the command post. Adams paced. He listened to frequent, invariably negative reports from the men on watch. Now and then, he issued a superfluous reminder for all, and especially those concentrated around Shaw's house, to keep out of sight. He drank coffee. He went outside, ostensibly to confirm the readiness of the command vehicle—a small van fitted with equipment for listening to and broadcasting on all the channels the police radio system used. Actually, he simply needed air, and the subarctic wind blowing across the lake was welcome to him.

Vogel arrived at ten, haggard and grumpy. He was twenty years older than Adams, and the long hours of the past few days had taken a toll. He heard Adams's brief report in silence and clumped away to his desk muttering about the overtime and paperwork required by all this crazy business.

Eleven o'clock: "Nothing to report."

Noon: "Nothing to report."

One o'clock: "Nothing to report."

A few minutes after one, Vogel came to the door wearing a bemused expression, and beckoned Adams to join him in the hall.

"Problems, boss?"

"Darned if I know. The Chief called a few minutes ago and said that the F.B.I. has been talking to him. It seems that McGuire and Tanner have asked for a conference, with Baker present, tomorrow morning."

"Is it Ashenden they want?"

When federal agents planned to make an arrest, they often informed the local police and sometimes requested assistance.

It was protocol to get in touch with the local Chief first.

Vogel snorted. "Well, they didn't name anybody. On the other hand, something that was said did prompt the Chief to ask me what we have on Professor Ashenden."

"Did Baker tell you what gave rise to that train of thought?"

"It wasn't anything definite, just something about University Research Center."

The radios in the room behind Adams had been chattering quietly. Now a voice came through enough louder than the norm to be startling.

"Subject in sight."

Adams looked at his watch. It was 1:17. Vogel raised his eyebrows questioningly, and Adams shrugged. He was a little surprised himself that action was beginning already.

"He's getting into his car."

"I'm on my way," said Adams.

In the van, Adams had both mobility and communications. He would be able to drive wherever the killer went and take charge on the spot. At the same time, he would be able to hear all reports and issue orders if he felt it necessary. Starting the motor, Adams followed the broadcasts attentively.

At first, the criminal's course was easy to trace, for he drove directly to the center of town. Near the corner of University and Main, he parked, left his car, and began to walk north on University Avenue. One block. Another. Halfway along a third block, he halted.

"He has joined the line outside the movie."

A movie at 1:30 on Sunday afternoon? Then Adams remembered. On Thanksgiving weekend there were special "family" matinées of Disney films.

Adams took up the microphone, swiftly scanning a mental map of the current locations of patrols.

"Car two and car eight: Park and proceed on foot toward the Odeon. Don't lose sight of him.

"Car sixteen: Cover the parking lot behind the theater."

Releasing the talk switch, Adams swore. He should have thought of that sooner. Shoppers went in and out of the lot all day; moviegoers used it evenings and weekend afternoons; residents of nearby apartment buildings left cars there overnight. No one would notice a car that remained parked for days, or even weeks.

Adams pulled away from the curb, reporting to Crane that he was heading for the intersection of Blake and Lincoln—Blake was the one-way street behind the theater, Lincoln the first cross-street north of the parking lot.

Bedlam!

Three voices tried to talk at once. He wasn't in the line. He wasn't in the lobby. They had lost him. Adams accelerated.

A fourth voice broke in, high-pitched with excitement. "I got him! I see him!"

"Report properly," Adams snapped.

"Yes, sir. This is car sixteen. Subject heading north on Blake in a gray Plymouth four-door, model year 1950 or thereabouts. License number YPS 700. The rear tires are bald. I didn't see the front ones, but I saw his face as he drove out of the parking lot."

"Car sixteen: Drop back. Don't let him realize that you're following him."

Adams didn't want to alarm the killer and start a chase in the busiest section of town.

"Car sixteen reporting. He's turning left on Lincoln."

"This is Adams. I have him in sight. He is proceeding west on Lincoln. . . . He has stopped for the light at University. . . . He is turning left, proceeding south on University."

West and south. A strange course, Adams thought. It was too early for the meeting on campus that Adams's cipher message had appointed. If the killer was planning to ditch the car, the sensible course would be to go east on Lincoln toward the highway, rather than to circle around on the most heavily traveled streets in Thorpe.

"All cars: Get him in sight, but keep your distance until he has passed the crowd near the theater. Then close in. Use extreme caution. Subject is probably armed. He is dangerous."

Adams turned south. Three blocks away, the Plymouth was turning right on Main Street.

Adams frowned. In that direction, to the west, Main Street dead-ended at the lakeside. No roads led south into the campus from that stretch of Main Street. Only one road went north, and that was the cul-de-sac, Lakeshore Drive. Unless the killer's reason had deserted him altogether, he couldn't be planning to get rid of the Plymouth out there. The only place to drive the car into the lake was straight off the end of the municipal dock. Otherwise, there was no—

"Oh, my God!" Adams whispered. "If she hasn't left yet . . ."

With dreadful certainty, he knew the killer's destination. For an instant, the thought was paralyzing. Then his foot went down hard on the throttle. With a sweep of one hand, he started siren screaming and lights flashing, and grabbed up the microphone.

"All cars: Subject proceeding west on Main toward Lakeshore Drive. Close in fast. Use your sirens. He must be stopped. Head for number 509 Lakeshore. Kate—" His voice cracked. He gulped and started over. "A Miss Kate Shaw lives there."

CHAPTER

29

Adams gave the orders, but he knew he was wasting his breath. There were policemen surrounding Mark Shaw's house, policemen on the campus, policemen coming from the east, policemen on University Avenue whose cars were facing the wrong direction. None was as close to the killer as Adams, and he was a quarter of a mile behind, not in a souped-up cruiser, but in a truck.

Adams turned the corner into Main Street with squealing tires, accelerated with a roar. The next corner was coming up too fast, much too fast. He stamped on the brake pedal, shifted gears, fought the wheel. The van fishtailed and slid all the way to the edge of the pavement before straightening out reluctantly. Down went the accelerator again.

There was the Plymouth. It was stopped right in front of Kate's cottage. The driver's door was opening. A man was stepping out. Adams pressed harder on the pedal and added the blare of the horn to the shriek of the siren.

The killer hesitated. Then his arm rose, pointing at Adams. Adams saw the round hole of the gun barrel, a flash of light, and a puff of dirty gray smoke. The windshield shivered, dissolved, and streamed back.

Adams tapped the brake and twitched the steering wheel to the left. In his Porsche, a four-wheel drift was a maneuver to be precisely controlled. God alone knew what would come of trying to tweak this behemoth around, but Adams had no choice. If he slowed down and stopped, he would be a sitting duck. If he rammed the Plymouth head-on at this speed, he would probably be trapped in wreckage, if he wasn't killed.

The van turned ponderously and listed alarmingly. The skid seemed to go on and on. When the collision came at last, Adams experienced it as a long screech of tearing metal, a thump that compressed every inch of his body and expelled the air from his lungs with a rush, a violent jostling that blurred his vision, and a sudden agony in his left side.

BLAM.

The van rocked under the impact of a heavy bullet. Adams threw off the safety belt and flung himself out and down. He hit the ground with a jolt that stabbed at the sore place in his side. Gasping, he rolled over, yanking out his gun.

Out of the corner of his eye he glimpsed a movement. His head jerked toward it.

"Kate! No!"

Her door was opening.

"Kate, keep away!" Adams screamed. "Go back! Kate, for your life, go back!"

He knew she couldn't hear him. His voice was drowned by the sirens of police cars speeding toward them. Adams leaped up.

Behind him, metal ripped again.

Adams whirled, and stared. The Plymouth was moving. Its bumper was gone. The trunk was crumpled. A mangled fender hung askew. The right-rear wheel wobbled crazily. It limped, like a wounded beast slinking away to find shelter.

There was no hole to crawl into. Before Kate's cottage the road was blocked by the van and two patrol cars halted beside it. Ahead, not more than a mile distant, Lakeshore Drive ended in a bog.

But the real beast wasn't crippled. He was trapped, but still dangerous.

Adams ran to the nearest cruiser and jumped into the back

seat. "Push the van out of the way with this car," he ordered the driver. "And give me that mike."

Quickly, Adams told Crane to send men up Lakeview Drive to head off the fugitive if he tried to escape up The Hill on foot. Then Adams organized the men gathering on Lakeshore Drive. One squad of two men must keep gawkers back. Four men were sent along the shore to flank the quarry and evacuate innocent bystanders from the beach and the Yacht Club. Adams led four more men straight ahead.

Topping a little rise in the road, Adams saw the gray sedan abandoned with its front wheels in the mud. Well up the slope, a lone figure was visible, climbing slowly. As the car Adams had commandeered stopped, a policeman appeared between two houses. The killer raised his gun, and the officer scuttled back out of sight.

The fugitive turned to face downhill. He took a step to one side, then stood still.

"Don't shoot," Adams ordered his men. "There are people in the houses up there behind him."

BLAM.

"Get down. He's shooting."

Adams ducked, ran to the Plymouth, and crouched beside it. He raised the bullhorn he had retrieved from the wrecked van, but the order to surrender was never spoken. The scene was changing. The Hill itself was changing.

Adams jumped up and ran, shouting, "Get back, you men! The mud is sliding again."

Almost imperceptibly, the earth stirred. There was none of the rumbling turmoil Adams associated with avalanches. This was a great ooze of what appeared to be solid ground. It was eerie. The land ought not to flow.

Only near the bottom of the slope did the smooth surface begin to break up. Here a gigantic crack gaped. There an immense wave rose and toppled over sluggishly in a monstrous parody of surf. All the while, the tumult remained soundless, and the silence was palpable and oppressive.

Adams could not have said when the slide ended. A terrifying subaudible whisper filled his ear after his eye no longer discerned motion.

A vast expanse of the earth's skin had crawled away, leaving a scar perhaps two hundred feet on each side. Miraculously, no house had fallen, although one had been left with the bare cement of a foundation wall suspended dizzyingly in space. The Yacht Club was unscathed, for the remains of Wednesdays night's landslip had diverted today's far greater one just a few feet to the north. The battered Plymouth stood undisturbed where it had been abandoned.

Of the killer there was no sign. At the first tremor, he had flung both arms wide in a desperate effort to keep his balance. A moment later, his feet had been sucked from under him and he had fallen on his back. Struggling ineffectually like an insect stuck in glue, he had been carried slowly, inexorably down.

"Spread out—"

BLAM.

The shot was curiously muffled, but there was no mistaking that deep tone. It was nothing like the whipcrack of a policeman's service revolver.

"Spread out," Adams repeated. "Keep down. Can anyone see him?"

A chorus of negatives responded.

Adams stood up. After a moment, he said, "Cover me."

Slogging through a morass toward a murderer with a .44 was not Adams's idea of good sport. If he had misinterpreted the last shot, he was presenting a target that couldn't be missed. He recollected vividly the effects that gun had on flesh and bone.

Soon, however, his thoughts were entirely occupied with the slogging.

The first few steps had been easy. Wednesday night's deposit was thin and beginning to harden. Going on, Adams found himself engaged in Sisyphean labor. The muck clung and slipped at the same time. To lift a foot required an effort both strenuous and nicely judged to keep the other foot from sliding. Adams inched ahead.

His breath came short and shallow. A rib must be broken, and these exertions were hardly the recommended therapy.

He confronted a ridge. It was less than eighteen inches high, but Adams had no confidence in his ability to surmount it. If he became mired to his knees, he would never get free without assistance. He glared at the mound, heaved his leg up, and thrust it forward.

He nearly trod on the shattered head.

Buried chest-deep, the body was held upright, but the head lolled back at an angle impossible in life. The slayer had slain for the last time, with a bullet into his own skull. Adams gazed unblinkingly, with no emotion of which he was aware. His only thought in the moment he stood there was that a tractor would be needed to get the body out.

Adams turned, lowered his head, and plodded back the way he had come. Reaction was setting in. He was trembling. His legs were weak. Every step brought a spasm of pain that forced a hissing exhalation between clenched teeth.

None of that mattered. His torment was in his mind. Five seconds later and the gun would have been at her head. "For your life," he had wailed, sick with the knowledge that he had failed to prevent the threat against her.

Adams became aware that the going was easier. One more step and he would reach dry, firm concrete. A policeman's hand gripped his arm. In the distance another man's voice spoke loudly but indistinctly. A woman's voice rose clearly.

"Let me by. Can't you see he's hurt?"

Kate's voice.

Adams lifted his eyes and saw her dart past the policemen who had blocked her path. Then her arms were around him and she was saying his name over and over.

CHAPTER

30

Hand-in-hand, Jeff and Kate walk off into the sunset.
Music up.
Fade out.

Unfortunately the world was not a Thomas Jefferson Adams production. The sun would not set at his direction. There were mundane matters to be seen to.

Arrangements had to be made for removing the body and the automobiles. The gray Plymouth must be examined and traced. After those tasks were delegated, Adams went to the hospital, where he discovered when he stripped to be X-rayed that he was black-and-blue from shoulder to hip and knee to ankle. Despite the seat belt, he had evidently bounced around in the van like a pinball. Not one, but two ribs had been broken. ("They're just cracked, not smashed," said the doctor cheerfully. They weren't his ribs. "You'll be fine in a few days.")

After his chest had been taped, Adams faced paperwork. Adding insult to literal injury was the necessity to explain and justify the wrecking of the van. That required four separate forms, all in triplicate, and Adams knew that most of them would be returned for corrections and additions no matter how careful he was.

Ordinarily, Vogel or Crane would have assisted, but they

were unavailable. Thorpe and its police were not yet done with threats to life. No one knew if the rest of The Hill was going to fall down. By the time the sun did set, residents of seventy-odd homes had been evacuated, roads had been barricaded, and policemen had begun patrolling on foot to prevent looting.

Adams might have postponed report-writing, except that on his return from the hospital he found on his desk an already approved request, in his own name, for a week of sick leave. Crisis or not, Vogel had made time to fill out the application and approve it. Adams meant to leave a completed case file behind when he departed.

Officers Turner and Warren weren't out on emergency duty, so they took charge of the gun, as well as the Plymouth and the galoshes, gloves, and hammer that had been found in its trunk. The weapon was the one that had killed Bauer, Overath, and Ritter; the boots matched the casts of tracks from the Feiths' grounds; the gloves were impregnated with the residue of black powder; the hammer bore traces of blood.

A description of the car had gone to the state police, who traced it to a downstate farmer, one Robert Weaver, whom they judged innocent of any more than a misdemeanor and stupidity. Weaver claimed to have sold the Plymouth for cash early in November to a man who called himself Jones or Johnson, or maybe James. According to Weaver, the purchaser had promised to take care of both his own application for reregistration and the notification of sale that the former owner was required by law to file. A good many people ignored that law and got away with it, but Weaver was going to rue his carefree ways, or so the tone of Trooper Mandel's voice suggested.

Then Agent McGuire called in response to a message Adams had left for him at the hotel. The F.B.I. man was as expressionless over the phone as in person, but Adams was pleasantly surprised when he consented immediately to explain the investigation of Ashenden.

"Embezzlement."

"You mean he was stealing government grant money from University Research Center?"

"Yeah."

"You're sure? I mean, you have solid evidence?"

"We've got him cold."

"Did he arrange the farce with the U.R.C. locks last spring?"

"Seems so."

"Why?"

There was silence for several seconds before McGuire said, "I think he was just making waves. He got into gambling. Like all these suckers, he planned to pay back out of winnings, only there weren't any. He seems to have hoped that stirring up a fuss would give him a chance to fiddle the records, or destroy them, or something. So far, he hasn't been willing to talk about that part."

"Oh. You've interviewed him."

"We arrested him right after you, uh, finished up your case."

"I see," said Adams, and he did. The feds hadn't known until then if Ashenden was a killer as well as a thief. Once certain on that point, they had felt free to move without first consulting the local officers.

Adams put a final question. "He couldn't have been spying as well as stealing, could he?"

"Nah." McGuire unbent suddenly. "We wouldn't let anything serious go on in a crazy place like that. That hairy kid what's-his-name—Morris somebody-or-other—is enough all by himself to make the security people nervous."

Al Morris would appreciate that, Adams thought.

"Okay. Thanks for the information."

All the loose ends had been knitted up. Even so, Adams was still typing when Vogel tramped in, dropped wearily onto a chair, and rumbled, "It's after seven. Are you planning to spend the night here? Don't you know your girl is waiting out front for you?"

"But—but I sent her home."

"Use your head, boy. She can't go home. Everybody has been chased away from Lakeshore, Lakeview, and God knows how many other streets."

"I know. I meant that I had sent her to my place."

"Well, she's here, and you better get a move on. Besides, I want you out of here so I can relax. Calamities happen when you're around." Vogel gave a startling hoot of laughter. "Smashing cars is one thing, but did you have to throw the whole damn hill at him?"

Before Adams could think of a suitable reply, Vogel hooted again.

"I guess you could say that the criminal really met his downfall, huh?"

"God, now I need that sick leave badly," Adams said. "And thanks, boss."

"Sure, sure. Listen, the state things are in around here, nobody is going to read your reports anyway. Beat it, will you?"

The desk sergeant had ensconced Kate on a chair, and her lengthy vigil seemed not to have been lonely. Two uniformed officers drifted away when Adams appeared.

"It's wonderful how much the men admire you," she said with a smile as Adams took her arm.

"That was the line, was it?"

"The line? I don't know what you mean."

"Hellion. You know perfectly well that every cop in Thorpe would call me God's gift to law enforcement if he thought it would give him a chance to spend time with you."

"What a cynic. Are you jealous?"

Adams halted and examined her closely. "You have that look which says mischief is afoot. What are you plotting?"

"You'll find out. Come on. I have had about as much exposure to a police station as I can take."

Outside, his Porsche, which had remained at Kate's since Thursday morning, was parked at the curb.

"Where's your car?"

"At your place. One of your nice young men drove it—he reminded me of a big teddy bear and I would swear he said his name was Koala, but that can't be right, can it?"

"Kovalló," Adams said absently. He was really suspicious now. Kate never simply chattered unless she had something on her mind that she meant to keep secret.

"Will it terrify you to let me drive?" she hurried on. "I brought the Porsche because of its reclining seats. I was afraid your ribs might make you uncomfortable if you had to sit up in my car."

Adams smiled. "Dear heart, it's all of three blocks to my apartment. I'd have survived."

"Yes. Well, um, I thought maybe we could go for a ride. Please."

She was determined not to disclose her scheme, he saw.

"All right," said Adams, lowering himself cautiously into the seat.

"And while we are driving you can explain the mystery to me."

"Oh, no."

"Oh, yes. You have to. The brilliant detective always explains at the end."

"Brilliant!" Adams cried. "I was so dumb I almost got you killed. I sent a blackmailing cryptogram. I guarded your father, the reputed former spy who might have broken the cipher and the witness who might have spotted the murderer's car.

"But it never so much as crossed my mind that anyone could imagine *you* as a blackmailer. All I did was feel sorry for myself because we couldn't spend night, morning, or afternoon together. I assumed you were safely out of the way with the Laceys, and never stopped to ask exactly what time you—"

"Jeff, stop it. You're flaying yourself for no reason. The worst did not happen."

"No thanks to me. I should have taken precautions."

"Very well. You won't allow yourself easy excuses. But I won't allow you to reproach yourself for failing to think about *me* in a cool professional manner. If that's a fault, my dear, don't ever cure it."

"Ah, Kate, I wasn't asking for reassurance."

"Do you really think I don't know that?"

Tilted back in the passenger seat, Adams couldn't see her face, but amusement became plain in her voice as she continued: "We made a deal once, and it has to work both ways. I'll stop you if I get bored. Now, start talking, okay?"

"Well . . . okay," Adams said.

CHAPTER

31

"Karl Feith decided to kill his parents when he learned late in October that they intended to break a twenty-five-year habit by staying home for Thanksgiving."

"But the messages—"

"Were fakes."

"The men weren't spies?"

"No, or if they were we have found no evidence of it, and it had nothing to do with the murders."

"Well, then, why did Karl kill them?"

"For his parents' money. The other men were extras— No. Less than that. They were mere props, stage scenery."

"Good God! He must have been insane."

"Perhaps. Dean Gage believes that something snapped under pressure at the time Feith failed his orals. Psychologists might argue he was warped in childhood by lack of love and warmth. Certainly Ernst Feith seems to have been, as a grad student put it, 'one cold fish' who heated up only when his temper erupted. Even Dr. Meadows, who had known all the men for years and called three of them by their first names consistently spoke of 'Dr. Feith.'

"I'm a cop. For me it's enough to say that Karl Feith lusted for money. A couple of years ago he treated himself to a summer in Europe, and he intended to go again. About the same time, he invested in a business, but one that showed a loss, not a profit. He wanted money. His parents had plenty, and by October he was ready to kill to get it.

"Meanwhile, the campus had been thrown into turmoil, which had been triggered, appropriately enough, by the activities of a couple of other crooks. First a flunking foreign student carried out an amateurish theft of documents. Then Ashenden tried to raise a cloud of dust to hide his embezzlement by removing the locks from University Research Center. But he had reckoned without the uneasiness with which scientists had begun to be viewed.

"When the demonstrations erupted, most people in Thorpe became convinced that U.R.C. was engaged in secret and probably frightful research which had attracted the agents of unfriendly nations.

"Karl Feith may have known better, but he saw that what others believed gave him an opportunity to make use of his parents' change of plans. If he simply went out and killed his wealthy parents, he would inevitably be a leading suspect. Every cop's instinct is to investigate heirs first. So Feith set out to distract attention from himself and onto a wholly fictitious James Bond kind of character.

"He needed material which implicated all the men in espionage, and which leaped into an investigator's view without seeming to do so. Seven Star Diaries served his purpose admirably. They had the innocuous appearance that real spies probably do cherish, but a cop confronted with five diaries, of which only one showed signs of ordinary use, was sure to doubt that they were innocent memo books. Adding tableaus and a couple of messages produced both a cipher that actually was difficult and the wherewithal to insure that sooner or later it would be cracked. And the messages themselves gave a sinister twist to his parents' change of plans for Thanksgiving, as well as to the Wednesday-night bridge games the four men had played for years.

"Next, he acquired an old car that couldn't be traced to him. He didn't need to obtain an untraceable weapon, since he could make use of Bauer's gun collection, which he had presumably known about from childhood. He did have to buy bullets, but he used Bauer's name. He disguised himself, but did so in a way that made the fact of disguise obvious. We were supposed to think that the mythical spy had bought the bullets.

"Feith couldn't create an alibi, but he did what he could to increase mystification by giving himself a sort of shadow of an alibi. He rumpled his bed, put some bottles and glasses on display, and filled an ashtray with two brands of cigarettes. When I asked him who had visited, he pretended nervousness, thereby disguising whatever real tension he felt and prompting me to chase around trying to find his bed partner.

"By the way, your pal Kovallo had the right intuition, although it sent us on a wild-goose chase. Kovallo wasn't able to believe that in this day and age anyone could be as fearful as Feith seemed at the prospect of exposure of a heterosexual affair. He suggested that Feith's problem was that his lover was male, which left us wondering, for one thing, if John Evans was AC-DC, sexually speaking."

Kate made a sound that was half gasp and half snicker.

"Yeah," said Adams. "Then what Crane called a regular three-dollar bill turned up, in the person of Thomas Fredericks, and that made it even harder for me to get rid of the false notion that Feith really had had a visitor.

"To go back to Evans for a moment, his request for help must have seemed heaven-sent to Feith. He was overjoyed to give his brother-in-law a false alibi that would never stand up under a police investigation. When it did break down, attention would focus on Evans. At the same time, the police might doubt that Feith would indulge in such a damnfool lie unless he was innocent of the murders.

"All of that business was only a little more dust to throw in our eyes. Feith's critical difficulty lay in finding a way to present the cryptographic materials without making it obvious that we were meant to find them.

"The method he chose was pretty feeble—as planned. He knew that shots in his parents' house wouldn't be heard. He hoped that if he fired four shots outdoors your parents would turn on lights or give some other sign of disturbance. Then he would run away, leaving his manufactured evidence behind.

"What actually happened was different, and its first effect was to strengthen Feith's fakery, but eventually it blew the masquerade apart.

"Your father was disturbed, all right, but instead of turning on lights he went straight out the door and headed for the Feiths' house. The first sign of a reaction that Feith saw was the appearance of your father at the end of the driveway, less than fifty yards away.

"Feith thought this gave him a chance to strengthen his plot. He fired a shot over your father's head, threw away the gun and cipher materials, and fled. The police were supposed to believe that he had been too frightened to keep incriminating evidence with him.

"In fact, he had created such a baffling mess that I couldn't believe anything.

"The first thing I noticed was Ernst Feith's study. Professionals search desks from bottom to top, so they can leave drawers open but out of their way. Feith's had been searched the other way around. It looked to me as if the ransacking was meant to misdirect investigators.

"Next I discovered that the Feiths had been killed by a gun using old-fashioned black powder. That made me feel that if the killer wasn't plain stupid, he was engaged in a very elaborate deception.

"Then I talked to your father. He said he hadn't seen anyone. But I thought that the evidence, planted or not, had to mean that the murderer had been in Ernst Feith's study when he spotted your father approaching. If so, he couldn't have got out of that brightly lighted house without being seen.

"Your father also said he had heard two pairs of gunshots. But I knew that the fatal shots couldn't have been fired in that pattern.

"By then I was disturbed, as well as confused. The witness was *your* father, and I got so nervous—"

"I know." Kate reached over and patted his knee. "I realized when you wouldn't stay and sleep on my sofa that you were more disturbed than you had said."

"There's not much I can hide from you, is there?"

"I hope not. Go on now."

"Well, strictly as a policeman, I was worried that your father had added flourishes of his own to the murderer's scenario, and that I'd never be able to sort out what had actually happened.

"During the next twenty-four hours, things got crazier and crazier. We found tracks of a car with three bald tires. We found a gun that belonged in a Wild West show. Karl Feith and the Evanses told nonsensical stories. The first cryptogram and tableau turned up. I learned that the Evanses had been roaming separately around town because John Evans was having an affair. His 'floozy' turned out to be so obviously out of his class that I suspected her of masterminding the plot. A couple of radicals scared me, and a couple of grad students distracted me with foolery about fireflies and featherless chickens. Ashenden wandered onstage just long enough to attract my suspicious gaze.

"And then things really went to hell. In the space of a couple of hours, we found three more bodies, four diaries, three tableaus, and another enciphered message.

"By the time Vogel sent me off to have Thanksgiving dinner and to drag you into the case, I was in a state of absolute befuddlement. If it hadn't been for you, I might still be benighted. You deserve at least as much credit as the not so brilliant detective for solving the case."

Kate laughed. "I never refuse praise, but I can't see that I earned any."

"Well, I'll wait for a more suitable occasion to describe in detail all that you did for my spirit.

"As for the case, you solved the cipher, which was the essential first step. In addition, you pointed out how convenient it was that the marks on one message showed us how to begin deciphering it. The point didn't sink in immediately, but while I was asleep my subconscious went to work and realized that we had been given all the pieces. We didn't have merely the minimum that permitted solution of the cipher. We had so much data that we couldn't help solve it.

"We had a Vigenère tableau and a cipher message that seemed to have been overlooked under Ernst Feith's blotter. We had a gun, as well as fingerprints on diaries, that would lead us to Bauer and Overath, and then to Ritter and the second enciphered message.

"I didn't notice right away how carefully the trail had been marked, because we didn't follow it as intended. Dr. Meadows found Bauer and Overath before the pointers led us to them. That was confusing at first but helpful later. Dr. Meadows gave me times I needed. She also persuaded me that the men really had played bridge as the scorecard indicated.

"Eventually, I came to see that no pieces were missing. Nothing had to be inferred. I had been presented with everything needed to show me that a spy ring had been in operation.

"The more I thought about the wealth of evidence, the less I believed in the conclusion it seemed to lead to.

"Then I remembered something you had said about Karl Feith. You remarked on the brazenness of denying that he had had a visitor, when evidence contradicting him was right in front of me.

"What you didn't know was that the glasses and ashtray that seemed to belie his story carried no fingerprints but Feith's. Either his guest managed to drink and smoke without leaving a mark, or else Feith was telling the truth while appearing to lie.

"Once I started thinking that Feith had been putting on a show, a lot of things began to make sense. We had found a very strange pattern of prints on the cipher materials. Each of the four diaries in the plastic bag had prints only on its cover. Each tableau and one of the messages had prints only on the front. And the other message—the one Ernst Feith had supposedly begun solving by putting lines between numbers—didn't have any prints at all.

"It may be possible for someone to use a diary and only touch the outside, or for someone to pick up paper without touching the back. But it was simply impossible for Ernst Feith to work on a message and to slip it under his blotter, yet not to leave a single print anywhere on the sheet of paper.

"I decided that the killer must have pressed the dead men's fingertips against the material—but that he had been just rattled enough so that he had forgotten to put Ernst Feith's prints on the message that mattered most.

"Here's another thing. We learned that a second gun had been used, yet it was clear that there had been only one killer. There was no reason for him to use two guns—except to try to confuse us about the number of killers we were hunting.

"In short, I came to see that the whole business had been staged, and that all the bits worked together to form a coherent whole. That made me take another look at the heirs. They were the ones who benefited from the Feiths' deaths, and they were the ones who benefited from diverting attention to a phony spy ring.

"John Evans had no alibi for the time of the Feiths' murders, but he was known to have been at the Yacht Club too late to commit the other murders. His wife had no alibi at all, but she could scarcely have planned in advance on having her husband go out and stay out as long as he did. They might, of course, have worked together, and I was unable to prove that they hadn't. I kept the possibility in mind, but it never became a probability for me.

"Karl Feith, on the other hand, was a bachelor, free to make plans without worrying about spouse or roommate. He knew guns and had had experience of killing the animals he hunted. Finally, he had put on an act that hinted at an alibi.

"I was pretty sure Karl Feith was the criminal, but I had no proof.

"Our evening of bridge didn't produce usable evidence, but it did reinforce my conviction that the four men hadn't been spies. At least, unless they played at an incredibly rapid pace, they had not had time to complete three hard-fought rubbers and still meet with a spy-master.

"The reconstruction of the murders was no more productive of real proof, but it did resolve the last conundrum.

"Wednesday night I had seen in Ernst Feith's study a ransacked desk beneath a window that showed the whole driveway. Your father had said that after hearing shots he went out, headed for the open front door of the Feiths' house, and was shot at.

"Thursday night I gave you an outline of events and you didn't notice that your father should have seen the killer. That seemed important, but I was too sleepy, and my mind was too clogged with other puzzles, to make sense of it then. Later, I realized that neither you nor your father had seen the mess in the study. Both of you had assumed unquestioningly that the murderer was already outside before your father was in a position to see him. When I discovered that the shots that had been heard must have been fired outdoors, I understood that your assumption was correct.

"The other fact I learned was that there had been no lights on in the front part of your parents' house on Wednesday night. I realized that the killer couldn't see their house at all from Ernst Feith's study. That was why he hadn't fired just outside the door of his family's home. He had felt he must go to a place where he could see past the trees and observe the lights he expected your father to turn on.

"So at last I knew the whole story, but I still had not a scrap of proof. My only hope was that Feith had in fact used the car with bald tires and that I could find it. Thanks to the University Regents, a routine and time-consuming search was out of the question. Desperation prompted me to send Feith a message in cipher to stir him up—in which, God knows, I succeeded only too well.

"The rest you know."

CHAPTER

32

"Brilliant, as I said," Kate commented after a pause. "And if I didn't know you'll have nightmares, I would be rather pleased that you came and rescued me in the nick of time, like the Seventh Cavalry in a movie."

"In real life, wasn't that the outfit Custer took to Little Bighorn?"

"You're incorrigible. You find the grim side of everything."

"Uh-huh. But never mind that now. I can't see much from this position, but I gather that we are on the highway. May I know, please, what you're doing?"

"I'm abducting you."

"Whatever for? You know I'll go anywhere you name, except away."

"Well, Vogel told me you're supposed to be off-duty for a week, and I thought . . ." She took a breath and said all in a rush, "I wanted to make sure that you wouldn't be able to hear that horrible buzzer if they tried to call you, and I figured that Southport was far enough away, so I reserved a room in a hotel, and I burgled your apartment of clothes and shaving kit, and—" She broke off with a laugh and a shake of her head. "I did all that, but I didn't feel like an idiot until now. I have just realized that I got so flustered worrying about how you would react that I gave the hotel my name. I suppose we will be registered as Mr. and Mrs. Shaw. Do you mind terribly?"

"Stop the car."

"Jeff! You aren't going to make me turn around, are you?"

"My darling floozy, I love you. I want to kiss you."

"Ah." The car slowed abruptly. "Now see what an obedient Kate am I."

Epilogue

All characters, places, and events that play parts in this book are imaginary, but some real ones are mentioned.

Kate Shaw's subjects are historical personages—indeed, though it pains me to say so, Ignatius Donnelly is beyond my power of invention.

During a political career that spanned the last forty years of the nineteenth century, Donnelly evolved from Republican to Granger and finally to chief ideologue and Vice-Presidential candidate of the People's Party. His writings include two political novels, *Caesar's Column* and *The Golden Bottle.* Although neither is much read now except by specialists, the former retains sufficient power to enrage one eminent historian. In *The Age of Reform,* Richard Hofstadter describes *Caesar's Column* as "childish" but "anything but laughable." Hofstadter sees anti-Semitism, "a kind of suppressed lasciviousness," and a "sadistic and nihilistic spirit." The book ends, says Hofstadter, in "an incredible round of looting and massacre which may have been modeled on the French Revolutionary Terror but makes it seem pale and bloodless by comparison."

If Donnelly's "nonfiction" has failed to overshadow reality, it has stirred some excitement. *Atlantis* and a book called *Ragnarök: The Age of Fire and Gravel* were popular when published. Paperback editions may be found today alongside the works of Velikovsky, von Däniken, and the laborers in the Bermuda Triangle industry.

The argument of *The Great Cryptogram* has been influential, even though the book is unreadable. William F. and Elizebeth S. Friedman have gently but thoroughly demolished the pretensions of Donnelly and other cryptographically inclined Baconians in *The Shakespearean Ciphers Examined.*

A quotation from the Friedmans' book is the source of the title of Kate Shaw's biography, and suggests a view of Donnelly rather more sorrowful and less angry than Hofstadter's. According to a commentator the Friedmans did not name, Donnelly displayed "a desperate gullibility which will accept almost anything as proof; a total lack of self-criticism; and a cheerful confidence in one's own ingenuity which will survive all the arguments of others. When men like Donnelly are born, they are given a kind of intellectual armor which will protect them from ridicule at the same time as it insulates them from reason. Perhaps it is just as well; to be at once ridiculous and sensitive to ridicule would be far more harrowing."

The groundnut scheme in Tanganyika was in truth ill-fated and remains well known among economists.

The existence of an Academy of Pataphysics in France (c/o Le Minoduart, 2 Rue des Beaux-Arts, Paris) may, or may not, attest to the reality of its field.

Seven Star Diaries, a.k.a. Success Diaries, are manufactured in Holland by N. V. Uitgeversmaatschappij Succes, who provided the 1968 edition from which I have quoted exactly.

Author's Note

"Code" and "cipher" are interchangeable in laymen's speech, but cryptographers distinguish quite sharply between them.

A code is a language. Coding or decoding is translation of meaningful units with the aid of a kind of bilingual dictionary, the code book. Many codes use five-number groups, each of which may translate a phrase, a word, or a prefix or suffix. Thus 84818 may mean "ship"; 84818 32054 may mean "ship sunk"; and 92356 may announce "war declared."

A cipher operates on the phonetic or alphabetic units of a message. Pig Latin, anagrams and the so-called Morse code are ciphers. The "key" is the set of rules by which "plain text" is converted to "cipher text" through transposition (as in Pig Latin and anagrams), substitution (as in Morse code), or both.

Only ciphers appear in this book.

A HARPER NOVEL OF SUSPENSE